# Abstract Love

samantha christy

*A*thena Books Publishing Group, LLC.
Saint Augustine, FL 32259


Copyright © 2014 by Samantha Christy

Cover designed by Letitia Hasser | RBA Designs

ISBN-13: 978-1500636654
ISBN-10: 1500636657

For my beautiful daughter, Kaitlyn, in hopes that one day you will find your more-than-enough love.

# Abstract Love

# Prologue

Everyone is watching me. Dozens of eyes are burning into me right now. They are wondering what I'm thinking, what I'm going to do if Jace doesn't walk through those large double doors soon.

My gaze travels from the doors back to the empty spot he should be occupying. Everyone else is in their place, waiting patiently, worried looks painted on their faces. No one is speaking to me, but I know what they're thinking. *Poor Keri, what will she do now?* They wonder if I will cry. Maybe they think I'll have a breakdown. I'm sure some think I will run through those doors in search of him.

People are starting to shuffle around anxiously, and I hear whispered voices in the conspicuously quiet room.

You could hear a pin drop in here.

Every so often someone will cough, or a cell phone will vibrate. The air is thick with unasked questions.

*Why wouldn't he show up?* After everything we've been through together.

The rich bellow of a horn from a nearby yacht pulls me from my thoughts. My eyes stare through the massive picture window at

1

the back of the room. The window that was the very reason I chose this location. The window that overlooks dock after dock lined with boats of all sizes in the marina that sits adjacent to this building. Boats that remind me of my dad and the stories he would make up about the three of us sailing around the world. Just him, my mom and me, and the adventures we would have in every port.

As I stare out the window, I feel close to him, but at the same time I miss him so terribly, wishing he could be with me on days such as this.

Then I hear the doors open and I abruptly spin around to see all heads turning with hopeful eyes watching to see if Jace will walk through. Then I hear the collective sighs when they see it's not him.

He's late. *Too late.* I close my eyes and allow my head to fall forward in defeat. I feel a strong but gentle hand on my shoulder. I look up to see the sympathetic eyes of my best friend who is trying to comfort me because he knows what everyone else here does.

Jace isn't coming.

# Chapter One

*Two months ago . . .*

Call them what you will. Breasts, boobs, jugs, tits, honkers, sweater stretchers, knockers, hooters, bosom, cans, girls, melons, rack. I'm obsessed with them. I can't stop thinking about them. I look at them all the time, and not just my own meager B cups, but breasts everywhere. I look at how they bounce, how they fit inside clothing, how they sometimes stress the buttons of a blouse or how they spill over the top edges of a tiny bikini.

I was never one of those women who was going to be defined by the size of my boobs. But at the thought of losing them, suddenly they are front and center. So to speak.

When Dr. Olsen informed me a few short months ago that I have stage two breast cancer, I grabbed them—actually cupped my hands over my breasts, as if I were somehow protecting them from the man who would want to slice them from my body. Luckily, I eventually—after twenty horrifying minutes—found out that more than likely I wouldn't lose them unless my treatment didn't work as expected.

So now I live my life by the numbers. Ninety-three—the percent chance I will survive the five-year mark. Thirteen—the number of cycles of chemotherapy I must endure. Eight—the number of eggs harvested from my ovaries in case the chemo fries my insides. Sixty-five—the percent chance I will lose my hair.

As I sit here in the chemotherapy clinic, it's the last number that is plaguing my thoughts today. This is my second cycle of chemo. My second week. This is when the hair loss most likely begins. I'm not a particularly vain person, but the idea of losing my long, wavy blonde hair that falls, ironically, to my boobs, scares the hell out of me.

I look at the people around me who share my weekly Monday morning time slot, and I inventory the amount of hair loss. Yup, I'd say more than half are completely without hair.

The women mostly wear scarves to cover their bald heads. One older lady, Grace, who also has breast cancer, wears a wig that is slightly misaligned with her face, but no one has told her.

Melanie, who, at thirty-eight is the next youngest patient to my twenty-four years, is stunning with her freshly shaved head. Last week she was complaining that clumps were falling out and today she showed up with a shiny bald head, refusing to cover it up. I admire her courage, knowing I wouldn't be able to embrace my hair loss as she has.

The two men here, in our group of eight, have managed to keep their hair so far. A fact I find decidedly unfair. Surely it wouldn't bother a man as much as it would a woman.

I reach down to retrieve my iPod from my purse and wince at the pain that rips through my arm as a result of my pulling at the IV line sticking into the back of my hand.

Stacy, the cute redheaded nurse, has mad skills when it comes to inserting the IV. She's so good that I forgot it was there, after the initial burning of the fluids entering my arm.

I don't mean to be anti-social, but given my age, I kind of feel like a fish out of water in here. Aside from Melanie, who is two seats down from me, I don't think there's another patient here under the age of fifty.

Last week being my first week here, they were all very nice and tried to make me feel comfortable. They gave me the run-down on the place.

Never drink the coffee, it sucks. Stop at Starbucks on the way.

The biscuits are to die for. It's true, I tried one.

Do not pass up a foot or shoulder massage when Trina, the clinic masseuse, comes around. They are heavenly.

But most importantly, never ever miss a chemo cycle.

There are only two reasons people miss a cycle. One, they've been in an accident on the way to the clinic, or two, they're dead. Or at the very least, laid up in a hospital bed somewhere near death.

So, the rule of thumb is to call in case of a missed appointment. That way the rest of us aren't worrying our asses off wondering what has happened.

I considered asking them to move me next to Melanie, but I don't. Today she's brought a friend with her.

We're allowed to have someone stay with us as chemo is a long, boring process. There are only so many things to occupy your time here if don't want to watch The Travel Channel, which is apparently what Steven, the man with colon cancer, wants to watch. From what I gather, he is the sickest one of our group. I guess it's an unwritten rule that we acquiesce the television programming to him. I silently pray that I never get to pick what we watch.

Two and a half hours in, I check the clock. It's a little after eleven. Only thirty minutes left to go.

The large double doors open, and we all turn our heads to see who is coming in, as it's such a rare occasion after a session begins that anyone enters the room through the main doors.

At first, I think it's a doctor. A very attractive, tall and muscular twenty-something guy walks over to the nurse's station. However, he lacks the confidence, and the white coat, of a physician.

He looks around the room with a blank stare on his face, looking at everything, yet nothing at the same time. He hands a paper to Nurse Stacy. She nods and pulls something up on the computer.

"Okay, everyone, meet Jace." She motions to him. "Jace, meet Keri, Grace, Melanie, Steven, John, Ann, Marjorie, and Peggy."

She points to us as she calls our names, running through the semi-circle of large, comfortable leather recliners that have become our homes every Monday morning.

"Jace will be joining us for eleven cycles."

She motions to his neck where I notice a bandage sticking up over his collar.

"Jace doesn't talk much, but don't let him fool you, I've heard he can still charm your socks off. So, watch out ladies." She winks at him.

Jace rolls his eyes and follows Stacy to his seat between John and Ann, on the other side of the room from me.

Some of the other patients speak up to make him feel at ease, but I stay quiet, as I'm still getting used to this myself. I try not to stare. It sucks that he has to be here, but at the same time I'm glad to see someone here who looks to be within five years of my age.

Grace, who sits next to me, looks over at me and raises her eyebrows before she whispers, "Well, what do you know, Keri, cancer comes in all shapes and sizes. And what a yummy shape that boy has." She giggles. "If I were forty years younger . . ."

While Stacy is taking his pre-treatment vitals and drawing some blood, I'm able to get a good look at him. He has light-brown hair that flops haphazardly in every direction, yet it seems perfectly groomed. His face has strong angles and a defined jaw, and when Stacy says something amusing, I see the tiniest dimple in his left cheek. He's wearing dark jeans that define his slender waist, and a snug polo shirt that clings to him like a second skin, showing off every ripple of his toned torso.

He is gorgeous.

I look down, chastising myself at my choice of clothing—my rainy-day sweatpants and oversized Florida State sweatshirt that used to be my dad's.

Apparently, Jace didn't get the memo to dress comfortably.

I selfishly worry that he might lose his incredible head of hair. Then I begin to wonder what he would look like bald. Well, it's a better pastime than watching The Travel Channel.

Fifteen minutes later, most of us are finishing up, but since Jace was late, he will run over into the next session.

I try not to look at him with sorry eyes, but I have to wonder if he has any idea what he's in for. He might look all delicious now, but by tonight, he may be begging for death. Not that chemo affects everyone that way, but it's why I chose to come on Monday mornings. It gives me a chance to recover in time for my weekend shifts.

I give him a small wave as I pass him on my way out. When I reach the door, I turn around and see him staring after me. I also see him quickly look away.

Outside the clinic, Melanie says, "Keri, you need to get Stacy to move you next to that prime piece of meat that just walked in."

"I work in a bar, Mel. I have a good feel for when and where to pick up guys, and I'm pretty sure the chemo clinic is not one of those places."

She shakes her head and laughs at me. "Girl, if you wait for lightening to strike, before you know it, you'll be as old as me, living with a bunch of cats."

"First off, you are not old. Second, how do you know I'm even single? And third, I'm allergic to cats."

"I don't even have to ask if you're single. I saw the way you were staring at Jace from the minute he walked in the door. Plus, this is your second time at chemo, and any guy in their right mind with a girlfriend as hot as you are would have come to support you by now."

Her words sting as we say our goodbyes. She's right. Almost everyone at the clinic had someone come with them either today or last week.

Not me. There's only one person who would ever come with me. My roommate, my best friend, my kindred spirit, the reason I'm not lying in a ditch somewhere. But my being here is the reason he's not. He's working double shifts to help pay for my treatments, and he even took on a temp job during the day.

Tanner is running himself ragged because of me. He wanted me to take a leave of absence from the bar altogether, but I couldn't let him shoulder the entire burden. Besides, by the time Friday rolled around last week, I had most of my strength back. He is my rock, my savior. And I'll bet if you asked him, he would say the same thing about me.

I also know he would have drooled over Jace, being that Tanner is gay.

I wonder if maybe Jace is gay as well. You never can tell. I mean Tanner is as much alpha-male as a guy can get. Women hit on him all the time and are sorely disappointed when they find out he's gay. I guess that's why he gets the best tips at the bar—both sexes are tipping him while I only get good tips from the guys.

Maybe I could set them up. Tanner is always trying to set me up with guys at work. I tell him not to bother. I'm never interested. I get everything I need from Tanner. Well, not sex, but everything else. Anyway, the sex part I can pretty much take care of myself, and from what I remember from the few guys I was with a long time ago, it wasn't that great to begin with.

No, Tanner is all I need. We complete each other in a way that I imagine most older married couples do. We finish each other's sentences, we know exactly what the other person will and won't order at a restaurant, we like the same movies and music, and we would do anything—*anything*—for one another.

So why then, as I lie here on the bathroom floor, head pressed against the cool tile after hours of gut-wrenching vomiting, am I doing nothing else but wondering if Jace is doing the very same thing?

Samantha Christy

# Chapter Two

By Wednesday afternoon, I'm feeling decent, so I decide to stop by The Freeway Station to help out. I can never stay away for too long. It's the reason I'm studying so hard to get my degree. It is the place that brought Tanner and I together.

Some people call them troubled kids. Unwanted kids. I was called that myself when I lived here for ten months. I was also called a 'long term.' There are kids who stay anywhere from a few days up to an entire year.

Most residents have gotten in trouble with the law and this was a way to keep them out of juvenile detention. For a lot of the kids it's simply that—a penance they must pay—a means to an end. But for me … for me it was my salvation. By the end of my stay, I vowed to get my high school diploma and go on to college so I could help kids just as I had been helped.

So now I volunteer whenever I can, which lately is only a few hours here and there.

Chaz, the head psychologist, and one of the most remarkable men I know, has been great to me. He was a counselor back when Tanner and I were here. He lets me sit in on intakes and counseling sessions. He has all but promised me a full-time position when I graduate.

"Keri!" He pulls me into a hug when he sees me walk in. "I'm so glad to see you here. How are you?"

"I'm holding up, Chaz." I look around the large empty house. "I was really hoping to see some of the kids today."

He shakes his head at me. "Most of them went to the beach. They'll be sorry they missed you."

I look at the ground, sad that on the one day I feel good enough to drop by, they aren't here. But I'm glad they're out having fun. I turn around to head into the kitchen to whip up a batch of cookies for them. On my way, I hear a chirping noise. I walk around from room to room until I figure out it's coming from the smoke detector in the main lounge area.

I look up at the ceiling and cringe when the thing chirps at me. "Chaz!" I yell over my shoulder towards his office.

He comes running out. "What is it, Keri?" He looks up at the ceiling to see what I'm staring at.

"It's the smoke detector. The battery is low and it's chirping," I say, as I feel the pace of my heartbeat increase.

"Oh, thanks. I think we have an extra nine-volt battery around here. I'll replace it."

"When is the last time you replaced the batteries?"

"I don't know," he says. "I would have to check the records."

"Well, you have to replace all of them." My breathing quickens.

"Maybe it's just a bad battery. That happens sometimes."

"No!" I raise my voice at him. "If this one is going bad, all of them could be going bad. Chaz, you have to replace them all. You have to do it. I don't care what the records say. This one is chirping, and the others could start at any time. You can't wait for the batteries to get low. You have to replace all of them."

Large arms come around me in understanding. "Keri, it's okay." He looks down at me sweetly, his large stature towering over my petite one. "I'll go out right now and get all the batteries we need. I'll replace them today. Don't worry, I'll get all of them. I promise."

He holds onto me until I calm down. It feels familiar, just like it did eight years ago when I was a resident, not a volunteer. Chaz has a soothing way about him. His arms envelop me. He's like a large teddy bear. I think it's one of the reasons I like him so much. He has a way of making the bad stuff go away. He is my mentor. My friend.

As we break apart, I feel smaller hands come around me from behind.

"Hey, Keri," Kimberly says into my back.

I turn around and give her a proper hug. "Kimberly, I'm so glad to see you."

I don't have to ask her why she stayed behind. The cuts on her arms are only the tip of the iceberg. She would never let anyone see her less than fully clothed in pants and sleeves, which is hard to do in this Florida heat.

Kimberly is the one I feel most connected to here. I was exactly like her as a kid, except instead of cutting, I used shoplifting to numb my pain. She, too, lost her parents, and after being shuffled from foster home to foster home, ended up here. Some of the other counselors have trouble with her, but she relates to me. I hate the fact that I can't be here more often for her.

We spend the next few hours baking cookies and brownies for the rest of the twelve residents. Then, exhausted, I decide to head home, but not before Kimberly catches me on my way out.

She gives me her shy twelve-year-old smile and hands me something. "This is for you. I made it. It's for when your hair falls out."

I examine the ... *hat?* I'm not really sure what to call it. It resembles one of those hats hunters wear with the floppy sides that cover your ears. I think she meant for it to look like hair. It's brown and green and yellow. And completely hideous.

"Kimberly, I love it!" My throat tightens and tears start to fill my eyes. "This is the most special gift I've ever been given. Thank you."

"I know it sucks and you don't have to wear it if you—"

"Are you kidding?" I interrupt, as I put it on my head. "You better be prepared to make some more, because once I show up at the clinic wearing this, you'll have to take orders."

She smiles proudly as I give her a hug and head out the front door.

~ ~ ~

Walking up the sidewalk towards the clinic for my third cycle of chemo, I take a mental inventory of how I felt this weekend. A little worse than the week before, that's to be expected. They told me I might feel weaker the further into chemo I get. But after the first horrible night of my treatment, and then a few days to recover, I felt relatively good and was able to complete my three weekend shifts.

I round the corner of the building and run smack into a wall. Well, it felt like a wall, but it's a person. And now I've got Starbucks all over my pants.

"Son of a bitch! Can't you watch where you're walking? My latte is all over me and now I'm going to be late and . . ."

I stop talking when I look up into the alluring green eyes of Jace, who has a horrified look on his face. His eyes are wide, and he looks like he wants to say something.

"What?" I bite at him.

He reaches into his jacket and pulls out a piece of paper and a pen.

*Oh, God.* I forgot he can't talk. Now I feel like a total bitch.

He scribbles something and then tears out the page and hands it to me.

> I'm sorry, Carrie, is it? I wasn't looking where I was going. If you give me your number, I can apologize properly via text. Because now we're running late.

I raise my eyebrows at him. "You're kidding, right? Do you get a lot of girls to give you their numbers by playing that card?"

He laughs silently then scribbles some more.

> Not like that. Have girlfriend. Really just want to apologize.

"Well, you have. Twice," I say, before turning to walk into the clinic.

After taking my usual seat, I pull out my laptop and start studying for my Contemporary Social Theory class. It's one of the three classes I'm taking this semester to try and finish my Sociology degree. I really hope I don't have to drop my classes and re-take them next year. I'm so close to finishing.

The main doors open thirty minutes into therapy. We all stop what we're doing to look and see who's coming in at this odd time.

When I see who it is, I look over at Jace, who just shrugs and smiles shyly.

Jace hands a few slips of paper to the guy in the Starbuck's apron carrying a tray of a dozen coffees. The guy looks around and stops when his eyes land on me. Then he proceeds to walk over and stand in front of me.

"He didn't say what kind of latte you wanted, so I have several to choose from."

I stretch my neck around the coffee guy to look at Jace, who is wearing a very large smile that is producing an adorable dimple in his left cheek.

Then I peruse the descriptions on the cups until I find the one I want. After I take the cup, the delivery guy hands me a piece of paper that simply says - *Again, sorry* - followed by a phone number.

I close my laptop and enjoy watching everyone else, including the nurses, pick a cup and savor their unexpected mid-morning treat, courtesy of Jace. Well, courtesy of Jace running into me and spilling coffee all over my pants. The pants that are not my usual comfy chemo attire. But for some reason, this morning, I was compelled to put on my favorite pair of worn jeans, the ones that make my butt look fabulous. I'm not sure why, because all I do here is sit on my butt for several hours, leaving no chance for anyone to admire it.

I pull out my phone and type the number scribbled on the slip of paper into my contacts. Then I type out a message.

**Me: Apology accepted. Keri.**

I know the instant he has read it. His eyes light up and a grin slowly creeps up his face. Wow, he is truly a sight to look at. For one brief second I'm sad that he has a girlfriend. Okay, maybe more than a brief second if I'm being honest.

> **Jace: Thank God. I'd like to pay to launder your jeans. It would be a shame to have those go to waste, Keri with a K.**

Oh! He did notice. Score one for Keri. With a K.

> **Me: Don't worry about these old things, they've had worse things than coffee spilled on them. But thanks for the offer.**

> **Jace: You're welcome. So, what's so interesting on your laptop?**

A little twinge races through me knowing he wants to keep talking after the whole apology thing.

> **Me: Stuff that's the opposite of interesting. Contemporary Social Theory. But it's a means to an end.**

> **Jace: You go to school? What's your major? No, let me guess …**

He stares at me for what seems like forever, those green eyes burning into mine as he cocks his head from side to side in contemplation.

**Jace: I've got it. Women's Studies. You want to champion the equal pay issue all the way to the top. Wait, you're not a lesbian, are you?**

He gets an eye roll from me for that comment.

**Me: Not a lesbian, but that shouldn't matter to you, mister 'have a girlfriend but want your phone number anyway.'**

I shake my head as I press send.

**Jace: To apologize! Geez! Yes, I have a girlfriend. But I thought since we are the only people here under forty years old, we could pass the time together.**

**Me: Melanie is under 40, but not by much. Okay, we can pass the time, but let's get the obvious out of the way, shall we?**

**Jace: Right. Stage 2. Throat. You?**

**Me: Also stage 2. Breast.**

I have to keep from reaching up to cup them. It seems like every time I talk about my boobs, I'm compelled to make sure they are still there. But somehow, I don't think feeling myself up right now would be the appropriate thing to do, especially not with him watching me.

I quickly pull open the lid to my laptop. I have to know what the numbers are. I Google throat cancer.

**Jace: You're Googling my cancer, aren't you?**

A blush sweeps up my face and I wrinkle my nose.

**Jace: That's adorable—don't do it anymore.**

Uh … okay. I go to ask him why not, but he beats me with a new text.

**Jace: What do you want to know about it?**

**Me: Well, I'm sort of obsessed with numbers.**

He nods his head in understanding.

**Jace: 80**

Oh, no. That's not nearly as good as my 93. My face falls. On the other hand, most people in this room have a much lower five-year survival rate than that.

**Jace: What else?**

I wish he'd just come out and tell me about his bandage. I mean it's so obvious, but I hate to be petty and ask about it, as I'm sure everyone else does.

He must see me eyeing his bandage because he types out a text.

**Jace: I had surgery a few weeks before starting here. It doesn't really hurt that much anymore,**

**but I won't know the full effects of the surgery for months.**

**Me: Full effects? You mean if they got clean margins?**

**Jace: No, they are fairly sure they got clean margins. I meant I won't know if I will be able to speak again.**

*Oh my God.* Suddenly, I feel a fool for mourning breasts that I still have. Breasts that could be replaced with plastic surgery. There is no replacement for losing your voice. I'm at a loss. I don't know what to say to him. I simply start typing.

**Me: Who needs a voice when you're as good looking as you are?**

I hit send before truly realizing what I said. I'm such an idiot. He's going to think I'm shallow and that I like him or something. I can't believe I just trivialized him not being able to speak. He's going to hate me. But when I look over at him, he's looking right at me with a smirk on his face. He starts to type out a text, never breaking eye contact.

**Jace: Keri, that is the best response I've ever gotten. Most people tell me how sorry they are and that I should learn sign language and crap like that. But not you, you are different. And might I return the compliment and say that while I think your breasts are quite attractive.**

**Not that I'm looking or anything. But you would still be smokin' hot without them.**

*Wow! I mean ... Wow!*

I don't respond. I can't respond. I realize Tanner has told me the very same thing. But he's required to, he is my best friend. He's supposed to lie and say that no, this dress does not make my butt look huge, and stuff like that. But I've never heard it from another man. Somehow it matters more coming from Jace, a virtual stranger. Yet I feel this instant bond with him.

**Jace: So, you think I'm good looking, huh?**

I don't answer. I just close my eyes and shake my head at my temerity.

**Jace: Don't worry, Keri. Like I said, I've got this great girlfriend ...**

And with that, he goes on and on about his girlfriend, Morgan, and how they've been together for years. Their families are close, and they practically grew up together.

The way he talks about her makes me admire him. He's proud of her. And by the end of our session, I truly believe he does simply want to pass the time with me. He's obviously fiercely loyal to Morgan.

I tell him about Tanner, since *he* is the most important person in *my* life. I'm not sure Jace believes he's merely a roommate. But there really is no point in bringing up Tanner's sexual orientation, so I just roll with it.

I look at the clock and see we're almost out of time. I'm surprised the time passed so quickly, and I'm glad we will have each other to stay occupied every Monday morning.

**Me: Did you have any reaction to your first cycle?**

I sit tight and await his response. People have a varied spectrum of reactions to chemotherapy. Not everyone gets sick like I do. I hope he didn't.

**Jace: Yes.**

I let out the breath I was holding and silently curse cancer for the millionth time.

**Me: That bad? The anti-nausea pills don't work for you either, huh?**

**Jace: Let's just say that while I was lying prone on my bathroom floor, I was wondering if you were doing the same thing.**

I flash back to last Monday night and wonder briefly if we were thinking of each other at the exact same moment.

# Chapter Three

I haven't heard from Jace all week. He hasn't texted me. Not that I expected him to. We were just passing the time during treatment, nothing more. But I have thought about him. A lot. Especially as I was enduring my weekly Monday night reaction to the chemo. And when I went to bed, I dreamed about a beautiful green-eyed man who couldn't speak to me with words, but somehow, I knew exactly what he was saying.

Work has gotten a bit more difficult, but I'm pushing through. Tanner insisted we work the same shifts so he could pick up any slack. Tonight, being Sunday, is a relatively slow night and Tanner brought a stool around behind the bar so I can sit down when I need to.

I sit and tell him, once again, all about my 'talk' with Jace last week. I don't know why Tanner keeps asking me about it. It's like he's analyzing it and trying to figure out if Jace is really after me romantically. I assure him that he isn't, but Tanner is still is watching out for me like any brother would surely do for a sister.

"He was checking out your boobs and your ass, that we know for sure," he says.

"Yes, but in a purely platonic way, and in a way that made me feel better about myself. Not in a creepy stalkerish way. Plus, he hasn't texted me once all week."

"Still, I think I should come with you to check him out."

I roll my eyes at him. "Tanner, you cannot take a day off from your new temp job to babysit me at chemo."

He scrolls through my phone, reading the entire Jace thread again. "Okay, as long as you keep letting me read your texts. But, Keri, as soon as I think he crosses the line—"

"I know," I interrupt. "I give you full permission to come check him out, kick his ass, or whatever over-protective things you plan on doing. But I can tell you right now, you won't need to. He's in love with this Morgan girl." I sigh.

"Oh my God, you just sighed!" He laughs. "You are *so* into him."

I reach out to slap him playfully, but he moves away, sending me toppling off the barstool and nearly hitting the edge of the counter on my way to the floor.

Tanner reaches out and stops me from doing a complete face plant. We are both laughing, but when we see what he has in his hands, things aren't so funny anymore.

This just got real. There in his hands are hundreds of strands of long blonde hair. *My* hair. I didn't even feel it come out when he caught me.

Tanner looks at me like he doesn't know what to do. If I didn't know any better, and if it weren't so dark in here, I'd say his eyes were welling up with tears that he was fighting to keep from spilling over.

"Keri, I'm so sorry, I didn't mean to hurt you."

He looks devastated.

"It's not your fault. You didn't hurt me. I didn't even feel it. I guess now we know I'm one of the sixty-five percent. I never wanted to be a minority anyway," I say with a weak smile, taking a teasing stab at his sexual orientation.

"You know I love you, and if you want me to, I'll shave my head bald tonight. We can do it together."

I don't doubt for a second that he would do it for me.

~ ~ ~

**Jace: Why the long face, sunshine?**

**Me: Do you want the smart-ass answer or the real one?**

He lets out a deep breath and stares right into my eyes. Okay, real then.

**Me: My hair started falling out last night.**

**Jace: Crap.**

**Jace: Hey, look on the bright side. You'll be the hottest bald, boobless chick I've ever seen.**

I laugh at the absurdity. I also know that only a fellow cancer patient could ever be allowed to get away with saying such a thing. I'm suddenly aware that we share a bond no one wants to share.

**Me: So, you've seen a lot of them, huh?**

**Jace: Shit, yeah. There are bald, boobless chicks all over the place. But they all suck ass on the hot scale. You would win hands down.**

**Me: OMG ... I'd like to thank all the fans who got me to where I am today.**

He laughs silently.

**Jace: You rock, Keri. You know that, right?**

**Me: You too, Jace. And thanks.**

**Jace: Anytime.**

The nurse goes over to adjust the flow on his IV and stays to talk for a bit. Well, she talks, he writes.

I study him and realize what I didn't when he first walked in. He looks thinner than he did last week. He's still all gorgeous and ripped, but he doesn't quite fill out his shirt and his face isn't as full.

I frown. Freaking chemo.

**Jace: What are you worrying your pretty blue eyes about now?**

I look up and he's smiling at me.

**Me: How do you know I have blue eyes? You're twenty feet across the room. Are you stalking me?**

**Jace: When I dumped coffee on you, you know, while you were chewing me out. I couldn't help but notice your intriguing blue eyes.**

I smile at him, but I'm unsure how to respond to comments like that knowing he has a girlfriend. An incredible girlfriend who he adores and who he has been with since childhood. A girlfriend who he described to me in such detail I could probably draw a picture of her.

Oh, crap … A girlfriend who just walked through the main door of the therapy room.

Jace follows my eyes over to her and I see the smile spread across his face. Then I see him look over at me for just a fraction of a second. But in that miniscule period of time, I thought I saw something on his face. Guilt? Regret? Sadness?

For the entire hour Morgan sits with him, I want to hate her. She's beautiful with her pixie cut brown hair, curvy figure and adorable giggle. She has perfect boobs, I'd guess a C cup, with exactly the right amount of cleavage—not too sweet, not too slutty.

Jace texts her and she whispers back in his ear. Near the end of her visit, she glances over at me and I feel like I've been caught staring. Because I have. Been staring. The entire time. But she simply smiles sweetly at me.

It doesn't escape me that she never even gives a look to anyone else in the room. Maybe she's afraid of old people. Or bald people.

Then before she leaves, she comes over and gives me a hug.

I raise my eyebrows at Jace while she is hugging me, hoping to get some kind of telepathic explanation for this when she says, "Keri, thank you for being someone Jace can talk to throughout this ordeal. He speaks very highly of you, and I know you all need a lot of support through your ordeals."

Is she afraid of the words cancer or chemo? *Ordeal?* Is that what this is to her? It's a life-changing, blood-sucking disease that could have a disastrous outcome, but to her it's an *ordeal.* I concentrate on this one tiny little blunder, because in every other way, Morgan is perfect.

"Here." She hands me a piece of paper with a phone number on it. "Anything you need, just call me." She nods her head at Jace. "He won't ask for help. And he doesn't talk about his ordeal much because he knows it scares me. But if you think he is in trouble, real trouble, please call me."

"Okay," is all I can say, because I've just been hugged by the girl who is with the guy I dream about every night. The guy who has me thinking of coffee dates and movie nights and playing footsie under the table at dinner.

And although I've tried to hate her. I've tried for sixty whole minutes to hate her. I can't. I'm kind of in love with her a little after everything Jace told me about her. And seeing her here with him— the way she responds to him—it's like he's her entire world.

I make a vow right here, right now, not to dream about him again. Morgan is great. She seems to love him. And he lights up when she's around. So, yes, I make a vow not to think of his floppy hair and the way he has to push it out of his eyes after he looks down to send me a text. Not to think about those strong fingers that pound his tiny keyboard, and what they could do to my body. Not to fantasize about those lips that move absentmindedly when he types the words that he texts me.

I watch her kiss him on her way out the door, and I know for sure—I'm jealous. How can I fall for a guy after only a few hours of texting? It's not normal. Not when I have my pick of guys throwing themselves at me three nights a week. Guys who I only smile at to be nice. Guys who only mean to me the difference between buying hamburger or ramen noodles for dinner, based on the tips they give me.

> **Jace: I'm sorry about that. I didn't mean to ignore you when she was here. I think I was just so surprised to see her show up that I completely forgot everything else.**

He looks up at me with guilty eyes.

> **Me: No need to be sorry, she's your GF, and it was great that she showed up. Why wouldn't you expect her?**

> **Jace: I didn't expect her to come because although she's great, she's having a hard time with this. I'm not sure she has even said the word 'cancer' yet.**

> **Me: Oh, yes. 'Ordeal.'**

> **Jace: Exactly! What's up with that? It's not like she will get cancer if she says it.**

> **Me: OMG, you are so right. People don't want to say it, like they think it will offend us if they say**

'cancer.' Like it's taboo or something. I want to scream at them—CANCER, CANCER, CANCER!

Jace: You're amazing, Keri.

Me: No, I'm not. I'm just a girl with ... wait for it ... cancer.

Jace: So, cancer girl, you never did tell me, what's your major? I'm pretty sure it's NOT Women's Studies now that I know you a little better.

Me: Sociology, actually. I'm in my last semester.

Jace: Are you able to keep up with your studies? I mean, through your 'ordeal?'

We lock eyes and crack up, making everyone else wonder what has been going on under their noses the entire time.

Me: Yes, so far school is fine. But I've had to cut my hours back at work.

Jace: What do you do?

Me: I'm a bartender.

Jace: That must be hard. Being on your feet all night.

**Me: It is, but Tanner works alongside me and steps in when I need a break. He has been great. He even took on another job to help pay for this.**

He purses his lips, like something I said made him mad.

**Jace: That's nice of him. So, what bar do you work at?**

**Me: It's a club, actually. A pretty nice one. I was lucky to land a job there a couple of years ago. It's called The Triple J. Have you heard of it?**

His mouth opens when he reads my text. He looks up at me in utter disbelief.

**Jace: You're kidding.**

**Me: So, you've heard of it?**

**Jace: You could say that. Nice place.**

**Me: I think I would have remembered seeing you there.**

His face grows slowly into a big smile.

**Jace: Oh, really? You would have remembered me? And why might that be?**

I roll my eyes and shake my head at him.

**Me: I could never forget a guy with such a big …
HEAD. Dork.**

I look up to see him do his silent chuckle. I realize in this instant how much I would like to hear his laugh.

**Me: You never told me what *you* do.**

**Jace: No, I didn't. But I can show you.**

Show me? Does he want me to go with him somewhere? Surely that would cross some arbitrary line of whatever this is that we have. Would I go with him if he did?

He is not sending any more texts but is tapping around on his phone for a minute. Then he looks up at me at the same time as I get a new text.

**Jace: Take a look.**

There is an attachment to the text, so I open it. It's a picture of an abstract piece of artwork.

**Me: You're an artist?**

He nods.

I've never understood abstract art. It just seems like blobs and blurs to me. I guess I've always thought abstract art was a label put on art made by those people not talented enough to be true artists.

I hold my finger up, indicating I'll need minute. Then I forward the attachment to my email so I can pull it up on my much larger laptop screen.

I peek over the top of my laptop and see Jace impatiently waiting to see my reaction. I take a few minutes to look it over. I'm trying to see how all the blobs connect and relate to the other blobs, when it hits me.

Wow! This is good. It's a painting of a man and a woman. The man is down on his knees holding up his hand and looking up at the woman. On the surface it looks like he could be proposing to her. But when I study it further, the deeper meaning becomes clear to me.

I look up at Jace as he holds his hands out while shrugging his shoulders. He really wants to know what I think of it. I giggle to myself while I take much longer than necessary typing out my text.

**Me: I want to know what Morgan thought of it.**

**Jace: Why don't you tell me what you think she thought.**

I roll my eyes at him.

**Me: Okay. Well, if you ask me, Morgan seems like a glass-half-full kind of girl, so she probably expected to turn around and get a ring slipped on her finger.**

He smiles and nods his head.

**Jace: Yeah, that was kind of awkward. Is that what you think of it?**

I shake my head as I look back at the painting on my laptop. No, not a proposal. This is not a happy painting at all.

**Me: I think it's much darker than that. I know we all sometimes see what we want to when it comes to art, but to me, it looks like the woman is confused or unhappy and the man is hurting. He is trying to tell her something, but he can't find the words and he's frustrated.**

I look over at Jace, and it looks like the blood has drained from his face. His chin might as well be on his lap and he cocks his head to the side and studies me with drawn eyebrows.

**Jace: Who ARE you?**

**Me: ???**

**Jace: Nobody, and I mean NOBODY, has ever understood what I've meant to represent in my paintings.**

**Me: Oh, really? You mean I was right? Do I win a prize or something?**

I smile and wrinkle my nose at him. He laughs silently at me. Then he closes his eyes and shakes his head like he's mad at himself.

**Jace: Quick, give me a side effect.**

**Me: What?**

**Jace: Give me a side effect of chemo.**

I look up at him like he's crazy and whirl my finger in the air around my ear.

**Jace: Just do it already.**

**Me: I think the chemo has started to eat at your brain.**

**Jace: Keriiiiii . . .**

I laugh at the way he can beg via text message.

**Me: Okay, okay. It burns when I pee. Now before you go thinking I've got chlamydia, I did check with my doctor and he says it's perfectly normal and is just the chemicals exiting my body.**

**Jace: That's good. Give me another.**

What the heck? Why does he want me to list side effects of chemo, didn't he go over all of this with his doctor?

**Me: My fingers go numb sometimes.**

**Jace: Hmm, me too. Come on, Keri, you can do better than that.**

Okay, but he asked for it.

**Me: One word. Diarrhea. Enough said.**

**Jace: Yes. Thank you! That's the one.**

He smiles like I didn't just text the nastiest thing to a guy that I can think of.

# Chapter Four

Wednesday, when I get home from volunteering at The Freeway Station, I see that Tanner left my mail opened on the bar—he has no boundaries. One thing in particular has a Post-It note stuck onto it. I read Tanner's handwriting.

Keri - Use this, you deserve it.

Upon inspection, I see it's a certificate for a complimentary spa day at a swanky place over in Clearwater. I call them and find out my name was placed in a drawing a while back and I've won a free spa day to include a mani/pedi, massage and facial—the full treatment.

After making sure they aren't going to charge me any hidden fees, I decide to go for it. Who turns down a free spa day? The massage alone sounds heavenly. Oddly enough, they're able to squeeze me in later this week due to a last-minute cancellation.

~ ~ ~

On Friday, I head into work feeling totally relaxed, thanks to my unexpected spa day. As soon as I walk through the front doors, Tanner grabs my arm and says, "Mike wants to see you in his office."

Oh, no. This can't be good. I've been late a few times. And I take more breaks than any other bartender. But I know Tanner has been doing a great job covering for me, and I'm not aware of anyone else knowing about my indiscretions.

I raise my eyebrows in question, but Tanner gives nothing away, shrugging his shoulders and going back to stocking the beer fridge.

The door to our boss's office is open, so I peek my head in. "Hey, Mike."

I try to sound a lot perkier than I feel, knowing that I'm probably about to get called out for numerous offenses.

"How are you holding up, Keri?" he asks.

Management knows about my health issues. I couldn't exactly cut back my hours and ask for shorter shifts without good reason.

"Pretty good, I think." I try to give him my best *please-don't-fire-me-I-have-cancer* smile. "Why, has someone complained?"

He just stares at me.

"Oh God, Mike. Someone did, didn't they? I'm so sorry. I know I probably take more breaks than everyone else, and last weekend I forgot to put the trash out back and—"

"Keri," he interrupts. "Nobody has complained. It's quite the opposite. We never get anything but words of praise about your work. In fact, I'm giving you a raise."

"A raise?" It comes out like I'm horrified rather than appreciative. "I mean, thank you, that is unbelievably great, and it couldn't have come at a better time. But ... why?"

He laughs. "Because you're good, Keri. We like you. You and Tanner know how to work the crowd. And when Mr. Jarrett suggested I check, I found it had been a while since both of you got a raise."

*"Both* of us?" I question.

"Yes. Tanner got a raise as well." He stands up to dismiss me. "Now keep up the good work and let me know if you need anything."

I walk back out to see Tanner waiting for me, bar towel over his shoulder, huge smile on his face.

I snatch the towel from him and snap him with it. "You knew!" I shriek at him. "You knew and you let me sweat it out, you jerk."

He grabs the towel from me and throws it down before grabbing me into a hug. "God, Keri, can you believe it? What timing!"

He walks me over to the bar where there are two shots of tequila waiting for us in celebration.

~ ~ ~

When Jace walks into the clinic I have to keep from visibly dropping my jaw at his appearance. If I thought he had lost weight before last week's cycle, that was nothing compared to the way he looks now.

His clothes are hanging off him. His thick floppy hair has thinned out. He is pale, and his cheeks look slightly sunken. Yet when his eyes meet mine, his entire face lights up and I can't help my smile.

I thought I would dread chemotherapy. And at first, I did. Before my very first cycle, I had just about gone crazy with worry. Would I get sick? Would I lose my hair? The weekend before my second cycle was even worse, because then I knew what would happen about six hours after I left the clinic. It was all I could do to drag myself here that second time.

But now, as incredibly absurd and deranged as it sounds, I find myself looking forward to chemo. And the sickly, pale, sunken face of the man I'm staring at is the sole reason.

**Me: If I ever saw a man in desperate need of a bacon double cheeseburger, I'm looking right at him.**

A smile spreads up his face when he reads my text. He closes his eyes momentarily before responding.

**Jace: Thank you! God, I'm so sick of everyone telling me I look great. They all feed me lines of crap. Do they really think I can't see the way I look?**

**Me: I know, right? Even Tanner, as great as he is, dances around the fact that I have to remove the rodent from the shower drain every morning. Like I don't know I've just pulled another handful of my hair off the floor.**

**Jace: I don't know, I'd have to agree with Tanner on this one. You look great. I was really thinking I'd get here and have to rub your bald head for luck or something.**

I laugh at him. Then I wonder what it would be like to have his hands on my head. To have his hands anywhere on me. It almost makes me wish I had lost my hair simply so I could feel his touch.

**Me: So far, I'm counting my lucky stars that it only seems to be thinning out, not completely falling out. Oh, plus I had a wonderful weekend.**

He raises his eyebrows at me.

**Jace: Tell me.**

I can't say how many texts I have to send him to get the entire story out. It probably takes a dozen to tell him all about my unexpected spa day and then the incredible news about my raise. The entire time I'm going on and on about it, he simply sits back and reads my texts, each and every one of them, with a big smile on his face like he's so genuinely happy for my good fortune when he, himself, is sitting here watching his own body fall apart before his eyes.

**Me: I just can't believe the timing of it all. I feel like the luckiest girl alive.**

Then I realize what I've said and glance down at the IV in my arm.

**Me: Well, you know what I mean.**

I look up to see him shaking his head at me like he can't understand me.

**Me: What?**

**Jace: I can't believe you're gushing this much over a day at the spa, something most women do on a weekly basis.**

**Me: Jace, you don't understand. I've never won anything. Not one single thing. Ever. And then to get the raise on top of that. It was unbelievable.**

He's staring at me now, and I start to fidget and feel a little uncomfortable.

**Jace: You are so different from other women, Keri. I've never met anyone like you.**

I'm not sure how to respond to his text. I think I understand what he's saying. I've never met anyone like him either. He's so honest, so down to earth and real. He gets me. I get him. We share this bond that others might not be able to understand.

**Jace: I never expected this.**

**Me: Never expected what?**

He lets out a deep breath and sends me a text without breaking eye contact.

**Jace: You. I never expected you, Keri.**

I study his text, and it hits me with such force that my breath hitches. He didn't expect me. Can he really feel the same way about me as I do him? Does he think about me when he's not sitting directly across from me?

He has a girlfriend. A pretty incredible one from what I've seen. Why would he think I'm anyone special? But as I stare into his eyes, I know I will never meet another man like him.

**Me: Ditto.**

He reads my text and closes his eyes. Then his chin falls to his chest as he exhales a long breath.

**Jace: Side effects, Keri. Now.**

**Me: What is it with you and side effects, don't you ever talk to your oncologist?**

**Jace: Please?**

I make a mental note to have Dr. Olsen talk to Jace's doctor.

**Me: Metal. My mouth tastes like metal. It's why I chew gum when I'm here.**

I reach in my bag and hold up my box-warehouse-sized pack of Trident.

**Jace: More.**

**Me: Body aches. I feel like I've run a marathon even when all I do is lie around in bed.**

I look up at him and he doesn't look happy as he is twirling a finger in the air to get me to continue. The guy can't get enough.

**Me: Mouth sores. Nasty ones. Like I've contracted the worst case of herpes known to the human race ... all in my mouth.**

He smiles and lets out a breath.

**Jace: Great, thanks. Now, tell me why you stare out that window all the time.**

Maybe I was wrong about him. He could be bi-polar or schizophrenic or something. I'm getting whiplash with the extreme direction changes in our conversations. I decide to chalk up his erratic behavior to the side effects of chemo. Maybe I should list *that* the next time he asks me.

**Me: The marina. It was the reason I chose this clinic. It reminds me of my dad.**

**Jace: Really. Do you go boating with him often?**

I give him a weak smile and shake my head.

**Me: No, we never went on a boat like one of those. We were far too poor for that. He had a small worn out fishing boat from a scrap yard that he and I refurbished when I was little. When we were fixing it up, he would tell me stories about places he wanted to take my mom and me. I was so young. I didn't know better and**

**I thought the small three-seat boat was seaworthy and would get us to exotic ports around the globe. When I became a teenager, I lost interest and didn't want to spend time with my dad on a dinky little boat my friends laughed at. Anyway, he eventually sold the thing. And then he and my mom died.**

I don't want to look up at Jace. I know what I will see. I'll see what I used to see anytime I told anyone. Poor little orphan Keri. So now I don't tell them. That way they will keep their pity to themselves. People throw enough pity my way without knowing *that* about me.

**Jace: What's it like?**

I look up at him, confused.

**Jace: Being without parents, what's it like?**

In the eight years since I lost them, nobody has once asked me that. They say they are sorry, that it must suck being alone. They all want to know how it happened. They ask how I'm coping and if I need anything. But no one has ever asked what it's like. Not until right now.

What's it like? I think about the past eight years and try to put it into words for him.

**Me: It's like trying to breathe only there's no air. It's like walking on a treadmill, not being able to move forward. I still can't get used to living in a world where they don't exist. I wake up and**

**make it from morning until night and then I do it again the next day. But it works for me. And Tanner is there to help.**

He stares at me again like he's trying to figure me out.

Luckily, Stacy breaks his gaze by handing him the 'graduation' card he needs to sign for Ann, who is having her last cycle today. It's a tradition to send them off with a card. Even if they will come back again later. Even if they know they're not tumor-free. It's just our way of saying we'll miss them; or get the hell out of here and go enjoy life.

Stacy is busy explaining this to Jace when I get a new text.

**Melanie: You know we all think you and Jace are getting it on when you're not here, right?**

My mouth drops open and I crane my head around to look at her.

"Mel," I whisper loudly over Grace, who separates us. "It's not like that. He has a girlfriend. You saw her the other day."

Melanie and Grace both look at me with raised eyebrows like I'm feeding them a load of crap.

"Really, we just talk ... um, text. We don't see each other or even text outside of the clinic."

"Mmm hmm," Grace murmurs and I roll my eyes at them.

Looking at Grace's wig makes me remember the cap Kimberly gave me, so I reach in and pull it from my bag, explaining to the two of them how it came into my possession. They love the story and insist I wear it when I'm here. Well, I did promise Kimberly. So I place it on my head.

**Jace: Uh, Keri, something died on top of your head.**

I laugh.

**Me: Deal with it. It's staying.**

I tell him about The Freeway Station and how I met Tanner there. I tell him how Kimberly is a lot like I was. Okay, so I may have omitted a few details like my propensity towards shoplifting and Tanner's juvie record. By the time I'm finished, my fingers are cramping from all the texting I've done.

**Jace: You're unbelievable, you know that?**

**Jace: No, you don't know that. That's what makes you so great.**

I blush at his words. My fingers are too tired to text, so I just sit and look at him. He waves Stacy over and gives her a note. A few minutes later, Trina, the masseuse, shows up.

"I heard you could use a hand massage, Keri," she says.

"Oh. Okay, thank you."

Trina is busy sending me into a trance by the way she kneads the tension out of my fingers. I can't text while she has my hands. All I can do is mouth words to Jace. *Thank you.*

He nods at me.

I startle when excited voices wake me and I realize Trina's ministrations must have put me to sleep.

When I get my bearings and realize where I am again, I see a massive bouquet of flowers at the nurse's station. Ann is looking inside them for a card.

"There isn't one," she says. "Oh, how will I know who to thank? These are the most beautiful flowers I've ever seen in my entire life."

Ann goes on and on gushing over the flowers. I look over at Jace to see him watching her. He has a huge smile on his face as he looks at her dancing around with the bouquet that is so large it almost topples her over.

We lock eyes and I realize what has happened.

**Me: You? You sent them. But why? You barely know her.**

**Jace: Why? Look at her. Do you see the smile on her face?**

I nod at him.

I've never heard the man talk. I've never had so much as a drink with him, if you don't count the coffee he got me that first day. I don't know him outside the four walls of this clinic. But one thing is for sure, Jace has stolen my heart.

Another thing's for sure—I'm in for a world of heartache.

# Chapter Five

On Wednesday afternoon, I stop by The Freeway Station to see if I can help cook dinner. They don't have a cook on staff. That job is shared by all the counselors, who are mostly men, so they pretty much hate it.

The residents are old enough to help with cooking and cleaning duties. But preparing a meal for twelve residents plus two or three staff is not easy and requires close supervision.

Today, I get the pleasure of cooking with Tyler. He's a fourteen-year-old four-time runaway who has major issues with his stepfather. He's here for a few months while his family seeks counseling to find a way for them all to live together. I'm pretty sure there was some sexual abuse going on in his home, but he won't talk about it and social services hasn't come to that conclusion.

We cook meatloaf and mashed potatoes, a house favorite. And since my appetite is back, I decide to stay for dinner.

Unfortunately, Tyler and another teenage boy, Anthony, don't get along very well and tension is high at the dinner table. I try to mediate their argument, but nothing I say is getting through to them.

I decide to take a different tack.

*Thwap!*

The room falls silent and all eyes look over at me in surprise.

*Thwap!*

Tyler and Anthony glance at me and then at each other as lumps of mashed potatoes slide down their chests where I flung them, leaving a gooey path down to their laps.

They stare at each other contemplating what to do when Anthony says to Tyler, "Together?"

"Heck, yeah!" Tyler responds.

*Thwap! Thwap!* The potatoes are now running down *my* shirt, dripping onto the floor. This sets off a chain reaction of mashed potato missiles flying across the table along with shrieks of shock and laughter that fill the house and send Chaz running into the dining room to see what has transpired.

When I see Chaz about to barge in and try to take control of the situation, I lock eyes with him, shake my head and hope he understands not to interfere with the madness that has ensued. Luckily, he heeds my warning and, rolling his eyes at me, quickly turns to make his exit.

An hour later, after a massive deep clean of the dining room and several loads of laundry, I walk through the living room to see Tyler and Anthony playing Xbox together, laughing at the way they keep killing each other.

Chaz pulls me into his office. "Keri, I heard about what you did in there, it was pure genius getting those two to make friends. Nice work."

I smile as I walk back to the laundry room to help Kimberly fold some clothes. My smile fades when I see the sad look on her face.

"Are you okay?" I ask her.

"I'm fine," she says. Then she sighs. "It's just that there's this boy at school. Adam. He is so cute and funny, and he smells so good." She frowns at the ground.

"But?" I say.

"But he doesn't like me. I'm stupid and ugly." She looks down at the scars that peek out from the cuff of her sleeve. "And he plays football and has parents and he doesn't even know I exist. Plus, I'm only twelve and I'm not sure it's okay to like boys yet."

I put down the shirt I'm folding and look her in the eye. "Kimberly, you are not stupid. And we all have scars, some of them are just more visible than others. They don't define you. It's okay to like someone, sweetie. I'm sure he knows you exist. Maybe he is afraid, like you are. And you know, even if he doesn't like you, it's okay. You will like lots and lots of boys before you find the one you really want. At some point, we all like a boy who doesn't necessarily like us back."

"Not you, Keri. You are so pretty. I'm sure you never liked a boy who didn't like you back."

I smile at her sweetly. "Thank you, Kimberly. I think you're pretty, too. And, yes, it happens to me. In fact, there's a boy I like right now, but he already has a girlfriend, so he can only be my friend. But that's okay, because I would rather have him only as my friend than not have him at all."

She looks at me thoughtfully. "Well, I never thought about it like that. Maybe I should learn some stuff about football so I can have something to talk to him about."

I hug her. "That is a great idea. I'll try to find you a book about it."

"Thanks. Now, can you tell me about the boy you like?"

I proceed to tell her about the 'boy' who goes through chemo with me. Well, I tell her as much as a twelve-year-old should hear, anyway.

After she has extracted from me all the information I wish to divulge, she touches a lock of my still long and wavy, albeit thinning hair and says, "Maybe you should let him borrow the hat I made you since his hair is falling out more than yours."

I smile at the thought of Jace wearing Kimberly's creation. "Yes, maybe I should."

~ ~ ~

Saturday nights are crazy at the club. There's always a high-profile band playing. In fact, they say if you haven't played at The Triple J, you aren't worth listening to. At least as far as local bands go.

Tonight, we have an all-girl band playing. Perhaps that's why we have an onslaught of men here and a lot of new faces I've never seen before. Two such men have been at the bar for a few hours. However, they seem a lot more interested in Tanner and me than in the band.

"So, Keri, how long have you been a bartender here?" one of the guys asks me, after picking up my name from other conversations I've had.

"About three years, I guess."

"And him?" He gestures to Tanner.

"Tanner got the job just before me. He's the one who recommended me. I had absolutely no bartending experience, but he taught me all about mixing drinks before my interview."

I try not to get too personal with patrons, but in my experience, the more they feel they know you, the better tips they leave. So, I play along.

The guys share a look. Then one says, "So, you're dating him?"

I laugh as I mix a drink for the waitress. It's only the five hundredth time we've gotten that question.

"No, not dating, but we do live together."

I like to let men know I have a protector of sorts, in case they think they can come back to my place, or God forbid, contemplate following me home.

"Oh, so you're available then?" the tall, buzz cut asks.

"No. Not dating and not available."

I walk away to fill another drink order.

Over the next few hours the two men ask us more questions about our job, our relationship, and life in general. We accommodate them as much as we feel comfortable, because we haven't missed the fact that they are tipping very well.

"Keri, Tanner, it was nice meeting you two. Hope to see you around more," says the one who I now know as Chris, as he reaches over to shake our hands. Then he puts a wad of bills into the tip bucket causing the two of us to go wide-eyed.

Tanner comes to the conclusion that the guys were from a competitor and they were sizing us up to see if they wanted to steal us away. I guess it makes sense with all the questions they were asking us. It wasn't like they were coming on to me or anything.

I'm just not sure either of us would entertain leaving The Triple J. Especially now that we recently got a raise. Not to mention they have been very accommodating of my health needs.

By the end of the night, I'm completely spent. Everything about my body hurts. I didn't get as many breaks as I needed. However, I still ride home with a huge smile on my face due to the enormous amount of tips we earned.

At home, the large tin can Tanner set on our kitchen counter the day I got my diagnosis, is filled almost to the top with cash. I don't miss the fact that he puts every dime he made in there, holding none back for himself.

# Chapter Six

I walk into the clinic a few minutes late. Jace is already here, but his back is to me because his chair faces the other direction. I see a ball cap covering what appears to be his bald head. I let out a sigh and close my eyes, trying to compose myself so I don't appear shocked when he looks at me.

"Hey."

I touch his arm as I come around his chair. I'm all too aware that my fingers are tingling from the sensation of being on his skin.

He looks up at me and I hope my smile doesn't look fake, but then again, how could it when I'm so genuinely glad to see him.

He gives me a small wave and then shrugs at me because he knows I'm seeing him for the first time without hair.

"Really?" I say, eyeing his Miami Dolphins ball cap. "You are aware that Tampa has its own professional football team, aren't you?"

I hear little bursts of air coming from his nose as he silently laughs at me. He looks up at me and gives me a big smile. I know he's thanking me for not commenting on the hair.

I'm probably staring at him too much, but it's rare that we get this close, so I take in as much of him as I can. He's pale. His clothes are baggy, and he is far too thin. I'd guess he has lost twenty pounds in the past month. Despite all that, he's gorgeous. Or maybe *because* of all that, he's gorgeous.

I walk over to my seat where Stacy meets me to do my pre-therapy vitals and blood draw.

"You really like him, don't you?" she whispers while she's working on me.

"What's not to like?" I whisper back. "But we're just friends."

"Right," she says with a wink as she finishes my blood draw.

"He's going to be okay, isn't he?" I look up at her with raised brows.

"Keri, he's young and strong. So are you. You both have the best chances at beating this. I'm confident everything will work out just fine."

She smiles sweetly at me and I wonder if she's still talking about our cancer.

**Me: Hey, Twiggy.**

**Jace: Only you would comment on my weight when I come in bald.**

**Me: You're bald? The only thing I see is that you're a traitor. Dolphins ... really?**

**Jace: I went to U of M so it kind of stuck with me. Went to a lot of pro games when I lived there.**

**Me: I guess I'll give you a pass. Just this once, but I may have to buy you a different hat.**

That reminds me of something. I reach into my bag.

**Me: Wait! I already have one. And Kimberly even said I should let you borrow it.**

He raises his eyebrows at me and smiles.

**Jace: Oh, she did, did she? And why did Kimberly know I was losing my hair? In fact, why does Kimberly know about me at all?**

Oh, crap. I'm so busted. Why did I have to open my big mouth? Now he knows I talk about him. And to a twelve-year-old, of all people.

**Me: Um, she was having boy trouble, so I tried to make her feel better.**

I re-read what I sent to him and sink into my seat. I'm just digging myself in deeper. I look up to see him smile. And darn it if that adorable dimple on his left cheek doesn't totally make me melt.

**Jace: Boy trouble? Kimberly was having boy trouble and MY name came up?**

My face must be so red right now that I'm surprised Stacy isn't running over here to take my vitals. I'm not even sure what I can say to recover from this.

**Jace: I'm just teasing you, Keri.**

He writes something on a piece of paper and gets Stacy's attention. Then she walks over to me and holds her hand out. "He wants the hat."

I look up at Jace in confusion.

**Jace: Give Stacy the hat so I can put it on. That way you can take a picture to show Kimberly you let me borrow it.**

I place the hat in Stacy's hand and watch in utter disbelief when he puts it on after she walks it over to him.

My first thought when he removes the ball cap is that I've never seen a more attractive bald man. I've never been into bald guys before, and I still question whether or not I would find any other bald man attractive, but he owns it. In fact, I don't even think he should be wearing anything on his head. He looks *that* good.

The next thing I think about is how absolutely ridiculous he looks with Kimberly's hat on his head. I've never met a guy who is so completely gorgeous, yet would allow his picture to be taken wearing, arguably, the most hideous hat ever made, making him look like a total geek. Just to make a twelve-year-old girl smile.

**Jace: Hello? Are you going to take the picture or aren't you?**

I snap out of my trance and take a picture of him with my phone. I look at the picture and I know immediately that this is going to be my favorite picture of any I have ever taken.

I fully expect him to remove the unsightly hat and give it back to me, but he keeps it on. And I can't help but giggle at his humility.

My heart is expanding with feelings for this man and I better do something quick to squash them.

**Me: How's Morgan dealing with everything?**

He shakes his head and looks at the floor before responding.

**Jace: She's having a hard time with it. I wanted her to shave my head so she could feel like she's a part of this with me, but she refused. But I don't think it's the hair—or lack of—that she's having the biggest problem with. It's the G-tube.**

They told me about feeding tubes before my chemo, the ones they put directly into your stomach that you pump liquid food into. Some people get so sick during therapy that they can't eat for months. However, I suspect his has more to do with his throat. He said it hurts a lot to eat so I guess he just hasn't been eating.

**Me: Oh. When did you get it?**

**Jace: Last week. I think it was inevitable really, and they told me I'd probably have to get one since it hurts like a mother to eat. But Morgan can't look at it. She can't even talk about it. Other than that, she's been good. She's had a lot**

**thrown at her with this. On the bright side, I've gained back five pounds this week.**

*She's* had a lot thrown at her? What about *Jace?*

**Jace: Enough about me, how was your week?**

**Me: It was pretty great, actually. I had a good day with the kids at The Freeway Station, and over the weekend, Tanner and I made a killing in tips. I just can't believe how things have started to work out for me. A few weeks ago, I thought all my credit cards were going to get maxed out from my medical bills. But now, I think I might be able to scrape by.**

**Jace: That's good news. I'm happy for you, Keri.**

**Jace: You know, I Googled your cancer, too. And there is one thing I've been wondering about. Do you have that cancer gene, Bracca or whatever?**

I'm about to text him back when I realize what he said. *He's been wondering about it.* He thinks about me. He Googled something for me. It's a small victory in my mind. And although it doesn't mean much, I like the fact that he wonders about me outside of these walls.

Then I think back to the visit with Dr. Olsen when he suggested genetic testing for the BRCA gene. I know he thought I had it since I'm so young. But given no woman in my family has ever had breast cancer that I'm aware of, the chances of me carrying the gene were small.

I feel my phone vibrate in my lap, so I look down at it.

**Jace: Um, Keri ... why are you touching your boobs?**

I look down in horror to see how I had absentmindedly cupped my breasts when I was thinking about the day I was told of my diagnosis. I must turn ten shades of red because my face is on fire. I refuse to look across the room at Jace.

**Jace: Hey, it's fine with me. In fact, I contemplated not telling you at all. But then I'd have to remove the IV and go take a cold shower. LOL.**

He winks at me when I look over at him. I'm beside myself with embarrassment and really wish I had something to throw across the room at him.

**Jace: So, Bracca gene?**

**Me: I'm so embarrassed. Sometimes that just happens when I think about losing my breasts. But, no I don't have the BRCA gene. Most people think I do since I'm only 24. Without it, there's only a five percent chance of getting breast cancer in women under the age of 40.**

**Jace: No need to be embarrassed. You and your numbers. Wow, you're only 24? I would have guessed you were older.**

**Me: Thanks, I guess. What about you, you never told me how old you are.**

**Jace: 27**

**Me: How is it that you ended up with throat cancer at such a young age?**

He looks at me like he's not sure he wants to have this conversation. But then he takes a breath and commits himself to it.

**Jace: Have you heard of HPV?**

**Me: I think so, but isn't that like an STD?**

**Jace: Yeah, kind of. Usually it's seen in women, and mostly it will simply go away on its own without any symptoms. But in rare instances it can cause cancer.**

**Me: Cancer in women? Then how did you get it in your throat?**

I look over at him. He is not texting me. He's just staring at me with raised eyebrows like he is waiting for something. Then it hits me. *Oh my God.* I get it. And for the umpteenth time today, I turn red.

**Me: Oh.**

He laughs silently as I try to look at anything in the room but him.

**Jace: You're adorable when you blush.**

I shake my head at him. Why does he keep saying things like that when he has a girlfriend? He's toying with my emotions. Or maybe I'm simply reading things into this that I shouldn't.

Tanner kids with other girls all the time, just like Jace jokes around with me. Maybe all guys are like that.

Does he even have a clue how I really feel about him? I hope not, because maybe then he would stop this—whatever this is. And even though I know it will hurt me in the end, I don't think I've ever wanted anything more than to keep this up.

**Jace: Do you want to see another one of my paintings?**

I snap my head up with wide eyes.

**Me: YES! Of course I do.**

A proud smile crosses his face and then he looks down at his phone and taps around until he finds what he wants to send me.

**Jace: This is the only other painting I've done since my diagnosis.**

When I get the text I, once again, forward it to my email so I can view it on my laptop. And, once again, Jace looks as impatient as a kid in a candy store.

I'm stunned by the abstract art he creates. The image is clearly a depiction of two people on a sea of blue surrounded by white blobs that could represent boats. My first instinct is that he painted this after my revelation about my dad and the marina. But I shake my head at my own bold assumption that he would possibly paint something that has anything to do with me. He has a girlfriend, I remind myself for the hundredth time.

**Jace: Well?**

**Me: I guess it could be two people swimming out in the ocean among some boats.**

**Jace: Could be. But is that what you really think it is?**

I study him for a moment, taking in his meaningful gaze. Then I scrutinize the painting some more. It finally dawns on me what it is. Or what I think it is. Or what my mind has decided it is. I abruptly look up at him.

**Jace: What, Keri? What do you think? Tell me.**

**Me: I think it's two people, lying prone on a cold, hard tiled floor, surrounded by gleaming white bathroom fixtures. Two people who are so exhausted from getting sick they can't move from the position they are in.**

He blows out the breath he was holding and nods his head. Oh, God, I was right. I look back at the picture and belatedly notice one of the 'blobs' has yellow hair. And then I notice the two people are holding hands.

**Me: Jace, it's wonderful! You are so talented.**

**Jace: I was inspired.**

We lock eyes for what seems like minutes. Nothing else exists in the world for me right now. In this moment, cancer does not control my life. I am free and my heart is bursting with unrequited feelings for the man sitting across the room from me.

He closes his eyes and types out a text.

**Jace: Side effects. Now, Keri.**

Way to ruin the perfect moment for me.

**Me: What is it with you and your side effects? Are you bi-polar?**

**Jace: Not bi-polar. Just feeling things I shouldn't. Things I can't.**

He stares at me some more and it hits me like a ton of bricks. I'm so stupid. Of course he knows the side effects of chemo. We all do. Why did I ever think he didn't? He has feelings for me. I'm elated and saddened at the same time. I'm not alone in this, yet I'm all by myself.

**Jace: I have a girlfriend, Keri.**

**Me: Yes.**

**Jace: I love Morgan.**

I take a deep breath. Of course he does. I'm fooling myself to think otherwise.

**Me: Yes.**

**Jace: But I feel this intense connection with you.**

**Me: Yes.**

All this time, when he's asked me for side effects, those are the times when his feelings for me have creeped up and he needs to have something to take his mind off me. Something terrible. Something gross. I don't want him to feel any guilt. So I play along.

**Me: Sometimes my pee is red for a few days after chemo. Oh, and my nails are brittle and flaky and they look like an old woman's. And my lips, they are so chapped I feel like I've been out in the sun for days without water. Yuck, I mean who would want to kiss that?**

I smile at him, but it's a weak smile. I know he suffers a lot of the same side effects. Despite that, I'm certain wild horses couldn't keep me from kissing his dry, chapped lips if given the chance.

**Jace: Thanks, Keri. You're a real friend.**

*Friend.* I look up at him and see him still wearing that frightful hat, and I think about what I told Kimberly just last week. I would rather have him as a friend than not at all.

**Me: Anytime. And you, too.**

# Chapter Seven

"He makes you spew out gross things about chemo so he can stop thinking about undressing you with his eyes?" Tanner asks, before finishing his beer and grabbing another.

We're having a Wednesday night movie marathon. It's one of his few nights off, so we rented some chick flicks, ordered Chinese food, and are sharing a six pack. Well, technically Tanner is having five and I'm having one since I'm not supposed to drink much.

"I wouldn't put it quite like that," I say, grabbing the last egg roll. "But he says he does it because he can't have feelings for me."

"Mmmm." He studies me for a second. "I read the texts, Keri. The guy wants you."

"Not really, Tanner. It's just that we share this thing. This horrible thing nobody else can relate to and it makes us feel closer than we would normally. But we have no connection outside of chemo." I sigh and wipe the beads of condensation from the side of my beer bottle. "I'm sure if we met on the street, he wouldn't even give me a second look."

"Keri, you really underestimate yourself, don't you? You are sweet and compassionate and you're super hot." He grabs my leg and gives it a squeeze. "And you know I'd totally *do* you again if I were straight, right?"

I lean over and kiss his cheek. "Thanks. I think."

I shake my head, remembering the one and only time Tanner and I hooked up, as I grab the empty food containers and walk into the kitchen.

I frown when I notice what's on the counter. It's another medical bill. They started rolling in last week when I got the bill for harvesting my eggs. That alone cost more than eight thousand dollars, plus my yearly storage fee.

Tanner insisted I do it even though it was expensive and might not even be necessary. He said it would be a shame to deprive the world of my 'hot genes.' Just another reason why I love him so much.

This bill is the first of many for my actual chemo. Not including the doctor visits and the extensive list of prescription drugs, which can cost even more than the chemo cycles. However, I'm completely surprised when I open it and find the amount due to be much less than I expected. This bill should cover four cycles, but I think they mistakenly charged me for only one. I show the invoice to Tanner.

"No, it covers all the dates of your first four. Look here." He points them out to me.

"But when I had my consultation, they said it would be much more than this."

"And your problem with this is?" He raises his brows at me.

"I just don't want them to discover their error after I've gone and spent the money on something else," I tell him.

"Then call them tomorrow. But if I were you, I wouldn't look a gift horse in the mouth." He throws the bill down on the counter. "Just sayin'."

"Tanner, we unexpectedly got raises. Then I won that spa day. We got off-the-charts tips last weekend and now this. It's not possible for one person to be so lucky." I shake my head at him.

His eyes open wide and then he furrows his brow. "Lucky? You think you're *lucky*, Keri?"

"Well, I—"

"What goes around comes around, sweetie," he says. "Look at how hard you work despite the fact you have cancer. The kids you help at Freeway? What you did for *me?* You are an incredible woman. This is pure karma and you deserve every good thing that happens to you."

I smile at my best friend as he leads me back out to the living room.

"I'm not sure what I did to deserve *you*, Tanner. But I'm so grateful you are in my life."

A tear slips out of the corner of my eye and trails down my cheek before he reaches out to wipe it.

"No. It's me who's grateful." He sits us down on the couch and pulls my legs into his lap. "Now quit crying and save the waterworks for our Tom Hanks/Meg Ryan marathon."

~ ~ ~

Monday morning has me feeling guilty about missing an entire shift at the club this weekend. I should have known better than to put in a day at The Freeway Station when I had a shift that night. It kills me that I can't do both.

Seven more cycles. Seven more weeks and if all goes well, I will start to get back to normal after that.

I'm running a few minutes late because I stopped by the club to see if I could take Shana's Wednesday shift since she was called in for my Friday one. She wouldn't hear of it, and I didn't try too hard to convince her. I know it would be a lot for me to work a full shift only two days after a treatment.

When I walk in, I'm surprised to see a woman sitting next to Jace. For a split second, jealousy courses through my veins and I want to stretch my leg out and kick her chair right out from under her. But Stacy is impatiently waiting for me across the room, so all I can do is nod and smile at Jace on my way by.

Stacy is doing my workup when she whispers in my ear, "It's his sister."

I let out the breath I didn't know I was holding in. I stare across the room at them while Stacy finishes up with me.

His sister is quietly talking to him and he is writing back to her. I look from one to the other and see that she has the same light-brown hair as he did, but the similarity ends there. She smiles, but her face is lacking the wonderful dimple that he has. And I can't be sure from this far away, but I think her eyes might be blue. Then I look at her tight sweater that enhances her large breasts.

She glances over to catch me staring, and I watch as a huge grin creeps up her flawless face.

As soon as Stacy is finished with me, Jace's sister walks across the room and pulls a chair up right next to mine.

She holds her hand out to me. "Keri, I'm Jace's sister, Julianne. But you can call me Jules. All my friends do."

She smiles brightly at me and I feel instantly at ease with her. "It's nice to meet you, Jules."

"I just had to come and meet the girl who has my big brother all in a tizzy," she says, not quite loud enough for Jace to hear.

My jaw drops and I turn my head towards her to look her straight in the eye.

"Oh, come on," she says. "You have to know he is totally enamored with you."

I bask in silent victory for about two seconds before I remember a tiny little detail. And it's called Morgan.

"Uh ... it's not like that. We simply pass the time here," I say, completely confused. "You do know about Morgan, don't you?"

"Of course, silly. And I love her. And I know Jace loves her. I'm just not sure he's *in love* with her. Maybe he thinks he is, but I see them together. They're more like best friends, siblings even." She shakes her head. "Ewww. I just had the worst visual." She giggles.

"But I've seen them together," I whisper. "She worships him. I know she's having a hard time with this, but he's always telling me how great she is."

My phone vibrates.

**Jace: Don't believe anything she says. Especially if she tells you how geeky and awkward I was as a teenager. Unless she's telling you I'm an awesome brother, in which case, totally true.**

I smile at him after reading his text. I study him and notice how his cheeks have filled out a little and he's not as pale. He is obviously putting on weight thanks to his new feeding tube. And he still dons that traitorous Dolphins ball cap.

**Me: Wouldn't you like to know what she's telling me? Your deepest, darkest secrets**

**maybe? Oh, and, Porky, lose the ball cap. You**
**don't need it.**

I put the phone down even though it almost immediately vibrates. Not only because I don't want to be rude to Jules, but I find myself in a position to learn things about Jace, so I decide not to waste precious moments.

I look up at Jules, who, like Tanner, has no boundaries and was apparently reading our texts. I raise my eyebrows at her.

She doesn't even blush or try to hide the fact that she was eavesdropping.

"You guys are so cute with your banter." She scoots her chair back over and holds up her hand to stop me from calling her out on it. "If we are going to be friends, Keri, you'll have to get used to the fact that I'll be all up in your business. Especially if you get with my brother. It's just how I am."

"First off, you would get along very well with my roommate. Secondly, I'm not going to be 'getting with' Jace. I told you, it's not like that," I whisper.

She cocks her head to the side and narrows her eyes at me. "So, you're saying you don't find my brother attractive?"

"It's not that—"

"So, you *do* find him attractive," she interrupts.

I blow out an exasperated breath. "Of course I do. I'm not blind. Even bald, thin and pale, he's gorgeous. And he's an artist. I mean, how sexy is that? But none of that matters. We aren't going to get together. He said himself that he can't have feelings for me."

She stares at me and I refuse to break eye contact. She needs to know I'm serious about this.

"Just like I thought." She nods her head. "You are crushing big time on my brother. It's okay," —she pops a stick of gum into her mouth— "most girls are. I get it. He's all 'dreamy'," she air quotes and then rolls her eyes. "And just because he says he *can't* have feelings for you doesn't mean he *doesn't* have feelings for you."

"But Morgan—"

"Will eventually realize that Jace is not the guy for her," she interrupts, not at all saying what I was thinking. "Listen, Keri, our families have been joined at the hip since before any of us were born. We all grew up together. Morgan is like a sister to me. It's practically an arranged marriage."

My eyes go wide.

She sees my reaction and puts her hand on my arm, laughing. "No, no, not like that. They aren't engaged or anything. What I mean is that our parents have pushed them together. They've kind of brainwashed them into believing they are perfect for each other. But if you could see them together, like on a daily basis, you would notice how they don't act like a couple hopelessly in love. My brother is twenty-seven years old and they've been together since college. So why aren't they engaged yet? I think deep down, Jace knows she's not the girl for him."

She looks down at her phone then says to Jace across the room, "Hold your horses, Number Three, I'm making a new friend over here."

"Number Three?" I question.

"He's named after my dad and grandfather. He's the third Jason. So, yeah, I started calling him that when I was little, you know, to piss him off, and it kind of stuck. He hasn't told you about our family?"

"Uh, no. He mostly just asks about me, I guess."

She turns her head toward Jace and gives him a mean stare with a shake of her head. Then she smiles at me and says, "Well, I like you even more now, Keri."

"Huh … why?" I ask.

Why would she like me more knowing Jace and I mainly talk about me?

"Never mind. He must have his reasons," she mumbles.

Then I remember one thing he does share with me. "Oh, but we do talk about his art. He's extremely talented. I'm not very cultured, and I've never particularly enjoyed art, especially abstract art, because I don't really understand it. But his paintings are incredible."

She nods, looking very proud of her brother. "Yeah. He told me you get it."

"I get it?"

"His art. He told me you get it. That you were dead-on in your interpretations of his paintings. That no one else has ever seen the deeper meaning to his art. That you two share some kind of cosmic connection."

Cosmic connection? I wonder about this for a minute while I sign the 'graduation' cards for Marjorie and Peggy that Stacy is circulating. Jace feels it, too? Then I frown. Because I know this all stems from the fact that we basically feel alone in this world. We both have cancer at a young age and nobody else can relate to us. I'm not naïve. I know that when relationships start under intense circumstances, they generally don't work out in the long run. Maybe if we both go into remission, we wouldn't have anything in common anymore. Nothing to build on.

I blow out a deep breath and curse myself for what I'm thinking. Because, for the first time, the *only* time, I—just for a split second—was glad I got cancer because it allowed me to meet Jace.

"So . . ." Jules pulls me back from my thoughts. "You were saying about this roommate of yours?"

I tell her about Tanner. Then we talk about school. By the time she's ready to say goodbye to Jace, we've become fast friends. She hugs me, gives me her number, and tells me that when I feel up to it, we should go out. She promised to stop by the club sometime.

I think it would be nice to have a female friend. I mean, I sometimes used to hang out with the bartenders and waitresses from the club on my nights off, but most of the time it's just Tanner and me. I vow to call her when I'm feeling better.

I look down at my phone and see the barrage of texts that came from Jace when I was ignoring him.

> **Jace: Porky?**

> **Jace: Uh, Keri, what did Jules just say to you? Your eyes went all wide.**

> **Jace: Believe nothing.**

> **Jace: Do you know how hard it is to sit here and watch you two when I know you must be talking about me? I mean, what could be so interesting?**

> **Jace: Porky?**

I laugh as I read them. It must have been killing him watching us together.

> **Me: Yes, Porky. I mean, go on a diet already. Geez, you must have put on ten pounds last week.**

**Jace: Eight, actually. And thanks for noticing. Not many other people did.**

I wonder if he's talking about Morgan. Does she even look at him? How can anyone not see how incredibly gorgeous he is?

I wonder about what Jules said to me. Maybe they do love each other but aren't really in love. But I'm not a fool, I know a lot of people spend their lives together simply because they think they should. Not every relationship is like a Tom Hanks/Meg Ryan movie. People don't always find their way to the perfect partner.

People get comfortable in a relationship and just stay there. I know, I saw it firsthand. My parents loved each other. I know they did. And they always got along, but I'm not sure they were really in love. They didn't hold hands or whisper things to each other when they thought I wasn't looking. They were high school sweethearts who got married. Because they thought they should. Because it was the next logical step.

Someone walks through the main doors, pulling me from my thoughts. I look up to see a delivery person. She has two baskets full of what looks like pampering products. She talks to Stacy, who directs her over to Marjorie and Peggy. They get wide eyed when the baskets are placed in their laps. They look at each other and then tear into the cards on top of the baskets.

"Oh, my goodness!" Peggy squeals. "It's a gift certificate to The J Spot. It's for a full day of pampering." She turns the card over and looks at the basket. "There's no name on it. What about yours, Marjorie?"

Everyone looks at Marjorie.

Everyone but me, that is. *The J Spot*. It's the same swanky spa over in Clearwater where I 'won' my spa day.

I look at Jace to see how much he's enjoying watching the two women revel in delight. The smile on his face is one of joy. It's so rare to see someone take pleasure in the happiness of virtual strangers. Is that why he sent it to me? But, how did he get my address? It must have been Stacy.

**Me: It was you. You sent me the gift certificate to the spa. But, why?**

**Jace: I have no idea what you're talking about, Keri.**

I look up at him and he smiles at me and then shrugs. I look into his eyes. Even from across the room, I can see the brilliant green of his irises. His text may have said he didn't send it, but his eyes—they are telling me something completely different.

~ ~ ~

Before work on Saturday, Tanner and I run some errands. We stop by The Freeway Station to drop off some baked goods I made for the kids. Tanner catches up with some of the residents there.

He used to come by more often, but since he has taken on so much more work to help pay my medical bills, he rarely gets to volunteer. I know he's having a hard time with it. I am, too. I know volunteering helps keep him on the straight and narrow.

Sometimes I feel he could slip back into his old ways, but then he'll work a shift at Freeway and realize how far he's come since we were there, and it's enough to keep him lawful.

I know how easy it would be for him to fall off the wagon and make some quick money. Especially since he knows I could use it.

But so far, he's been keeping to his renewed set of moral standards, even though he's breaking his back to help me out. I pray he will continue on this path. It would kill me to know I was the one who sent him back to the dark places he came from. Especially because he's doing all this to pay me back for helping him out years ago.

After The Freeway Station, we go to the salon to get Tanner a haircut. I always offer to do it for him, but quite frankly, I think he has a crush on Kevin, the stylist who cuts his hair. So he shells out forty bucks—that he can't afford—every month just to have Kevin run his hands through his hair. I roll my eyes as I watch Tanner getting his cut with a huge smile on his face.

I'm sitting in the vacant stylist chair between Tanner and a girl getting her hair done for a school dance. She's adorable. She must be about sixteen. She's telling her hairdresser all the details about her night ahead. I think about how carefree her life is. I never went to any school dances at her age. I was the freak who bounced between foster homes until I landed at The Freeway Station.

Suddenly, my stomach rolls. I become overwhelmed by the smell of the electrical element of the hair dryer and the stench of the flat iron as it heats up only a few feet from where I'm sitting. I jump out of my seat and run to the door.

"Keri!"

Tanner runs out after me just in time to see me hurl in the bushes lining the sidewalk in front of the hair salon. He rubs my back as I wretch until there is nothing left in my stomach.

A woman comes out of the salon and offers him a bottle of water and some napkins to give to me. He thanks her, and when I can stand up straight again, he helps me organize my disheveled appearance.

"I'm sorry, Tan. It was the smell . . ."

"God, Keri, you don't have to be sorry. It's okay. I get it. I was pretty much done anyway. I'll go pay Kevin and we can get out of here."

I nod, mortified that I just tossed my cookies in front of a dozen strangers who are now staring at me from inside the large front windows of the salon. Just one more thing to make people feel sorry for me.

I kick the large cement column next to the bushes.

Samantha Christy

# Chapter Eight

I'm already hooked up with poison dripping into my veins when Jace walks through the door. I immediately notice he's put on a few more pounds. I also notice that he has decided to go au naturel and not cover up his bald head. He smiles at me as he pretends to spit into his hand and rub it on his head. He is obviously in a good mood today.

My heart skips a few beats, and I realize just how much I was looking forward to seeing him. Chemo has become the highlight of my week. I wonder how many people can say that. It's crazy. Especially knowing what I will feel like tonight. But even the thought of throwing up so much that it feels like someone has reached an arm down my throat and pulled my stomach out through my esophagus, doesn't keep me from walking on air all weekend in anticipation of Monday morning.

**Jace: Why the big smile? That happy to see me?**

Oh, crap. He caught me daydreaming. About him.

**Jace: Kidding. But I'm happy to see you. Do you think it's strange that I actually look forward to chemo?**

Did he really just say that? I re-read the text. I swear the man can read my thoughts sometimes.

**Me: Not so much.**

I stare at him and he nods in understanding. Then we both turn to see strangers walking through the main doors. Stacy greets them, shuffles around some files, and turns to introduce them to us.

"This is Eileen, who is joining us for sixteen cycles. And this is Jenny, who will be here for twelve."

They both look to be in their fifties. My eyes immediately go to their breasts as everyone says their hellos.

Jenny has an ample chest, highlighted by the pretty blouse she's wearing. But it looks like Eileen might have had a double mastectomy. Either that or her boobs are really, really small. I close my eyes and pray for the latter.

Then I suddenly realize I'm putting on another public display of self-affection. I quickly look around, relieved nobody caught me cupping my breasts like an internet porn star. Least of all Jace, who hands a written note over to Steven as they hold a conversation.

Steven is old enough to be Jace's dad. That gets me wondering about his parents. He never talks about them. They haven't ever been here to support him. If I had a child, you can bet that no matter how old they were, I'd be here. Just like Melanie's mom comes to almost every visit. Just like John's dad pops in now and then, and my guess is that his dad has got to be pushing ninety years old. Yet he still shows up.

When I see Jace and Steven have finished talking, I send him a text.

> **Me: You never talk about your parents. Is it because mine are dead and you don't want to make me feel bad? Because it's okay to tell me about them.**
>
> **Jace: No, that isn't why. There isn't much to say. I love them, but I'm not much like them. Sometimes it feels like Jules and I are adopted.**
>
> **Me: What do you mean you aren't like them?**
>
> **Jace: I guess I would say they are ostentatious. And that might be putting it mildly. Don't get me wrong, I love them. And I know they love me, in their own narcissistic way. Let's just say my mom didn't come today because she had an important meeting with her gardening club. Not that she gardens. In fact, I've never seen her even so much as chip a nail. But she does it to be social. And my dad, he's off for a long golfing weekend with his so-called friends who are really just fellow narcissists.**
>
> **Me: You are definitely adopted.**

He laughs at my quick response while stretching out his fingers from his fast typing. I can't imagine Jace being raised by such people.

He is the opposite of a narcissist. In fact, I've never seen someone do so many anonymous deeds simply to make others happy. I have a hard time believing they are as bad as he portrays them. They must have done something right to raise such a selfless man.

I'm about to ask him what his parents do for a living when the main doors open and in walks Morgan, carrying a couple of drinks from Starbucks.

My heart sinks. And then it practically implodes when I see her give him a kiss. He works his hand around her neck and holds her there for a beat. Then he kisses her on the tip of her nose when they part. It's such a sweet gesture, and if I weren't teeming with jealousy right now, I might get all gooey inside.

She whispers something to him, and he closes his eyes briefly before he reaches around and pulls a ball cap out of his back pocket and puts it on his head. He glances my way after he puts on the cap, and he gives me a small shrug.

Morgan is all smiles when she walks over to me and hands me a tall Starbuck's latte.

"Jace said you're a big fan, so I thought I would bring you one to thank you for being such a good friend to him. Plus, I still think he feels guilty about spilling one all over you." She smiles sweetly back at him and he locks eyes with her.

I, on the other hand, am not all peaches and freaking cream inside. *Jace talks to her about me?* I'm so incredibly bummed that he shared the whole latte experience with her. I can't believe I thought—even for a second—that what we had here was anything more than a simple friendship. A mild flirtation even.

I can't believe my eyes when Morgan pulls a chair up next to me.

"Do you mind if I sit with you for a few minutes while I drink mine? I think the smell makes Jace nauseous."

Ahhh … I wondered why he didn't have one of the drinks he had delivered that day.

"Did Jace tell you what he did for my birthday? He is so sweet," she practically sings out.

"Oh, you had a birthday recently? Happy Birthday!" I try to sound genuine knowing I'm probably about to turn green with envy when she tells me what he did. "No, he didn't get a chance to tell me yet. What did he do?"

She giggles. "Oh my God, when I walked out to my car after work on Friday, about a million balloons spilled out when I opened the door. They were all filled with helium, so they came out and went into the air in a trail of pink floating up into the sky." She sighs at the memory.

"There was only one balloon left when I got into the car. It was taped to the steering wheel with 'pop me' written on it. So I popped it and there was a note inside telling me where to meet him for dinner."

She smiles over at Jace and I swear I see him blush, knowing that she's talking loud enough for the entire room to hear. He looks helpless and he can hardly object to her story—being that he's tied down to his IV and can't speak.

I look around to see the entire room listening to her. Melanie and Grace are both looking at me with heavy eyes.

"Wow, that sounds really nice." I try to sound enthusiastic.

I think back to the only two relationships I've ever had. If you can even call them that. James was the guy I stayed with after I left Freeway. I thought he merely wanted to take care of me at first. He was so nice, giving me little gifts all the time. But then I realized the pattern. He would give me a gift and then he would expect something in return. I played along for a few months because he made me feel special. The first time I didn't give him what *he* wanted, he kicked me out.

Connor, on the other hand, didn't want anything from me … at first. He was sweet and funny and was the perfect guy for me. I even thought he might put a ring on my finger. That is until I helped Tanner out of his predicament. Then it became clear, especially after I found the hidden articles and newspaper clippings. All Connor ever wanted was money.

After that, at only nineteen, I swore off men. That's when Tanner and I moved in together. He was all I needed. At least that's what I've told myself for the last five years.

Now—now I want so much more. I want someone to fill my car full of balloons just to see the smile on my face. But the thing is, the *more* I want can only come from one person. The very person I can't have.

"It was spectacular. I met him at Bern's Steakhouse," Morgan says, pulling me from bad memories of past boyfriends.

I wrinkle my nose. I know how expensive that place is.

"The whole night was incredible. And you know Jace, he isn't normally that extravagant, so it was a total surprise."

She goes on and on to describe their entire evening in detail, completely unaware that I am slowly dying inside every time she tells me about something romantic he did or said.

I look over at Jace. He looks sad. Guilty even. Not that he has anything to feel bad about. I chastise myself for being stupid enough to fall for a guy who is obviously in love with his girlfriend. What he did for her was over-the-top romantic.

I think back to last week when I had my talk with Jules. She's wrong. He *is* in love with Morgan. Men don't do what he did for women they don't love.

Morgan finishes her coffee and gets up to walk across the room. But she gets pushed out of the way by Stacy, who is making a beeline to Steven, who fell off his chair and is lying lifeless on the floor. Drops of blood drip down where the IV ripped out of his arm.

"Oh my God!" Morgan cries out.

"Call an ambulance!" Stacy shouts over her shoulder to the nurse's station.

We all sit in distress, watching her do her best to revive him. There is nothing we can do, we are literally held captive by our IV lines, helpless in a situation that cries for help.

Camille, the older nurse who usually just sits and handles paperwork, rushes over with a defibrillator that they quickly hook up to Steven's chest.

I hear an ambulance siren in the distance. Jace and I lock eyes. Both of us look defeated. We are powerless bystanders, witness to a terrible situation. He's holding on to Morgan tightly, her head pressed against his chest, refusing to look at the chaos when the EMTs burst through the doors with a barrage of medical equipment.

Finally, Steven groans and coughs and there is a collective sigh of relief followed by tears of joy when we see his arms moving.

I see Jace reaching out to Morgan as she peels herself away from his body, crying and running out of the clinic. "I can't be here," are the last words I hear her say to Jace when she makes her exit.

The EMTs put Steven on a gurney and wheel him past us to the main door of the clinic. I hear a muffled, "Don't worry, I'm okay," come from him as he speaks from under the oxygen mask on his face.

Stacy addresses all of us after they've left. "Sometimes this happens, folks. Steven is very ill and maybe the chemo was just too much for his body to handle. But I've seen plenty of patients come back from collapses like his. So, don't worry."

She smiles weakly at us and turns to walk away. It's not lost on me that her hands are shaking a mile a minute.

The clinic is eerily quiet after Steven's departure. I notice that John and Melanie are watching the television. It's on The Travel Channel, of course, and maybe that is their way of paying tribute to Steven.

**Me: Is Morgan okay?**

**Jace: She just texted me. She said she was sorry, but it was all too much for her, so she had to leave. She said to tell you goodbye.**

**Me: I'm glad she's okay. I think we all got traumatized a little from it. I hope Steven will be alright. He's just so sick. What if ...**

I stop typing and send the text. What I wanted to say is what if that happens to him? What if *Jace* collapses right here in front of my eyes? If I count up the total days that we've known each other, that we've talked, I won't even use all my fingers. So, then why does the thought of him lying lifeless on the floor in front of me make me stop breathing?

**Jace: Keri, please don't worry. What happened to Steven won't happen to you. You are young and not as sick as he is. You're going to be fine. We're both going to get through this. I promise, we'll get through this. Together.**

He thinks I'm worried about myself. He has no idea, does he? No idea that the reason my heart even beats is because he is sitting across from me. I re-read his text. *Together*—I know he's talking about chemo, about our cancer. But just for a second, I wonder if there isn't a deeper meaning.

**Me: Okay.**

I nod at him. I need to stop my mind from picturing his lethargic body on the floor. I need to stop my heart from wanting what I can't have.

**Me: It was really nice what you did for Morgan for her birthday.**

He rolls his eyes at my text.

**Jace: Thanks. Do you know how much shit I took from my friends for putting a hundred pink balloons in her car? But she was happy, so it was worth it.**

There he goes again. Thinking nothing of himself but doing something simply for the enjoyment of another. I have to laugh at the thought of him trying to put all those balloons into her car. Then I think about the way Morgan told the story. She was giddy. He made her so happy doing what he did.

**Jace: I'm sorry you had to sit through the entire regurgitation of the evening.**

He looks over at me with a pained look on his face.

**Me: No need to be sorry. She's your girlfriend.
You have every right to be doing wonderfully
romantic things for her. She's a lucky girl. And
Bern's Steakhouse? Geez … you must have sold
a painting to afford that place.**

He winces and shrugs a shoulder. I can tell he doesn't want to
talk about it.

**Jace: Tell me more about The Freeway Station. I
Googled it and found out that most of the kids
who go there get placed there because they're
in trouble with the law.**

I nod. I know where he's going with this.

**Me: You want to know why I was there, don't
you?**

**Jace: Only if you want to tell me. Plus, I need to
know if you're a serial killer, that way I'll know
never to be in the same room alone with you.**

He laughs. Then his eyes go wide and he stiffens.

**Jace: Oh, God, Keri. Your parents didn't get
murdered, did they? I'm such an insensitive
asshole.**

I shake my head and giggle. Then I realize he's the only man
who has ever made me laugh when thinking about my parents. What
is it about him? He makes me want to open up and share my past

with him. Well, some of it anyway. Some things I still don't talk about—like my parents.

I try to think of reasons not to tell him how I landed at Freeway. There aren't any really. He's not my boyfriend. He's not going to *be* my boyfriend. Plus, if he finds out about my record, he may be so turned off by me that he won't even flirt with me anymore. Maybe that's a good thing. I don't know if he realizes he is toying with my heart here. Of course, it might just all be in my head. Then again, I have to assume his sister knows him better than I do.

I'm not going to win this argument with myself, so I decide to go ahead and lay it out there.

**Me: When they died, I stopped feeling. I became emotionally shut off. They said I had PTSD. Nothing made sense to me anymore. I lived life as a zombie. At times people had to almost force me to eat. I didn't sleep either, I had too many nightmares. I was shuffled around from foster home to foster home because my mom was an only child and my dad's only living relative was not capable of caring for me. I hated everybody and everything. I couldn't stand it when I saw people who were happy and laughing. But I also couldn't stand it when I saw people sad and crying. I never cried, not right away anyway. Not for a very long time. I was numb. Emotionless.**

I look up at him prepared to see the pity in his eyes. But instead I see concern. And then he smiles at me. The smile practically touches his eyes and makes the green in them almost sparkle. Then he reaches up and removes the baseball hat from his head and sticks it back in his pocket. I know he wasn't wearing it for himself. He was wearing it for Morgan. He's willing to stand up and show the world that the things happening to him don't define him. He gives me the encouragement to continue.

**Me: One day I was out walking around the neighborhood and I wandered into a convenience store. I was thinking how my life pretty much couldn't get any worse than it already was, so when I was looking at the magazines, I decided to put one of them inside my jacket. I mean, what was the worst thing that could happen? They would arrest me and lock me up? It wasn't going to be any worse than the prison I was already in inside my head. I walked out of the store and turned the corner and just started running. After a while, I looked back to see that nobody had followed me, and I started laughing. It was the most incredible feeling I'd had in months. It was the ONLY feeling I'd had in months. It was exhilarating. I had to do it again. Every day after that, I went into a store. It didn't matter what kind of store. Clothes, candy, makeup. I even stole a hard drive once and I didn't even own a computer. It wasn't about what I was stealing. It was the high I got from the act itself. But then after a while I got careless and started to get caught, landing me at The Freeway Station.**

I close my eyes and think about my first days there before I continue to type.

**Me: They wouldn't let me go out of the house without an escort. I wasn't even allowed to go into any stores for months. It was excruciating. I was an addict and they were keeping me from my drug. It was Tanner who saved me. He was placed in the house a month after I was. He made me feel again. He made me feel, so I didn't need to shoplift anymore. Well, he and Chaz, the guy who runs the place now.**

I finish my story and look at the ground. Then I close my eyes. I know what he must think of me. A common criminal. Not good enough to be among the good people in this very room. A juvenile delinquent who only escaped jail because the numerous retailers refused to press charges.

My phone is silent. I know I've stunned him. I'm afraid that when I open my eyes, he won't look at me the same way. I told him my story so he *would* look at me differently, so he would know what a terrible person I was and leave my heart alone. But I know that isn't what I want. I know it's wrong of me to want his affection. It's wrong of me to want what isn't mine—what belongs to another woman.

"Keri," I hear the whisper in my ear, and a pulse of electricity shoots up my spine. It's not even a whisper, more like a small burst of air that sounds like my name.

My eyes snap open and I turn to find Jace sitting next to me. I look up, stunned, at Stacy who is holding his IV bag. She must have helped him over.

I jerk my head to the side and stare at him. He can talk? Well, not talk, but whisper ... sort of.

I'm frozen to my chair, eyes locked on his when he leans closer to me. My eyes go wide. He looks like he's going to kiss me. Right here in the chemo clinic, he's going to kiss me.

My heart is beating so hard I think it might come right through the front of my shirt. I feel lightheaded and silently pray I don't pass out. His hand comes up to rest on my shoulder as he leans into me even further. I shiver under his touch.

I brace myself for the feel of his lips. Even though I know how wrong this is. It's like watching a train wreck. I know it's going to happen, but I can't do anything to stop it. I know he has a girlfriend, but there is nothing I want more than to feel his lips, his hands, on me.

I close my eyes in preparation. I lick my lips and take in a deep breath. And then I feel it—bursts of air in my ear. "You're amazing," he whispers.

It's not the kiss I was expecting, but that doesn't make it any less sensational. The way his hot breath flowed over my neck when he whispered, makes my body betray me as tingles of pleasure work their way to my core. I can imagine him whispering those same words into my ear after making love to me.

"Okay, Casanova. I need to get you back into your chair before I get fired for breaking the rules." Stacy pulls his elbow to get him to stand up and follow her across the room.

Once he's situated back in his chair, we stare at each other. Neither of us breaks our gaze. I try to re-play what just happened over and over in my head knowing it might well be the closest I ever get to feeling what my body craves from him. His spicy, rugged scent still floats in the air around me. I ingrain it into my memory.

A tear falls unbidden, down my cheek. As I raise my hand up to wipe it away, I see Jace clearly involved in some internal struggle. He shuts his eyes tight and shakes his head. His hands turn white as they grip the arms of his chair. I instantly feel ashamed. I'm a horrible person, making him feel like this. Making him have inappropriate feelings for someone who is not Morgan.

**Me: Are you okay?**

I see him blow out a deep breath and shake his head infinitesimally.

**Jace: No. I'm not okay. I can't feel like this. I'm so confused, Keri.**

His emotions are clearly raw. He doesn't have to explain. I know what he means. I need to stop whatever this is that I'm doing to make him feel this way. I need to give him space to love Morgan. She is his girlfriend. Not me. And here I keep crossing the line.

**Me: It's okay, Jace. It's okay to love Morgan. I get it. You don't have to worry about me.**

**Jace: But that's the thing. I do worry about you. Not just worry, but I think about you. All the time. How is it that I love Morgan, but you are all I think about? I didn't know I could feel this way about two ... I'm just so sorry, Keri.**

I can see how guilty he feels and how it hurts him—just like *my* heart hurts because it's breaking. He needs a side effect. *I* need a side effect. I inhale deeply through my nose and then I give him what he wants. What he needs.

**Me: Okay, so you know how I sometimes pee red after chemo, right? Well what I didn't tell you is that occasionally I pee in the shower.**

He jerks his head up at me and raises his eyebrows.

**Jace: What?!**

**Me: You heard me. So once, after chemo, I was simply too tired to get out and use the bathroom, so I was just sitting on the shower bench … and … well, I must have looked like a stuck pig the way the red flowed out of me and down the shower drain.**

I look up at him, embarrassed about the revelation, but I knew it had to happen. He reads the text and a slow smile creeps up his face.

**Jace: Does Tanner know you pee in his shower?**

**Me: First of all, how do you know we use the same shower? And second, yes, he does. And he loves me anyway.**

I look up to see him read the text and then his face falls slightly as he takes a deep breath.

**Jace: You said he knows about your hair in the drain, so I assumed you shared.**

**Me: Yeah, well, we do share a bathroom. It was hard enough to find a two bedroom we could afford, let alone the luxury of separate bathrooms.**

He looks physically pained after he reads my text.

Then Stacy sees that his bag is empty, so she goes over to disconnect him and get him ready to go. He stands up to walk out but taps out one last text and then leaves without looking back.

**Jace: Thanks, Keri. You really are something else.**

# Chapter Nine

It's been three days since chemo. You'd think I'd be over it by now. The feel of his breath on my neck, the smell of his cologne in the air, the burning of his eyes into mine. Yet, here I lie in bed, a sheen of perspiration covering my body as I wake up from yet another dream about a certain man with green eyes whispering declarations of love into my ear as he makes passionate love to me. My skin is on fire, just as if he were here, touching me. I can't help but stay in bed a little longer to release the tension he built inside me in my dream.

When I finally walk out into the kitchen, Tanner cranes his head and looks behind me.

"What?" I ask him.

"I'm just looking for the guy who made you moan, that's all."

He smiles at me, handing me a cup of coffee.

My face instantly heats up and I try to brush him off. "Oh, yeah, I guess I had a dream or something."

He shakes his head and stares at me with pursed lips, then says, "If that's how you want to play this, Keri."

I pick up the pack of coffee filters off the counter and throw them at him.

He bats them out of the way, and they fall to the floor. "Hey, what did I do? All I'm saying is that I'm glad someone has awakened the beast. It's about time you started acting like the sexual being that you are."

I think about how long it has been since I've wanted to go to bed with a man. Connor was the last man I slept with and that was almost five years ago. I've been fine since then. I haven't needed anyone but Tanner and some girlfriends from work. I haven't *wanted* anyone. Until now. Until Jace—the one man I absolutely can't have. I frown.

"It doesn't matter, Tan. He's with Morgan and that's that."

I plop down on a chair at our small kitchen table and stare into my coffee mug.

"Keri, I don't care if he's with the Playmate of the Year. I read his texts and that man is seriously crushing on you."

"We've known each other for exactly six days. Six Mondays of texting cannot possibly constitute any kind of deep feelings. We share this bond, that's all."

I'm not sure if I'm trying to convince Tanner or myself.

"Whatever," he says. "I'm going to ask for some time off soon to come with you and check this guy out for myself. No arguments."

He gets up from the table and tucks in his dress shirt. He looks gorgeous, all dressed up for his office job. His tanned skin pops out against the stark-white shirt. Most people would kill for a natural glow like he has. It comes from his mom, who was part Cuban. Top it off with his brown eyes and dark hair and he's quite a sight. I almost feel sorry for all the women who won't get to adore him.

"Tell the gang at Freeway I said hello," he says on his way out the door.

~ ~ ~

At The Freeway Station, I get a big hug from Kimberly when I give her the book I bought for her that explains football in the most basic of terms. It's the least I can do to try and help her win over Adam. She immediately takes it to her room and starts reading.

I'm laughing along with Todd, a counselor who works mostly the night shift, when Chaz comes running out of his office with a huge smile on his face.

"I can't believe it!" he cries. "We may be able to add another bedroom or two to the house. Do you know what that means? Two to four more kids who we could help. We may even be able to fund another position with this."

Todd and I look at each other and then over at Chaz. "What's going on?" I ask.

"We got a huge donation. It was targeted exclusively for Freeway. This is phenomenal. I mean we get donations all the time, but this is … well, just look here," he says, holding the ledger out for us to look at.

I have to count all the zeros twice. Whoa! A million dollars! For Freeway? Our little house that holds twelve kids got a million-dollar donation?

The three of us have an impromptu dance party. We hug and laugh and try to imagine how wonderful it will be to take in more kids. Some of the residents hear the commotion and come out to celebrate with us.

"Can we get that basketball hoop now?" Anthony asks.

"How about some decent outdoor loungers so I can work on my tan?" asks our newest resident, fifteen-year-old Shelly.

Chaz looks at them thoughtfully. "Why don't we make a request box. You can write down what you want, within reason, and put it in the box. Then we'll draw from them and see what we can do."

This excites the kids to no end, and they all run for their rooms to start making their lists. I follow a few of them up the stairs to greet the kids I haven't seen today.

I peek in the room that Tyler sleeps in to see him sitting at his desk working on homework. I come up behind him and say, "Hey, kiddo." Then I wrap my arms around him in a hug.

He jumps out of the chair, breaking my hold on him, and in the process, he plants his elbow right into my cheek, sending me to the floor. He runs over to his bed, tripping over his chair, causing even more commotion which has everyone flying into the room to see what has happened.

Tyler looks back in horror to see me lying on the floor, holding my cheek.

"Oh my God, Keri. I'm so sorry."

He comes over to help me up and his eyes go wide when he sees my face.

"Crap, I think I may have given you a shiner. I'm really sorry. With my earbuds in, I didn't hear you come in the room and you scared me. I'm so sorry I hit you."

Chaz and Todd make it up the stairs to find Tyler and me sitting on his bed. After explaining to everyone that it was just an accident and I had unknowingly snuck up on him, making him jump up and plant his elbow in my face, everyone seems to be placated enough to go back to what they were doing.

Downstairs in the bathroom, I check out my face and see the beginnings of a bruise up near my eye. It's quite a sight with black and blue mixed in with splotches of red. At least he didn't break the skin. They warn us during chemo to steer clear of injury because it will take longer to heal. I hope that doesn't apply to bruises. This one is flat-out ugly.

Chaz gives me a bag of frozen peas to hold on my eye and then he pulls me into his office to fill out an incident report. Once I detail the entire scenario for him, we both realize what more than likely happened. My heart sinks and my chin falls to my chest.

"This is classic male sex-abuse victim behavior, isn't it?" I ask him, even though I know the answer.

He nods his head. "Keri, you know we've all suspected Tyler's stepfather. But all this has to go through the system. If Tyler won't talk about it and we can't find proof, there is nothing we can do for now but try and keep him here."

I cringe when I think about this fourteen-year-old kid who panics when someone comes up behind him because he has probably been assaulted by a trusted male in his life.

"Chaz, would you let me talk to him? Maybe he would open up to me. You know I've been through all the training. I think I'm ready."

He bites the inside of his cheek while he ponders my question. He nods at me. "I think you're ready, too. But not today. He looks pretty shaken up by what happened. Give him some time. If I can't get anywhere with him in the next week, you can have a shot."

I smile, knowing Chaz trusts me enough to talk with a young kid about his probable sexual abuse. I'm a little relieved that I won't be doing it today, however, so I can have time to go over some of my training notes before I talk with him.

~ ~ ~

By the time my shift rolls around on Friday, my black eye is about as bad as it gets. I contemplated wearing sunglasses to work, but I think it would be impossible to mix drinks in the relative darkness of the bar while wearing them. I only hope it's dark enough in here so most people won't give it a second look.

Tanner understands completely, having been both a resident and a volunteer at Freeway. Most other people, however, will probably not be as quick to accept what really happened.

I decided to just go with something a little simpler, so if anyone asks, my story will be that I ran into a door.

"Hey, Keri!" I hear from the other side of the bar as I'm placing a tray of drinks up for Shana.

I turn around to see Jules. I smile and tell her I'll be right there.

I'm not sure why I'm so happy to see her. It's not Jace, but I guess it's the next best thing.

Jace hasn't come in here even though he knows I work here. Then again, why would he? We don't even text outside of chemo, so socializing is surely out of the question. But he did say he was familiar with the place. Maybe he's just staying away to keep a safe distance because of Morgan.

I tell Tanner I'm going to take my fifteen-minute break now, and Jules and I head over to a quiet corner table. Before we sit down, she pulls me into a hug. "You look great, Keri," she says.

My smile falls as I guiltily say, "I'm lucky. My hair has only thinned out and I've barely lost five pounds. Unlike some people."

When I look back up at her she notices my eye and gasps.

After a few minutes of explaining to her that I did not get mugged or even intentionally hurt, we move on to other topics of conversation.

"So, that gorgeous creature is your roommate, huh?" she asks, pointing over to Tanner. "Are you sure you're not dating him? And if not, why aren't you?" She laughs, fanning herself at his deliciousness.

I think back to our conversation at the clinic and I guess I never told her Tanner is gay. It's not like I introduce him as Tanner, my gay roommate. No more than he would introduce me as Keri, his heterosexual friend.

"Yes, I'm sure we're not dating given the fact that he's gay."

Jules chokes on her drink and then a smile creeps up her face. "Well played, my friend."

"What do you mean?" I ask.

"What I mean is that my big brother may already have green eyes, but they've been darkened a shade by thinking you're dating Tanner, not just living with him as a roommate."

I rack my brain to try and remember if I ever said anything to Jace about Tanner being gay. We talk about him a lot and I did tell Jace that Tanner is the one who saved me back at Freeway. I guess he could have interpreted that to mean we were a couple.

The fact is, we did hook up once, but that wasn't how Tanner saved me. He saved me in many other, more important ways.

"What? That's crazy. He's not jealous. He has a girlfriend."

"Maybe that's why he hasn't brought it up with you. It would make him seem like a hypocrite, now wouldn't it? But believe me, my brother is crazy over the fact that you go home to Tanner every night. I swear he stares at his phone all the time like he wants to text you, but my guess is he hasn't. Has he?"

I shake my head and lower my eyes to the ground.

"Keri, I like you. I like you a lot. And I think if you'll give it time, he will come around and see that Morgan is not the one for him."

*Time?* Time is something I don't have. We only have three more cycles together. Three more Mondays. It almost makes me wish we had more because then I'd know for sure I would see him again. I know it's ludicrous. Even when I only say it to myself, in my head, it sounds crazy. But he has made me that way. I'm crazy about him.

"Hey, Julianne, how are you? I don't ever see you around here anymore," my boss says to her as he walks by us, leaving for the day.

Jules looks over at him. "Mike, nice to see you too."

He gets pulled away by a waitress and I lean over to ask Jules, "How is it that you know Mike?"

She looks a little uncomfortable. "Um—"

"Hey, Keri," Shana says, walking up to our table, "Tanner says he needs some help with the big group that just came in."

I look over to the bar and see people two-deep waiting to be served.

I jump up and tell Jules, "Sorry, I have to get back to work. It was really nice seeing you again."

She stands up with me. "Let's hang out when you feel up to it. I think you and I are going to be great friends."

I smile at her as I make my way back to the bar, selfishly thinking that if we are friends, I might still get to see Jace when chemo ends after all.

# Chapter Ten

When Jace sits in his chair and gets a good look at me, a look of alarm washes over his face as his eyes go wide and his fists ball up. He immediately starts texting me, hampering Stacy's efforts to get him hooked up to his IV.

**Jace: Keri, what happened to you? Are you okay? Whose ass do I have to kick? It's not Tanner is it?**

I'm silently basking in the knowledge that he's being protective of me, and I try to keep a huge smile from taking over my face.

**Me: I ran into a door.**

He looks up at me and shakes his head. He's mad. Really mad. He can tell I'm lying to him. I can see that he's about to get out of his chair and confront me. Oh, hell, I'd better be straight with him. I guess he didn't think my explanation was so funny.

> **Me: I'm fine. It was an accident at The Freeway Station. I snuck up on someone I shouldn't have, and he accidentally caught me with his elbow. It's nothing, really. No ass to kick, but thanks for offering.**

It takes me a few more texts to fully explain what happened and I can visibly see him relaxing as he reads them all.

When everyone has arrived and has been hooked up, Stacy gives us an update on Steven. I look over at his vacant chair as she tells us that he has been in the hospital since last week's collapse. He's stable but very sick. She has a card for us to sign on our way out.

> **Jace: We should do something for him. Maybe send him a nice meal if he can eat. Hospital food sucks.**

> **Me: Why are you always being so nice to virtual strangers? It amazes me the things you want to do for these people you don't even know.**

> **Jace: Why does that surprise you? I'm no different than you. Look at what you do for all those kids at The Freeway Station. When you get a new kid, do you help them any less just because you don't know them yet?**

He has a point. I do love helping kids. Sometimes I can't wait to go there and just talk to them. When I see a face light up because someone is taking the time to pay attention to them, it makes me both happy and sad at the same time. Happy that such a small gesture on my part can make a difference, and sad because these kids have missed out on so much.

Thinking of Freeway reminds me of something, and a huge smile creeps up my face as I tell Jace the great news.

**Me: You'll never guess what happened. It's a miracle. Someone donated a million dollars to Freeway. It's the largest single donation we've ever gotten, and it will allow us to expand and take in more kids.**

**Jace: Wow! A million bucks. Nice. I'm so happy for you.**

When I look over at him, he has a look of genuine happiness on his face. It amazes me that this man has so much compassion for other people. I always thought artists were quirky egocentric types who stayed secluded away in their art studios. Jace isn't anything like that. At least I don't think he is.

But it dawns on me that I really don't know what he's like. I mean, I know he's a talented artist who cares about others. And I know he has this incredible girlfriend and sister. But for the most part, we always talk about me, not him. I feel so selfish.

**Me: So, tell me about you. I know you have pretentious parents, a great sister and girlfriend, and you're kind of talented at**

hidden-meaning paintings. But there has to be more to you than that. What do you do when you aren't painting?

He smiles when he reads the text. He studies my face for a minute and then works his bottom lip with his teeth like he's contemplating something.

Jace: When I'm not painting, I work for a foundation. It's an outreach program that helps less fortunate people. We work a lot with kids. We also help deliver technology to areas devoid of it.

Me: I knew it! I had a feeling you were a humanitarian. And why painting? What got you started in that?

Jace: I didn't always want to be an artist. I still don't even consider myself one. I just like to paint. But I didn't really know I had a knack for it until college. I was nineteen and took an art class at UM. My professor told us to go out in the world and look at current events, to find something that made us feel emotions like we'd never felt and draw on that to get our creative juices flowing. And it worked. I knew after the first painting that I had found my passion. It's amazing what can happen when you find that one thing. That thing that inspires you.

When I look up from my phone and our eyes meet, my heart skips a beat. But it does more than that. I could swear it comes out of my chest and collides with his halfway across the room. He's looking at me like *I'm* the one thing. The thing that inspires him.

Then he breaks our stare to look down at his phone. He starts to tap on it, but after a while, I realize it's not me he's texting. I see a hesitant smile come up his face. Then he silently laughs as he reads another text before he, again, texts someone back. Someone who's not me.

After several minutes, he looks guiltily back over at me.

**Jace: Sorry. That was Morgan.**

My heart crawls back into its proper place as I realize I was reading too much into things. He has a girlfriend. It's Morgan—*she's* his inspiration. He looked happy just now when he was texting with her.

I don't know why I keep allowing myself to see what obviously isn't there. Jace and I have a connection, a bond we share because we have cancer. Nothing more. We're helping each other get through this and that's a good thing. But that's all it is.

**Me: How is Morgan?**

**Jace: She's okay. The whole thing with Steven really shook her up. I know she's trying to deal with it, but she can't stand it when I forget to wear a hat, and she won't be in the same room when I use the feeding tube. I think some people simply aren't strong enough to step up. You're lucky you have Tanner.**

He looks a little sad now. It must be hard to have a girlfriend who he's been with forever who can't or won't help him. And then there are his parents, who haven't lifted a finger to come here and support him. I can't imagine.

I like to think if my parents were alive, they wouldn't leave my side for a single second until they knew I was okay.

**Jace: Quit feeling sorry for me, Keri. I'm fine. Morgan and I still go out and have fun like before. It's just that now she won't talk about the future. I think she is scared to jinx it or something.**

**Jace: So tell me, what's in your future? Where do you see yourself in five or ten years?**

I know most girls my age would probably see themselves married with kids by then. I was never one of those girls. I never wanted to define myself by the man I was with. But when I imagine what my future might be like, right now in this very second, the only person I can see is Jace. But I can't tell him that.

**Me: I guess I see myself working at Freeway. Chaz has pretty much promised me a full-time position when I graduate. Maybe I'll even go back to school for an advanced degree and someday run my own place.**

**Jace: What, no husband, no kids?**

**Me: I'm not sure I can have kids.**

**Jace: Oh, right, the chemo. Yeah, they told me there is a small chance I wouldn't be able to father children after. That's why I had my sperm frozen. Just in case. I couldn't take the chance.**

I'm stunned. He wants kids that badly? Most guys in their twenties wouldn't even be thinking about how they would feel later in life if they couldn't have a baby.

My mind immediately goes haywire with thoughts of what he had to do to provide his sperm. My face heats up, the hair on my arms stands up, and all kinds of sensations make their way through my body.

I try to shake off my impromptu mid-morning fantasy by texting him back.

**Me: Yeah, I did too. I mean, I had my eggs frozen.**

He looks up at me in surprise.

**Jace: I know how expensive that is, even more so for you with the egg retrieval.**

**Me: Yeah, about eight thousand dollars in all. Plus storage. But Tanner insisted on it. It's why he's working so hard at three jobs.**

Then I remember the medical bills and how they were lower than expected.

**Me: But don't feel too sorry for me. Apparently, someone at the billing office screwed up and**

**only charged me for one chemo cycle instead of four, so it's not like I can't pay rent or anything. I keep forgetting to call the billing office about that.**

**Jace: Keri, I don't feel sorry for you. And are you crazy? Don't call them, just count your lucky stars. Are you sure Tanner is just your roommate?**

**Me: That's exactly what Tanner said about the bill. No, he's not just my roommate, he's my best friend.**

I think back to the day Tanner came to Freeway. The day we first met. I was in my room lying on the bed staring at the ceiling. I did that a lot. Most of the kids would watch TV or listen to music. Not me, none of that did anything for me. Music just made me mad because of all the feeling involved. I had no feeling left in me. I was numb.

Tanner stood in the doorway and introduced himself. We weren't allowed to go into the rooms of opposite sex residents. It's kind of funny though, because he was gay. So that rule really didn't apply to him. But at the time, he wasn't sure he was gay, he was struggling with it. His mom had kicked him out because he was caught making out with a guy in school. Also, because he got arrested for selling drugs.

We became fast friends. Every time Tanner saw me staring at a wall or spacing out, he would try to engage me in conversation. Others had tried that as well, but after a while, I guess I seemed like a lost cause.

But Tanner was persistent, and he wore me down. He made me listen to hours and hours of stories about his miserable childhood, and in some way, it made mine not seem so bad.

Not that I'm trivializing losing my parents, but up until the moment they died, I had the ideal childhood. My dad taught me how to ride a bike when I was six, and he let me help him refurbish the old boat from the scrap yard. My mom took me shopping for training bras at age eleven and taught me how to drive her stick-shift when I was fifteen.

Tanner never had any of that. He was raised by a woman who jumped from one man to another. In fact, he doesn't even know who fathered him. He grew up around men who would hit him to shut him up so they could have sex with his mom.

We would hang out in the back yard of The Freeway Station at night, looking up at the stars. He would put thoughts in my head about how life could be if we got out of there and took control of our own destiny.

Eventually, when they let me out of the house unsupervised, he would take me down by the train yard. We would sit underneath the railroad overpass and wait for trains to come by. The feeling I got when that happened was indescribable. It was so loud, with the echoing of the engine and the rail cars as each of them thumped over our heads. The trees would sway and the wind from the train would kick up dirt and leaves, swirling them around us. It was exhilarating, like being caught up in a tornado for a few minutes.

It was the first time I felt anything after my parents died. From that day on, every chance we got we would go to the train yard. And that was the beginning of my healing.

My phone vibrates, bringing me back to the here and now.

**Jace: So, Slugger. You want to see another painting?**

**Me: Yes!**

I open it up on my laptop and it takes me a minute to realize what he's painted. Then I roll my eyes and shake my head as I type out a text.

**Me: If you ever tell anyone what this is, I will kill you.**

**Jace: Oh, so you get it? Good, I was hoping you would. It was definitely one of the highlights of chemo for me.**

I look back at the picture of his abstract painting on my laptop screen. To the unsuspecting eye, it appears to be a woman with arms crossed over her chest, almost like pledging allegiance on both sides, or she could be meditating, or maybe even praying. Her eyes are closed, and she has wild colors in her hair. But I know better. And I hope he doesn't sell this one, because I would hate to walk into a restaurant or office building and see a picture of me, feeling myself up, plastered on some random wall.

And even though I know *he* was wearing it that day, Jace chose to paint Kimberly's hideous hat on my head just for good measure.

# Chapter Eleven

Tanner studies Jace's latest painting on my laptop. "I don't get it. How is this a painting of *you?*"

I try to explain it to him, but I can't understand why, even after I point everything out, he still can't see it. But that doesn't keep him from once again playing the over-protective friend that he is.

"He made a painting of you grabbing your boobs, Keri. And he said it was his best moment at chemo. That settles it. I'm going with you next time."

I roll my eyes at him, but I give in all the same. I knew he would come sooner or later. And I'm glad someone will finally be there to show some support. I'm sure the others feel sorry for me as I'm the only person who hasn't had anyone come with me.

I wonder what it will be like when Tanner meets him. Will they get along? Not that it really matters. Because in a few weeks this will all be over, and I might never see Jace again. After all, what excuse would I have to see him? Plus, he has Morgan. But then I think back to what Jules said about giving it time. Does she really think he'll eventually break up with her? I try to imagine what that would be like, Jace being available.

I spend the rest of the week hoping that when Tanner meets him, he will see all the wonderful qualities in him that I do.

~ ~ ~

As Tanner follows me into the chemo center this morning, we are still talking about the large amount of money in tips we raked in this weekend. On Saturday, one of the waitresses put a wad of bills into our tip jar telling us it was from one of the cute guys in her section who asked her to do it. He must have really liked our drinks. Either that or he really liked one of *us*.

I'm one of the first patients to show up this morning. I planned it this way so Tanner will be sitting down and completely across the room from Jace when he shows up. I agreed to have him come and check him out, not give him the third degree. It's chemo for Christ's sake.

As the other patients trickle in, I see the surprised looks on their faces when they see I've brought someone with me. I also see a couple of raised brows. I'm not sure if it's because Tanner is so handsome, or if maybe they think I'm trying to make Jace jealous. Like that could happen.

I think I see Melanie drool a bit when she walks in. It doesn't take long before I get a text from her.

**Melanie: Keri, what is it with you and hot men?**

**Me: Roommate, Mel.**

**Melanie: Can I come live with you? Forget what
I said about you growing old with a bunch of
cats, you go girl!**

I laugh at her and proceed to introduce Tanner to her and Grace.

Stacy tells us Steven died in the hospital a few days ago and if we want to sign a sympathy card or make a small donation in his honor, we can do so today.

We all look around at each other. People are sad, most are silently crying. I wonder if anyone else feels like I do, guilty about feeling just a tiny bit relieved that, because it was someone else who died, statistically our chances of living just got a little better. *Jace's* chances just got better.

I shake my head at myself for thinking such things. I look up at the TV to see someone has turned on The Travel Channel. I don't think anyone else wants to pick a program. I don't blame them.

"What time is Jace supposed to show up?" Tanner asks, checking his watch.

I look at the clock on the wall. It's not quite nine o'clock, and he sometimes comes in a little late, but never this late. "He usually gets here about a quarter to nine. I'm sure he'll be here any minute." My foot taps the floor as I anxiously await the man who infiltrates my dreams to walk through the door.

Tanner is making small talk with Grace. What a twenty-four-year-old gay man has in common with a seventy-year-old former kindergarten teacher is beyond me. But he has her giggling like a schoolgirl, and their banter is keeping my mind occupied. It is not, however, keeping my eyes from looking at the slow movement of the minute-hand on the clock that is mounted on the wall over the nurse's station. The clock that now says ten after nine.

He's late.

I look at my phone as if a text will magically appear telling me why he hasn't shown up. I wonder if I should ask him where he is. But there seems to be an unwritten rule that we only text within the walls of this building. I would be breaking the rule if I texted him right now. Would he even want me to? Maybe he wants to leave what happens here at the door. What happens in Vegas and all that. I'm a chemo distraction, a way to help him through a bad situation.

Then I scroll through my texts and read what he wrote a few weeks ago. When he told me that he thinks about me all the time. Surely that means outside of the clinic. I didn't just imagine his feelings, he pretty much admitted them to me, right? Or maybe I'm reading too much into his texts.

I look over at the nurse's station and see Stacy watching me. She gives me a weak smile and looks up at the clock. She obviously hasn't heard from him either. I try to engage in the conversation between Tanner and Grace that also now involves Melanie. Anything to keep my eyes off the clock.

An hour into our session I realize nobody is talking anymore. Everyone is watching me. Dozens of eyes are burning into me right now. Eyes that keep glancing between Jace's empty chair and Steven's. They are wondering what I'm thinking. Wondering what I'm going to do if Jace doesn't walk through those large double doors soon. I'm not sure I've ever wished for something so hard in my life. Maybe not even when I was waiting to see if my parents were alive. Oh, God. I close my eyes and realize what I've been fighting for weeks now. Even though it's not possible. Even though I've known him such a short time. Even though he can never return my feelings.

*I love him.*

My gaze travels from the doors back to the empty spot he should be occupying. There is his chair, across from mine, sitting painfully vacant.

Everyone else is in their place, waiting patiently, worried looks painted on their faces. No one is speaking to me, but I know what they are thinking. *Poor Keri, what will she do now?* They wonder if I will cry. Maybe they think I'll have a breakdown. I'm sure some think I will run through those doors in search of him.

Tanner is holding my hand to comfort me, his large fingers entwined with mine, his thumb rubbing soothing strokes on the back of my hand.

People are starting to shift around anxiously in their seats and I hear whispered voices in the conspicuously quiet room. You could hear a pin drop in here. Every so often someone will cough, or a cell phone will vibrate. The air is thick with unasked questions.

*Why wouldn't he show up?* He seemed so good last week, healthier. He had gained weight and wasn't quite so pale. But a lot can happen in a week. I look over to Steven's deserted chair and close my eyes in painful contemplation.

The rich bellow of a horn from a nearby yacht pulls me from my thoughts. My eyes stare through the massive picture window at the back of the room. The window that was the very reason I chose this location. The window that overlooks dock after dock lined with boats of all sizes in the marina that sits adjacent to this building. Boats that remind me of my dad and the stories he would make up about the three of us sailing around the world. Just him, my mom and me, and the adventures we would have in every port.

As I stare out the window, I feel close to him, but at the same time I miss him so terribly, wishing he could be with me on days such as this.

I wonder what he would do to comfort me. In the sixteen years he was with me, I can't remember anything more than a simple scrape of the knee that he or my mom had to tend do. What are parents supposed to do in times like these? When my heart is breaking. When my lungs struggle to breathe.

Then I hear the doors open and I abruptly spin around to see all heads turning with hopeful eyes watching to see if Jace will walk through. Then I hear the collective sighs when they see it's not him.

He's late. *Too late*. I close my eyes and allow my head to fall forward in defeat. I feel a strong but gentle hand on my shoulder. I look up to see the sympathetic eyes of my best friend who is trying to comfort me because he knows what everyone else here does.

Jace isn't coming.

*Drip … drip … drip ….*

My eyes focus on my IV bag as I watch the rhythmic dripping of the poison as it mixes with the fluids coming into my body. I'm counting the drips, trying to keep my mind occupied so I don't keep going over the words that were spoken to me on my first day here.

'There are only two reasons people don't show up for chemotherapy …'

# Chapter Twelve

I sent Tanner on his way. He can't miss any more work or they'll fire him. But I don't think I'm in any condition to drive, so I sit on a bench outside the clinic. I watch the motorboats, sailboats, and yachts come and go from the harbor. I sit here and daydream about sailing far away with my dad, away from things like cancer and chemotherapy. Away from the heartache I feel right now.

It's just after noon, and I can't take it anymore. I've tried to respect the boundaries of our relationship. But he has to know that I'm worried about him, that everyone at the clinic is worried about him. So I look down at the text I composed, but didn't send, over two hours ago.

My finger lingers over the button that will send it to him. The button that will violate our unspoken rule to keep things casual and within the walls of the clinic. The button that may lead to my heartbreak. I press send.

**Me: Jace, where are you? Are you okay? You're supposed to call if you miss a cycle, it's rule number one. Please let me know if you are still alive. I'm sorry, I know I'm not supposed to text you, but I don't think I can go home until I know you're okay.**

I do some more boat watching before I check the time again. It's been thirty minutes since I sent the text. My head slumps forward.

I hear the excited cries of children running from their parents' car to find their boat. I raise my head to see their father carry a large cooler, and their mother, a beach bag stuffed with towels and toys. I watch them walk down the ramp to the dock, climb aboard their private boat, get it ready, and sail happily away from the hustle and bustle of the street that parallels the marina.

Oh, what I would give to be one of those children right now.

I look at my phone again. I've already broken the rule, I've violated the agreement, so what will another text matter?

**Me: So help me, if you don't respond to this text, I'm going to kill you the next time I see you if you aren't dead already.**

My stomach rumbles and I know I only have a few hours to get something to eat before I can't eat for another day. I reluctantly get up and walk to my car, feeling defeated.

Hours later, sitting on my couch, waiting for the chemo to hit me hard, I get tired of waiting for his response and make a split-second decision to call him. Before I chicken out, I dial his number, wondering if he can even answer the phone without being able to speak.

Then it hits me.

*Voicemail.*

As the phone rings I realize that more than likely, I am about to hear his voice for the very first time. I'm about to hear the voice of the man who whispers in my dreams. The man I love but can't have.

It's on the fourth ring now and I brace myself. My heart is pounding so hard I think it might escape my chest, and my breathing is shallow. My hands are shaking so badly I pray I don't drop the phone. Then the ringing stops and I hear it. Oh, God.

> **Hey, you've reached Jace. Obviously, I can't get to the phone right now. I'm probably at the loft painting. Maybe Jules has got me running some ridiculous errands for her hobby of the week. Or I could be working at the foundation. Who knows? But if you can leave me a message, I'll get back with you. Maybe not today, but probably sometime this week, or at least as soon as I get around to —**

The message stops and the beep sounds. My chin is on the floor. A tear rolls down my cheek. I can't speak past the lump in my throat, so I hang up the phone.

His voice—it sounds even better than I imagined. It's deep and rough and as sexy as I've ever heard a man speak. His message was so long it got cut off.

Realization dawns on me and I shake my head as more tears fall.

He was cupping his breasts.

He must have recorded that right before his surgery. My shaky fingers dial his number again. It's almost as heart-wrenching to sit through the message a second time, but I commit to giving him a piece of my mind.

"Jace, what the hell? You can't just not show up for chemo! What's going on? You have me scared to death. If you don't text me, I'm going to think you're dead on the side of the road or something. Please text me back."

I hang up the phone and run in the bathroom to throw up.

My bathroom is a shrine of sickness on Monday nights. There is a cooler full of ice, a few magazines, a pillow, a stool for me to sit on so my knees don't get sore when I'm retching over the toilet, and a few bottles of water—that I usually end up vomiting back up, but they feel good going down. Oh, and my phone so I can listen to music to drown out my hurling.

I get a couple of texts from Tanner, who moonlights at another bar on Monday's because The Triple J is closed. He offered to stay with me, but after that first Monday, we realized if I brought everything in here that I would need, there wasn't any reason for him to stay and watch me get sick over and over. But he still checks up on me and that is sweet of him.

I'm about halfway into my Monday Madness, or so I've dubbed it, when I get a new text. A text from Jace. I don't know if I should rejoice or be pissed that it took him so long.

**Jace: Keri, I'm so, so sorry. I didn't even think. Today was so messed up. Morgan broke up with me. She said she can't take my being sick anymore. We had a big fight right before chemo when I went to ask her to come with me. Long**

**story short, I threw my phone down and it broke. I just picked up a new one. I didn't know you were so freaked out. I'm really sorry. You're probably getting horribly sick about now and I hate that. Oh, and don't ever think you can't text me. You can. Whenever you need to. I'm here for you. Rules don't apply to us.**

I read his message three times. He's okay. Not dead on the side of a road. Not laid up in the hospital. Not even sick with the flu. Thank God.

Rules don't apply to us? What does that mean? Rules about not texting outside of chemo? Rules about him having feelings for me? Rules about calling if you miss an appointment? I just don't get it.

And … Morgan broke up with him? I can't even imagine. They've been together for what, five or six years? And she goes and dumps him because he has cancer? Who does that? Sweet little Morgan. He painted such a good picture of her. She seemed so genuinely nice, bringing me coffee and giving me her number, asking me to look out for Jace.

*Morgan broke up with him!* Even in my sickness, a small voice shouts at me in my head. *Yes!*

Wait, no. I can't be excited about this. *She* broke up with *him*. She broke his heart and he's probably in a world of hurt. He smashed his phone because of her. He can't get into another relationship. If he did, nothing good could come of it, it would be a rebound relationship. I'm nobody's rebound girl.

I hang my head. Why couldn't he have broken up with her? No, this is not good. Another wave of nausea hits me and I'm down for the count for a few more hours.

Later in bed, exhaustion sets in, but I tap out a reply to Jace anyway.

**Me: Glad you're okay. Don't let it happen again. What are you going to do about your missed cycle?**

I press send and then sleep pulls me under.

~ ~ ~

In the morning, I sleep late and wake up to see that Jace sent a few texts. One from last night and another from earlier this morning.

**Jace: I'll call tomorrow and see if they can fit me in. I'm glad you're not so sick that you couldn't text me back. Try to get some good sleep.**

**Jace: I wanted you to know I'm in for chemo this morning. They wanted to get me right in so I could stay on schedule. Is there any more news about Steven? Stacy isn't here today.**

I send him back a message telling him about Steven. Then I frown, wondering if there's another young woman in his session today. Someone like me. Someone who he connects with, who he likes to text, and who will *get* his paintings.

I drag myself out of bed and into the shower to wash off the sickness from last night. The entire time, I worry that he is texting someone else. Someone prettier, funnier, and not with a tainted past.

What if he switches to Tuesdays for his last few sessions? I realize I'm acting like a jealous girlfriend and swear not to think of it again when I pick up my phone to see several missed texts from Jace.

A big smile spreads across my face.

> **Jace: Oh, Keri. That's awful. I'm sorry to hear that. But he was very sick. That won't happen to us. We should send something to his family. No wonder you were so freaked out when I didn't show up.**
>
> **Jace: Keri, are you there?**
>
> **Jace: I was kind of hoping you would keep me company. It's not the same as you being here, but I'll take it.**

I check the time of the last text. It was only ten minutes ago. I look at my clock to see it's only ten thirty which means he still has at least an hour left. I smile and begin tapping on my phone.

~ ~ ~

When Tanner gets home, he gives me the third degree about my interaction with Jace this morning. I show him the texts of course, and it takes him about ten minutes to read through all of them.

Jace and I talked the whole rest of his session, making my fingers go numb. The texts were all very benign. No flirting. No crossing boundaries. No mention of Morgan. Just two friends passing the time. I'm amazed at how much we could find to talk about when his ex-girlfriend and both our parents were not topics of conversation.

"So, what are you going to do now?" Tanner asks.

"About what?"

He gives me a 'duh' look. "About Jace. What are you going to do about him? He's suddenly very available. Oh, and look ... so are you!"

I roll my eyes at him. "No way, Tan. We're talking about a guy who was so distraught, he missed chemo and didn't even call to let anyone know. That's the first rule. And he forgot. And he smashed his phone. She broke up with him after six years and he smashed his phone. That is not a guy who wants a new girlfriend."

"So, you aren't going to be jealous if he goes out and gets laid to get over her?" He raises an eyebrow at me.

"Gee, thanks. As if I weren't screwed up enough over the Morgan thing, now I have to worry about every other red-blooded girl on the planet." I blow out a big breath.

"Nah ... he probably won't tell you about it if he does, so don't worry your pretty little head."

I throw a couch pillow at him.

Then I go back to my room, lie down on my bed and worry about Jace going out to find some one-night stand to get over Morgan. When did I become so jealous, petty and insecure?

Oh, right—the same damn day he spilled the latte all over my favorite jeans.

# Chapter Thirteen

The first thing I notice about Jace when he walks through the clinic doors, other than the fact that he is sans baseball cap, is that he looks really good. He's obviously put on weight. He's still not filling out his shirt, but I'd guess he's put on about half the weight that he had lost.

It's been two weeks since I've seen him. I can't stop staring at him while Stacy gets him all situated. Then I get a little sad. After today, he only has one more cycle. One more chance for me to see him and share this connection we have.

I selfishly think about my own last session a week after his. I'll be lonely without him to keep me company. If Tanner hadn't taken last Monday morning off to come with me, I might have asked *him* to come, but I can't now. He needs that job. Even though I haven't had to use my credit cards yet, we're still barely scraping by with the rent after paying all my bills, even the ones that weren't as much as I thought they would be.

**Jace: Hey. It's great to see you after two long weeks. You're looking good.**

Long weeks? Does he mean the weeks were long because he didn't see me, or because of what he's been through with Morgan? I could go crazy trying to figure him out. If he were only as clear to me as his paintings are.

**Me: You, too. How are you? I mean, are you doing okay?**

**Jace: Are you asking about my health or my breakup with Morgan?**

I'm not sure how to answer that, especially when deep down, I'm celebrating the fact that they haven't gotten back together since we last spoke.

I guess I want to know about both, but anyone can clearly see he's looking better, so it must be obvious I'm asking about Morgan. But I don't want to upset him.

On the other hand, I really want to know how he's dealing with it. Do I even have the right to ask? I mean, I'm not sure what the boundaries of our relationship are. I know we texted early last week, but that was just because he missed his appointment. He didn't contact me after that. He is still basically keeping me within the confines of the clinic.

**Jace: We're friends, aren't we?**

**Me: What?**

**Jace: I consider us to be friends. I know we just talk when we're here, but we've become friends, right? And as friends, you can ask me anything. Go ahead, I know you want to.**

**Me: Okay then, friend. I can see that you look healthier today. I'm glad for that. But, yes, I want to know how you're doing after your breakup.**

**Jace: I won't lie and say it's been easy. We were together for years, and friends before that. She's keeping her distance. My parents are livid, they told me I have to do whatever it takes to get her back. But what's the point if she can't deal with all of this? I think maybe she'll come around once chemo is done and I start getting stronger and looking normal again.**

I think of how I had Morgan pegged all wrong. She seemed like such a sweetheart, but what kind of woman leaves a long-time love when he's down? And after what he just said, it sounds like he will go back to her if she decides she wants him again.

I can't help but close my eyes in disappointment. I'm not even sure I'm disappointed for myself, knowing he won't be available, or for him, spending a life with someone who runs away when things get tough. What about 'in sickness and in health' and all that? If they get married, is she planning on leaving that part out of their wedding vows?

**Jace: I know what you're thinking, Keri. But don't. Morgan is a good person. It's just that**

**some people aren't capable of handling things like this. She's not as strong as you are. But that doesn't make her a monster.**

He's defending the woman who just stomped all over his heart. The woman he loves, but who left him in his greatest time of need. The woman he will take back the minute she comes calling.

My heart sinks. I know I didn't expect to live happily ever after with the guy, but I guess I thought that maybe, eventually, we might have something.

I have to push my feelings aside. He says we are friends. I can do friends. Like I told Kimberly weeks ago, if that's the only part of him I can have, I'll take it. It will just have to be enough.

**Me: I'm sorry you are going through this. I mean, having cancer is bad enough without having to cope with a breakup. I'm sure things will all work out for the best.**

**Jace: Thanks, I hope so.**

**Me: So, Tanner showed up last week. He wanted to meet you.**

His eyes snap up to meet mine and he raises his eyebrows while a smile overtakes his face.

**Jace: Oh, really? And why would Tanner take time off to do that?**

Oh, crap. I didn't even think about what I said before texting him. Why would Tanner want to show up here and meet Jace if I hadn't been talking about him a lot? I try to come up with an excuse when my phone vibrates.

> **Jace: It's the bald head, isn't it? Chicks dig it. And the clean-shaven look 24/7 … Ahhh, the benefits of chemo. I mean, why wouldn't you tell your roommate how you can't keep your eyes off me? And when I wear Kimberly's cap, I mean watch out—People Magazine hottest man of the year!**

I'm turning three shades of red as he teases me. Then I laugh at his ridiculous comments. And I marvel at the way he remembers Kimberly's name, even though we only talked about her once, weeks ago.

I pull up the picture I took of him wearing Kimberly's cap. I think I've looked at this picture a hundred times. It's what gets me through Monday Madness. I prop my phone up on the edge of the tub and stare at his silly picture. And when I feel like I'm about to die if I vomit one more time, I think about the man who has lost all his hair and had a feeding tube surgically implanted in his stomach; all after a doctor cut out a portion of his vocal cords.

Jace is the one thing that gets me through it. Not Tanner's texts, not knowing that I may come out of this with my breasts fully intact. *Him*, he is my inspiration.

> **Jace: Hello? Earth to Keri.**

> **Me: Sorry. Well, he kind of looks at my texts. All of them. All the time. He has no boundaries.**

**Jace: Have you met my sister? They sound like kindred spirits, those two.**

I laugh. I thought the same thing when I first met Jules.

**Me: I know, right? Anyway, he just wanted to meet you. He's kind of like an over-protective brother.**

**Jace: Brother, huh?**

Oh, right. I guess I still haven't told him Tanner is gay. I contemplate not saying anything, but it really doesn't matter in the overall scheme of things. Despite what Jules has told me, Jace doesn't want me. He couldn't possibly sit around and think about texting me. He only wants Morgan. He said it himself, we are just friends.

**Me: Didn't I ever mention that Tanner is gay?**

He closes his eyes and lets out a sigh. Then he looks up at me and he stares at me with pursed lips as he types out his reply.

**Jace: No. No, you failed to mention that. So when can I meet him?**

**Me: Well, he can't come back here. He already took last Monday morning off and he can't miss any more time away from his temp job or they'll fire him.**

I look over at him as guilt washes over his face. I know he feels terrible for missing his appointment, especially after finding out about Steven. I wonder if he will ever know how completely wrecked I was when he didn't show.

**Me: But you could always come to The Triple J some night to meet him. We work every weekend night together.**

He looks uncomfortable with what I just said. Stupid me, does he think I'm asking him to hang out with me socially?

**Me: Or he works Tuesday and Thursday without me if you wanted to pop in to meet him then.**

**Jace: Why would I possibly want to meet him when you aren't around to introduce us? I would love to stop by and see you work. I'll just have to check my schedule.**

**Me: Okay, great. He'll be happy to meet you.**

I'm silently basking in the new knowledge that I'll get to see him at least one time outside of these walls. I wonder if that will open the door to seeing him other places.

**Jace: Do you want to hang out with me for a while when we're done here today? You know, to enjoy our last moments of feeling okay before we want to crawl in a hole for the rest of the night?**

I'm still reeling over the fact that he said he'll come into the club. And now he wants to do something *today?* My heart leaps for joy. But at the same time, I know nothing can come of this, other than a friendship, so I try to keep myself from getting too excited. Can I be with him, in a much closer proximity than we are now, without having my heart break? Without falling even more for him? No, I'm not sure this is such a good idea.

**Me: I'm not sure that's a good idea.**

His face falls.

**Jace: It's just coffee, Keri. There's a place around the corner we can walk to. It's quiet and they make a killer latte. Come on.**

I know he can never be mine. I know he belongs to another. Still, I can't imagine him falling out of my life in a few short weeks. So even though I know it will hurt my heart, I say yes.

**Me: I guess a coffee would be nice. Doesn't it make you sick anymore?**

**Jace: Nope, not anymore. That was only when my stomach was empty and I couldn't keep food down. I'm better now.**

Jace gets pulled into a conversation with John and they end up 'talking' the rest of the session. But he still sends me a text every so often to let me know he's not ignoring me. That tugs at my heartstrings just a little bit more.

After chemo, I walk out of the clinic with Melanie. We see Jace sitting on the bench outside the building. When he stands up and walks towards us, Melanie winks at me as she heads for her car.

It's not what she thinks. I know everyone in the clinic thinks Jace and I have something going on. They are sorely mistaken, but I think they're all amused by it, and if it helps make their time at chemo a little bit better, then who am I to set them straight?

Jace motions for me to follow him. We walk away from the parking lot where he leads us to a paved path that winds around a building. On the other side of the building and around the corner is a small coffee shop. It's quite out of the way, and I didn't even realize it was here.

"How did you know about this place? It seems so secluded. It's adorable."

I take in the quaint little mom-and-pop coffee shop with its hand-painted glass windows and soda-shop booths.

When I look up at Jace, he's studying me with a strange look. "What? Is there something on my face?" I wipe at my mouth.

He pulls his phone out of his pocket and types on it.

**Jace: It's just that I hardly ever hear you talk. I forgot what your voice sounds like since we only text each other. You have a great voice, Keri.**

I think about what he said. I realize I sit all the way across the room from him. And when I talk to other people at the clinic, it's in hushed voices or whispers mostly. In fact, the only times I can remember speaking to him are when he spilled my latte on me, when I commented on his Dolphins ball cap, and when I yelled at him via voicemail.

I guess when you don't have a voice, you pay special attention to those who do.

I wouldn't call my voice anything special. In fact, I hate when I hear myself on a recording because I think I sound like a twelve-year-old. But I understand where he's coming from. I'm always looking at other women's breasts, so I can hardly fault him for commenting on my voice.

"Thanks. I always wanted one of those deep, sultry voices you hear in old movies. But unfortunately, my voice never grew up along with the rest of me."

He shakes his head, disagreeing with me.

**Jace: It's perfect, Keri. It suits you.**

He holds the door open for me and we walk up to the counter where he hands a slip of paper to the Barista. I smile when I take a peek and see that he had already written down my order.

He grabs a bottle of water and places it on the counter.

"What, no coffee for you?" I ask him, pulling out my wallet.

He gently pushes my wallet back inside my purse, pays for our order, and texts me.

**Jace: No, it still hurts to drink hot things.**

He follows me over to a booth and motions for me to sit down. Then, surprisingly, he sits right next to me, not across from me as I thought he would.

He smiles and leans into me, like he's going to kiss me. My heart beats wildly as he draws closer. Then he grabs my chin with his fingers and turns my head away and whispers into my ear, "Is this okay?"

And I melt. I'm a pool of hot melted lava on the floor of the quaint little coffee shop. Just like when he whispered to me a few weeks ago, his breath on my neck, the closeness of his body, and the touch of his fingers on my face have all caused sparks to race up and down my body.

I hope I don't look as affected on the outside as I'm feeling on the inside. I try to compose myself, but it's hard with that spicy, rugged scent of his filling my nose.

"Yes, it's fine. So, you can whisper? How long will it be before you know if you can speak?"

It's a question I've wanted to ask so many times. We just had the one conversation that first day when he told me it could be months before he would find out the outcome of the surgery. It's been about that long, so I'm hoping for some good news.

He doesn't lean into me again. He types out another text instead.

> **Jace: I can whisper a little bit, but it's hard. I'm not sure when I'll know. I think it just takes time. But I do get sick of texting sometimes. Plus, I really wanted an excuse to sit next to you.**

My heart can't take this. The up and down. The yes and no. The back and forth. I'm trying to put up a protective shield around it. A barrier against these feelings I'm having.

"Say something, Keri," he whispers in my ear. "Let me hear you."

We spend an hour or so talking, texting, and whispering about everything. About nothing. And when we get up to leave, I'm certain that I'll never feel for another person—ever—the way I feel about this man.

# Chapter Fourteen

As I drive home, I realize he never told me how he found out about that coffee shop. Maybe Stacy told him about it. Then again, you'd think after ten weeks of chemo, I'd have heard of it as well, given that everyone knows I like coffee.

My phone vibrates in my pocket. I excitedly hope he's decided to break the rules and contact me—just because. He did say 'rules don't apply to us.' I'm still not sure what that means.

When I check my phone, I see a number I'm not familiar with, so I wait until I'm home to read it.

When I finally read the text, I'm surprised to see who it's from.

> **Morgan: Keri, it's Morgan. Jace gave me your number a while back, just in case. I'm sure you've heard by now that we're no longer together. But I still love him, and I need to know he's okay. Can you tell me how he's doing? Oh, and please don't tell him I asked.**

Why is she asking me? Me, of all people. Isn't she friends with Jules? Wouldn't Jules know more about his condition than I do? My first inclination is to lay into her. Ask her how she could possibly leave a man as compassionate as Jace. How does she even think she has the right to ask me about him? Because she brought me a latte once? I want to tell her to go to hell.

I'm contemplating what to say when I get another text from her.

> **Morgan: I know I don't have a right to ask, but I'm asking anyway. I'm not a very strong person, Keri. I've always relied on others, especially Jace. You are different. I think that's why he's been able to get through this ordeal without losing hope. You have inner strength he can draw from. Thank you for being such a good friend to him.**

Well, crap. What am I supposed to say to that?

Just when I want to hate her, she goes and makes me like her again. Even though I still fault her for breaking up with him, I guess I can understand how some people can't handle certain situations.

I see it all the time at Freeway. Parents send their kids to us because they can't deal with them. They need a break from the constant battle in their heads over what is best for their children. Most of them genuinely love their kids, but they need time apart to figure things out.

Maybe Morgan just needs a break. Maybe after she steps back for a while, she will realize that being with him, even though he has cancer, is better than being without him. It's this possibility that scares me the most.

If there's a stronger emotion than love, I don't want to know about it. I already love him. I already don't want to live my life without him in it. I already know I will never have this bond, this connection with another living being.

I thought Tanner was my soulmate. I was wrong. I wonder, however … can Jace be *my* soulmate even though I'm not his?

**Me: Hi, Morgan. He looked much better today. He's put on a little more weight. He even told me that if he keeps his weight up for two weeks after chemo, they will remove the feeding tube. That's great news.**

Damn it! Why was I so nice to her? Why did I give her any details?

Maybe so she won't ask him directly.

I struggle with what I will tell Jace the next time we talk. I have no loyalty to Morgan, especially after what she's done. We both love the same man. But by not telling him, am I being selfish? He loves her and he would want to know that she is asking about him.

~ ~ ~

Monday Madness is in full bloom. The silver lining is that I only have two more cycles after this. I've made it this far. The light at the end of the tunnel is getting brighter. I can do this.

I'm lying on my pillow with a cold washcloth plastered to my head, trying to hold down the water I just drank. I'm staring up at the corner of the tub where my phone is displaying that wonderfully hideous picture of Jace, when a text message pops up. I reach out and pull the phone down to me.

**Jace: I don't know why I didn't think of it before. But every Monday night when I get sick, I swear I won't go back to chemo. And the only reason I go back is because of you. You get me through chemo. So, I thought maybe if you were up for it, could we try to get each other through this as well?**

**Me: Sure, Monday Madness will be a fraction more tolerable if we can share the misery.**

**Jace: Monday Madness? Is that what you call this? It sounds like some kind of reality show.**

**Me: Oh, don't get me started on stupid reality shows. I think the worst one is that guy who is building some kind of fortress in the middle of nowhere so his family can ride out the apocalypse. I mean, really? You have an extra couple of million lying around and that's what you do with it?**

It takes a while for Jace to get back to me, and my heart hurts. I know he hasn't forgotten about me. He's getting sick. I'm not sure that anyone who hasn't been through chemo sickness can really understand what happens.

Most people probably think it's like getting food poisoning— that you just throw up for a while and then you're better. Frankly, that's what I thought would happen before my first time.

It's so much worse. At least for me. And apparently for Jace. For me, it's like someone sticks a sharp knife into my stomach, and then twists it, and for several minutes I pray I will throw up soon because it's the only thing that will bring me some relief. And in between the frequent bouts of nausea, there is flop sweating, diarrhea, hot flashes, chills, and blurred vision.

It lasts about four or five hours, and every time, I think I can't possibly survive it anymore. Every time, just like Jace, I tell myself I won't go back to chemo. And every time, like Jace, I go back. I go back to see *him*. I put myself through this hell just so I can share a few hours with him once a week.

I thank God for Jace. I truly believe I wouldn't have stuck it out if it weren't for him.

Fifteen minutes later, when I'm dealing with another wave of nausea, I hear my phone receive a text. As soon as I'm able, I read it.

> **Jace: I hate that show, too. So, Keri, what would you do if you had an extra million bucks burning a hole in your pocket?**

> **Me: That's easy. I'd probably give it to The Freeway Station. Either that or maybe I'd start a whole other house exactly like it.**

> **Jace: If you were anyone else, I'd say you were full of shit, feeding me bull because you know I work for a charitable foundation. But I believe that is exactly what you'd do with it. Have I told you lately how great I think you are? Thanks for helping me through this.**

> **Me: Ditto. I'm not sure I would have made it this far going it alone.**

I don't hear from him for another half hour or so as we each battle with our on-and-off waves of sickness. We go on like this all night, periods of texting and then not. And it does make it slightly more bearable. What's that saying ... 'misery loves company?' It's *so* true.

When I hit the five-hour mark, I know I'm about done. My throat is sore, my abs feel like they've been through a killer workout, even my teeth hurt. And as exhaustion sets in, I send him one last text.

**Me: Same time next week?**

**Jace: I wouldn't miss it for the world. There's no one else on Earth I'd rather puke my guts out with than you, Keri. And I mean that from the bottom of my heart.**

This makes me smile. Smile, at a time when my body wants to just give up and die.

# Chapter Fifteen

Two things have kept my mind occupied this week. The first is the daily battle within me not to pick up the phone and dial Jace merely to hear his voice again. The voice that's now in my dreams along with his whispers. But the one thing keeping me from actually doing it is the idea that he might feel the same way about me if I lost my breasts. Would he crave them as I crave his voice? I mean, if we were together, that is. The difference is—I could replace my breasts.

I fell in love with him knowing he may not get his voice back; before I even heard his voicemail greeting. I convince myself it's not important. I need to be a good friend and let him know it doesn't matter to me. Because it doesn't. I could live my whole life with him whispering in my ear.

I wonder if Morgan could say the same thing.

The other thing that's plagued my thoughts is what to do for Jace's 'graduation.' It's not like I can afford very much. I can't simply sell a painting and send someone on a spa day like he can.

After much contemplation, I think I've come up with something. I just hope he doesn't think it's an idiotic idea.

**Me: How excited are you that this is your last cycle?**

**Jace: Pretty psyched. But bummed there are still people here who have more to endure.**

I look around the room at the faces that have been here since I started. Since Jace started. John, Grace and Melanie were all prescribed more treatments than either of us. From what I can tell, not one of them has experienced Monday Madness the way we have, so I guess there's that. But it by no means indicates chemo has been a walk in the park for them.

**Me: Are you free after? I'd like to take you somewhere to celebrate your graduation.**

**Jace: Keri, you don't have to do that. Please don't feel obligated to do anything for me. I really didn't expect you to.**

Oh, God. He doesn't want to hang out with me again. I feel so stupid. For all I know, he's back together with Morgan. It's been a week since we've talked. A lot can happen in a week.

I sigh and look at the ground. I try not to look as wrecked as I am. I don't need him knowing the extent of my feelings for him.

**Jace: What I meant to say is ... Yes, I'm free to celebrate. But only if you let me do the same for you next week.**

Relief washes through me, and I can barely contain my excitement over the certainty that we get to spend almost two entire days together.

**Me: Deal.**

**Jace: So, where are we going?**

**Me: You'll have to wait and see.**

**Jace: Is it someplace quiet so when I whisper to you, I'll be able to smell that incredible shampoo you use? What is it anyway? Some kind of flower?**

I'm reveling in the fact that he wants to be close to me. That he remembers my scent just as I do his. That his whispers could possibly affect him, even by some small measure, the way they affect me.

Jace spends the rest of the session making me crack up by trying to guess where I'm taking him. Then, as the graduation card circulates and everyone is saying their goodbyes to Jace, I start to get nervous about my idea. I hope he isn't disappointed. Maybe I should have just planned to take him to lunch instead.

I'm waiting outside the clinic for Jace to finish up when hot breath washes over my neck from behind.

"Where to?" he whispers.

I can't move for a few seconds. I pray my legs will continue to hold me up and provide support for my body. The body that has turned into a melted, quivering mess merely from his whispered words.

"I hope you don't mind riding with me," I say.

I point in the direction of my less-than-impressive car. He smiles and motions for me to walk ahead of him. At my car, he sneaks around me and tries to open the door for me, but my key fob doesn't work anymore.

Embarrassed by the state of my old car, I put my key in the lock and say, "Sorry, I have to get in and unlock your side for you."

He simply shrugs at me like it's no big deal. I look out my window at the other cars in the lot and wonder which is his. Then after he gets in, I explain how I had to trade in the nicer car I used to have for two heavily used vehicles when Tanner's car died shortly after my diagnosis. He needed a way to get to the temp job he got that was going to help pay for my treatment.

I don't tell him the nice car was my only indulgence from the money I got when I turned eighteen. With the money that wasn't mine; wasn't even my parents'. Money I did nothing to get other than watch my mom and dad die.

On the way to our destination, I realize we can't have a conversation unless I want to jeopardize our safety by reading his texts. He must understand this, as he keeps his phone tucked safely away in the pocket of his jeans.

It takes twenty minutes to get where we're going. Twenty minutes of what I thought would be uncomfortable silence.

I was wrong. I've never felt so at ease with another person.

We catch each other stealing glances and then laugh. Every so often I'll speak to him, like when we pass by my apartment complex, or the gym I belonged to before I got sick. I get a huge smile and a raised eyebrow from him when I nonchalantly mention passing the salon that does my waxing.

When I pull into a parking lot, Jace gives me an amused look and gets out his phone.

**Jace: You brought me to the Tampa Museum of Art?**

I nod bashfully.

**Jace: But you hate art.**

"But *you* love it. Plus, it's not that I hate art, I've just never taken the time to understand it. Anyway, I've developed a new appreciation for it lately."

**Jace: Is that so?**

"Yeah. Some guy I know likes to hide messages in his art." I roll my eyes at him.

**Jace: They're not hidden, they are as clear as your beautiful blue eyes. If you just know what to look for.**

I feel the blush creep up my face from his compliment.

"Anyway, I thought maybe you could teach me a thing or two."

Suddenly, a thought pops into my head. "Hey, they don't have any of *your* paintings here, do they?"

He laughs, little bursts of air coming through his nose.

**Jace: I'm flattered you think I'm talented enough to have a piece displayed here, but no. And, I'd be honored to share my knowledge of art with you, Keri.**

"Oh, well, good. I know it's cheesy and all, and you've probably been here a thousand times before, but—"

The touch of his fingers on my arm causes me to stop speaking. The heat from his hand radiates through my body, right to my core. He almost instantly removes it and starts texting.

**Jace: This is anything but cheesy. I think it's the most thoughtful thing anyone has done for me in a very long time. I can't even remember the last time I was here. College maybe. Thank you.**

He grabs my hand and pulls me along the sidewalk. The way he's holding it is not very intimate, our fingers are not entwined, but that doesn't keep electricity from shooting up my arm, straight into my chest.

At the ticket booth, he releases my hand to reach for his wallet. I shake my head and say, "No. This is my treat. You have to let me pay."

It's only a ten-dollar entrance fee. Five if I show them my student ID. It's not like I bought him a spa day or a gigantic arrangement of flowers or anything.

He looks at me like I'm crazy for even thinking of paying.

"Please?" I ask. "Let me do this. I got unbelievable tips this weekend. I'll let you pay next week."

He smiles and then nods in agreement.

We spend about an hour perusing sculptures, paintings, pottery, and photographs. I guess I thought an art museum would simply have a bunch of pictures on the walls.

Jace gets so excited texting me about ancient pottery. Apparently, he took a course on that very thing in college. I never knew there were so many classes of artisan pots, here organized by styles of design and purpose.

We see many abstract paintings, and I'm just as confused as I thought I would be. How is it that I only get *his* art?

Suddenly, and without warning, an alarm sounds overhead. It pierces my ears and drives a knife straight into my heart. It's so loud it even overtakes the sound of blood pumping through my ears.

A fire alarm.

Through my sheer panic, I hear bits and pieces of a woman speaking over a loudspeaker. "Ladies and Gentlemen, please follow the signs to the nearest exit and promptly leave the building. Be assured there is no immediate danger, but there is a small fire in our main control room in the basement. Again, please follow the signs to the nearest exit and depart the building immediately. If you need assistance, please find a Docent in a red jacket, and they will help."

I'm completely unaware of my surroundings. My instincts tell me to run, get out as quickly as possible, but my legs are no longer taking directions from my brain. Instead of fleeing, I find myself cowering in a corner, shaking uncontrollably and on the verge of passing out because I'm hyperventilating.

Strong arms come around me and lift me up, carrying me through a dimly lit stairwell and out into the bright sunlight.

Sometime later—I can't tell if it's been minutes or hours, I'm still in Jace's arms and we're sitting on a park bench across from the museum.

People are staring. I wonder if they saw my panic attack. I look up at Jace and expect him to be disappointed in me for such childish behavior. But all I see when I look into his alluring green eyes is a caring, compassionate man.

He leans in close and whispers in my ear, "Keri, are you okay?"

I'm sure I must look a sight. I can feel the wetness on my cheeks, and my mascara must be terribly streaked. Then I see that I must have wiped my face on Jace's shirt, and I'm absolutely horrified at the black marks staining his nice polo.

"Jace, I'm so sorry. I ruined your shirt."

I close my eyes and take in a deep breath. Then I reluctantly move myself off his lap and into a position sitting next to him on the bench so he can remove his phone from his jeans.

**Jace: I guess now we're even, since I ruined your jeans.**

I'm so embarrassed. I can't understand why this seemingly perfect man is wasting his time on someone like me.

"Why do you even bother with me, Jace? I mean you and I have nothing in common, no connection other than cancer. Why are you always so nice to me?"

He looks like he's angry as he types on his phone.

**Jace: Why do I bother with you? Keri, I think you underestimate yourself. You are a kind and caring person. And we're friends. Friends are nice to each other. And I can't explain it, but I really feel like our connection goes deeper than just cancer. It's okay, whatever it is that caused you to panic, it's okay. I'm here for you. I'm not going to think any less of you no matter what you tell me.**

I haven't told anyone since Tanner. I didn't even tell any of my foster parents or the counselors at Freeway. Social Services explained it all to them. I've only ever told Tanner, just the one time, and we never talk about it … *ever*.

I'm not sure why after knowing Jace only a short time, I feel compelled to tell him my secrets.

I take a deep breath and brace myself to say the words I haven't spoken in years.

"My parents were killed in a fire."

# Chapter Sixteen

**Jace: Oh, Keri. That's terrible. The alarm going off ...**

He stops texting and grabs my hand. He doesn't waste time telling me how sorry he is and that everything will be okay. How does he know that hearing those words does nothing for me? I understand people say them because they don't know what else to say, but what he's doing right now, holding my hand in silence, comforts me more than a thousand words ever could.

The world goes on around us, people walk by, cars drive down the street, street vendors peddle their food, but I'm wrapped up in a protective bubble with Jace right now and I feel like nothing can hurt me. Not even telling him my story.

"It was awful. The night of the fire. We weren't even supposed to be at home. But I had gotten into trouble the night before. I had snuck out of the house to meet up with some friends. So, I was grounded, and my parents had to cancel their plans."

Jace squeezes my hand, urging me to continue.

"It was really cold that winter, especially for Tampa, and we lived in an old house where the heat sometimes didn't work properly. So, my mom turned on the small space heater down in the living room."

Jace closes his eyes briefly and then pulls his hand away and wraps his arm around me. I feel the tears well up in my eyes and I struggle to get more words out.

"I don't remember anything about being inside the house. Except the smell. I remember the awful electrical burning smell. And the horrible taste of soot in my mouth. And the sound of the sirens, I remember those. They said a firefighter found me crouched in the corner of my bedroom. They said I was lucky my room was the farthest away from the fire. My parents' room, however, was right next to the living room."

I stop to take a few deep breaths and then I realize Jace has pulled my head over to rest on his shoulder. My tears are running down onto his shirt, the shirt that is already ruined with my mascara, so I don't bother moving my head. It feels so right to be here. I fit up against his body like I belong there, like we're two pieces of a puzzle.

"When I came to in the hospital, they said my parents were found passed out and badly burned in the hallway. They had been trying to get to me. I was allowed to see them briefly, to say goodbye as they were both dying from burns and smoke inhalation. All I could do was tell them how sorry I was for causing us to all be at home. If it weren't for me, maybe that space heater wouldn't have caught the couch on fire. Maybe we would have all just come home later and gone straight to bed to get warm under the covers."

Jace puts his hand under my chin and lifts it up so I have to look at him. He simply shakes his head. I know he's telling me it's not my fault. That it could have happened even if I hadn't snuck out and gotten in trouble.

Logic tells me this, but it doesn't help assuage the guilt I have over it. I lay my head back onto his shoulder and feel his lips gently press against the top of my head. I close my eyes at the incredible feeling.

"The worst part was the media. They jumped all over the story of the poor little girl who was orphaned in the fire. Some photographer took a picture when I was being rescued. It was a picture of the firefighter carrying me out of the house, with the house in flames behind us. I think he won some award for it. But it made me the talk of the town. They didn't use my name, because I was a minor, but everyone knew who I was. Everyone wanted to talk about it, to ask me about it. That's when I pretty much stopped feeling. I became numb and shut down. Until I met Tanner."

My head is still on his shoulder and I don't remember moving my hand, but somehow it ended up right over Jace's heart. The heart that is beating wildly right now. I think it's beating as fast as my own. I look up at him to see his face pale. His eyes are wide, and he looks utterly shocked.

He leans into me and whispers, "When was this?"

"Eight years ago. I was sixteen."

I can feel his entire body stiffen.

He moves me slightly to get to the phone in his pocket.

**Jace: I need to show you something. Will you come with me to my loft?**

He texts me his address and I drive us to his apartment that's in an up-and-coming urban area of the city.

I'm not surprised at all by the feel of his place. It screams stereotypical artist. It's basically one very large open area that is organized chaos with lots of paint, canvases and easels. There's a partition at one end of the room that must lead to his bedroom.

The first thing that hits me when I walk into his apartment is the smell. Mixed with the smell of paint is Jace's spicy, rugged scent I've come to crave. I'm tempted to leave my jacket here, so that when he returns it, I can have something with his scent.

Before we get too far into the loft, he sits me down at his entry table and holds up his finger at me to wait a minute. Then he pulls out his phone and starts typing.

**Jace: I'm not sure if you remember a while back when you asked me how I started painting. I told you about a class I was taking when I was nineteen. The teacher had told us to find something that inspired us and just let our creativity run wild. Well, I found something. Something that touched me deeply. Something that still inspires me to this very day.**

He looks at me while I read his text. Then he nods and holds his hand out for me to take as he helps me up from the chair. He leads me over to the living room area of the loft where there is a huge fireplace and exposed brick wall. He motions towards the painting over the fireplace and I turn to look at it.

It's a large abstract painting, probably four feet wide and at least as tall. The colors he used were incredibly bright. The yellows, oranges and reds in the background look like a glorious sunset, and in the foreground, a silhouette of a man carrying a woman.

Then it hits me, and I stumble back, thankful there's a couch directly behind me to break my fall. My hand comes up to cover my gasp as I realize Jace painted a picture of *me*. Eight years before we even met, he painted a picture of me. A picture that has a prominent position in his home. A picture of me, at age sixteen, being carried by a fireman out of my burning house.

I stare at the blurry painting through my tears. Hot breath tickles my neck as I hear Jace's whispered words. "Deeper than cancer, Keri."

I turn to look at him in utter disbelief, but he is typing away on his phone.

> **Jace: I've thought about the girl in this painting every day for eight years. I've felt a connection with her. Somehow, it doesn't even shock me that she is you. I knew we shared something more. You were my inspiration. You got me into painting. When I'm feeling sorry for myself, I look at it and think of what the girl in the painting had to endure and it makes my problems pale in comparison. It was you, this picture, your story that got me to go ahead with the surgery and chemo, even when I didn't want to. So, you see, you saved me, Keri.**

I look up at him as a tear slips from his eye. I lean over to catch it and he grabs my hands and pulls me to him. He looks into my own teary eyes with passion and purpose as he draws me in closer. Then his gaze travels to my lips, which I absentmindedly wet with my tongue. He's going to kiss me. I don't think I've ever wanted anything more in my life than to feel his lips on mine.

When our lips touch, my world stops. Everything inside me is focused on the way his lips feel, the way they fit perfectly up against mine, the way his hands cup my face and take charge of our kiss—take charge of me. As my lips part for him, everything is perfect. My life is perfect. Except for the little voice screaming at me in my head.

I abruptly pull away, leaving him confused. "Jace, I have to tell you something. I should have told you before now, but I can't keep quiet any longer. Morgan contacted me last week. She wanted to see how you were doing. She says she still loves you, but she can't be with you because she isn't strong enough."

He shakes his head and blows out a heavy breath. I have to ask him. I have to find out the answer to the question racing through my head. "If Morgan asked you to go back with her right now, would you do it?"

I hold my breath as I look at him. He closes his eyes and runs a hand over his head still devoid of hair. He looks pained, frustrated, torn. He doesn't whisper or text anything, yet his hesitation is all the answer I need.

I sit back on the couch, painfully breaking our contact as I say, "It's okay, Jace. I know you love Morgan. I know that you and I have these feelings, but we don't have to act on them. I won't act on them. I won't be second best. But I want to be your friend. If you still want that, too."

He stares at me for a second, then he pulls me into a hug, wrapping both his arms around me, enveloping me in his body, in his scent. "More than anything," he whispers in my ear.

He goes into the kitchen and puts on a pot of coffee for me. Then he comes back with some sandwiches for us to eat while we talk.

I tell him about the outpouring of sympathy that came my way after my parents died. About the survivor's fund the local paper set up that collected almost a hundred thousand dollars for me to have access to when I turned eighteen. Then I tell him about how I used almost all of it to help Tanner out of a situation, leaving both of us penniless. The whole time, Jace listens patiently, never asking me about details, occasionally reaching over to squeeze my hand when he thinks I need encouragement.

"Don't you want to know why Tanner needed such a large sum of money?" I ask.

**Jace: No. It's not your story to tell. It's his.**

I wonder who else knows the extent of this man's compassion and understanding of others.

It's been hours since we left the clinic. I know I'd better head home before Monday Madness rears its ugly head once more.

Jace tells me his sister dropped him off at chemo this morning so there's no need to go back to get his car. As I drive home, dreading the hours to come this evening, I hold onto the silver lining of being able to go through it with Jace, together.

I re-read the last text he sent me when I get home.

**Jace: I'll talk to you in a few hours. We can do this. You're my inspiration, Keri. Let me be yours.**

# Chapter Seventeen

I'm feeling particularly good for a Wednesday. Maybe it comes from knowing I only have one more cycle of chemo. Maybe I'm still reeling from Jace's shocking revelation. I know I'm excited about being able to spend time with him even though we can only be friends.

As I'm walking into The Freeway Station, I get a text from Jace.

We're not at chemo. We're not going through Monday Madness. I haven't just left him a message threatening bodily harm if he doesn't get in touch with me. No, this text is simply because he wants to talk. And knowing this makes my heart race uncontrollably.

> **Jace: So, I'll bet Tanner really wants to meet me now, huh? I'm assuming he read all my texts already.**

> **Me: You know he did. And yes, he wants to meet you. If that's still okay with you.**

**Jace: That's actually why I'm texting you. I wanted to see if it was okay if I swing by the club on Sunday.**

I smile at the prospect of two of the most important men in my life meeting each other. I hope they will become friends. Maybe we can even all go to Scrabble Night together. I wonder how silly Jace will think we are when he hears about Scrabble Night.

I've missed those intense Monday night games since I got sick. Monday is the only night the bar is closed, so most of the staff get together to let off steam. It's kind of like Poker Night, but with little wooden pieces instead of cards. I can't wait to go back.

**Me: Sunday is a great time to come. Not so busy and my boss won't be hanging around.**

**Jace: Sounds like a plan.**

We continue to text like old friends for a few minutes until I have to go inside for my shift.

Today is an important day. Today is the day I've been training for. The day I will have Tyler all to myself in hopes that he will open up to me about his sexual abuse. Chaz has tried for a few weeks now to get through to him but has been unsuccessful. As promised, he's giving me a shot. He's told me not to expect much as Tyler vehemently denies everything.

I decide to take him to the beach. We spend the afternoon boogie-boarding and pigging out on ice cream. I think he knows why I've brought him here, just the two of us, but he hasn't let on.

When we're both exhausted and lying on our beach towels on the soft sand, I take a deep breath and prepare myself for the conversation. "Tyler, you can talk to me or not talk to me, it's okay. But you need to know that whatever you tell me is not going to change the way I feel about you."

I remember Jace saying those exact words to me just days ago, so I decide to share my experience of that afternoon with Tyler. Sometimes kids will open up if they know you have a painful memory as well. I tell him all about the fire alarm and how I panicked. And how I didn't know how badly I needed to share my story with someone. And that I needed to realize the world wouldn't end if I did. My world didn't end, in fact, quite the opposite. I tell him about the painting Jace had done of me all those years ago and how that made us connected somehow. Just as Tyler and I have a connection because we both ended up at Freeway.

He sits up on his towel and looks over at me. "Can I see the painting sometime?"

"You can see it now if you like. I have a picture of it right here on my phone."

I took the picture Monday afternoon to add to my collection of Jace's other pictures he sent me. Pictures I look at during Monday Madness, along with the one of him wearing that ridiculous hat.

I hand my phone over to Tyler and he studies the painting. He enlarges it on my little phone and scrolls over each part of it, taking it all in. Then he looks up at me. "That must have been the worst day of your life, Keri."

I nod. "It was."

He continues to study the picture. Then, without making eye contact with me, he says, "The day *he* moved in with us. That was the worst day of my life."

Over the course of the next hour, Tyler tells me all about his stepfather and the horrid things he did to him over the months they lived under the same roof. By the grace of God, he even agrees to speak with the police. But only if I go with him.

Back at Freeway, I cry in Chaz's arms for hours. Happy tears because Tyler opened up to me and his nightmare will end. Sad tears because something that awful could happen to an innocent child.

As I fall asleep in my bed, I have a feeling that I may have finally found my place in this world. It was Jace. His kind words and acceptance inspired me and gave me the courage to step up and help another. And peace washes over me.

~ ~ ~

I'm not sure why I'm so nervous. I've been a bartender for three years, so I can pretty much make drinks in my sleep. But today, I changed clothes three times, finding precisely the right Triple J shirt—the slightly immodest one that, when combined with my Wonder Bra, usually brings in more tips than normal. I paired it with my favorite pair of worn jeans. The ones that make my butt look fabulous. The ones Jace spilled my latte on.

He's coming here tonight to meet Tanner, and my hands are shaking so badly I'm afraid I'll drop someone's drink.

Why do I feel like my dad is meeting my boyfriend for the first time?

I guess it's because Tanner is the closest thing to family I have, and Jace is the closest thing to a boyfriend. In my dreams, he *is* my boyfriend. In my dreams, he sweeps me off my feet, takes me to his loft and makes passionate love to me in front of that massive fireplace of his—underneath the painting that cements our bond.

But my dreams are the only place I will allow that to happen. I know where his heart is. I know if I allowed myself to have a physical relationship with him it would wreck me. He isn't the kind of man

170

you can sleep with and get over. He's the kind of man you marry. He's the kind of man you compare all other men to. My fear is that I will never find one who measures up.

Tanner lifts an eyebrow at me when Shana returns a second drink to me that I had incorrectly made.

"What?" I snap at him, leaning my back against the bar.

He holds his hands up in surrender. "Nothing. But you kind of seem on edge tonight. Are you really that nervous over me meeting him?"

"Yes. No. I don't know." I blow out a breath while I look at the ceiling. "It's just that I haven't seen him since we kissed last week, and I don't want it to be all weird when we see each other."

Tanner gets a smirk on his face. "You mean all weird like if he were to be standing behind you right now overhearing everything you just said?"

My eyes go wide and my face heats up as I look into the mirror behind the bar and see that Jace is sitting on a stool, directly behind me on the other side of the counter.

Tanner gives me a supportive arm squeeze and turns me around to face Jace, which is a good thing, because I think I'm too mortified to move my own legs.

Jace has a huge smile on his face as I introduce them.

"Jace, this is my roommate, Tanner. Tanner, this is my, um … friend, Jace."

They both crack up at my awkwardness, causing me to blush even more.

"Nice to finally meet you Jace," Tanner says, shaking his hand. "Hey, if you want to talk, come on over to my end of the bar, this is Keri's side. Do you want to text my phone?"

Jace nods and Tanner scribbles his number on a napkin. Jace then holds up his finger letting Tanner know he'll be over in a minute. Then he gets out his phone and starts typing.

**Jace: It's nice to see you. You look great by the way. We won't let things get weird. Friends, right?**

"Absolutely," I say. "Hey how excited are you that you don't have to go back to chemo tomorrow?"

**Jace: I can't even explain to you what it feels like, Keri. Just know that you'll feel the same way after tomorrow. I'm going to head over there and talk to Tanner now.**

"Great. You know where I'll be."

He smiles at me as he gets up and walks down the long length of the bar to the very end, by Tanner's waitress station.

The next hour of my life is spent wondering what they're talking about. I mean, there's not enough about me to fill up an entire *hour* of conversation. Sure, Tanner is working while they talk, but still it's enough to drive a person crazy.

Every now and then, they will both look over at me simultaneously, usually with a smile or while they are laughing.

Jace catches me stealing glances at him and my face heats up every time. I'm more than aware, however, that for him to catch me looking, he had to be doing the very same thing.

Throughout the night, when Tanner walks off to help a customer, Jace will sometimes send me a text.

**Jace: So, as a friend, I feel that I can tell you this.
Every time you bend over to get something out
of the beer fridge, I can't help but remember the
latte I spilled all over those jeans. I'm glad you
got them clean. It would be a shame to waste
them. Oh, and those guys at the other end of the
bar? Believe me, they noticed, too.**

Although I could care less about the guys at the other end of
the bar, his text makes me want to high five someone, knowing that
*he* is affected by me.

Then again, that's not the problem here, is it? Our mutual
attraction is evident. The thing that keeps me from jumping into his
arms and holding on for dear life is something my mom told me
when I was little.

She had some good advice. I didn't know it at the time, of
course. But tonight, as I see Jace looking all gorgeous and starting to
fill out those tight shirts of his again, I can hear her voice in my head.

"When it comes to men, never settle, Keri. Never settle for
second best and never *be* second best."

I wasn't sure what she meant until I was older, until I started to
ask questions about her and my dad. I knew they loved each other,
but it just seemed like something was missing. One day, a few
months before they died, she told me the story.

*"Your father and I were high school sweethearts. We
were each other's first love, first kiss, first everything. We
had planned out our life down to the last detail, even
down to what we would name our children if we were
blessed with any. When he had a hard time getting
accepted into college, he panicked and didn't know how
he was going to support a family. So, as you know, he*

*joined the Army. He was away for almost ten months a year those first few years. It was hard, but we got through it. And when he was finally able to get his degree and get an honorable discharge, we picked right back up with our plans. That's when we had you. But what I didn't know was that when he was overseas, there was a woman, a nurse stationed where he was. I guess they grew close and even requested the same tours. He mentioned her, of course, as he did all his army buddies, and I was grateful that he had people he could lean on. Over those years, he never wavered in his love for me. He never gave me a reason to doubt him. Then one day, after we had been married for about ten years, a package came in the mail for your dad. I only caught a glimpse of what was inside. It was some pictures, an old army medal, and some personal effects. He asked me for privacy and I never questioned him about it. After a few days, he confessed everything. They'd had a love affair. Not a physical relationship as far as I know, but a love affair no less. He even let me read the letter that was included in the package. A goodbye letter to him, her one true love, because she was dying of cancer. I asked him why he stayed with me and he said it was because they both had someone else who was in love with them back at home and they couldn't hurt them. Your father asked if I was going to leave him. Of course I stayed, I stayed for you, and I did love him, I still do love him. But my only regret is that I didn't know. I thought he loved me, I thought he loved me enough. But Keri, being loved enough isn't adequate. Be loved* more. *Make sure you are loved* more *than enough."*

So, as I watch Jace and Tanner talk, smile, and become friends, I know that even though we share these intense feelings, I will never be loved enough by him. Not in the way my mom was talking about.

I feel sad for her that she never got to have a deep, enduring, passionate love from the man she loved. I feel sad that she didn't get her more-than-enough love.

I vow not to let the same thing happen to me.

# Chapter Eighteen

I can't wait any longer. I open Tanner's door and crawl into bed with him. I was too exhausted last night to bother him with my questions. But now I've been up for hours, and it's all I can think about.

I nudge him. "Tanner, you awake?"

"No," he says, pulling the covers off me and rolling onto his side.

"Come on, Tan. It's only fair that you let me see them."

In the darkness, he reaches over to his nightstand and grabs his phone. Then he practically throws it at me.

"Now get out," he yawns.

I smile triumphantly as I carry his phone into the kitchen and scroll through it while I drink my first coffee of the day.

I try to piece together the conversation they had, but it's hard only seeing Jace's half.

**Jace:** I know you are. She's a great girl, incredible even. But you already know that. I felt instantly connected to her and I've since found out why. I want to be her friend. I want to be there for her, just like you are.

**Jace:** I love Morgan.

**Jace:** No, we're not, but I still have feelings for her.

**Jace:** Yes, I'm not going to lie and tell you I don't.

**Jace:** There is definitely something between us, but like Keri told me last week, it can't work. We can only be friends.

**Jace:** If I do, man, you have my permission to kick my ass.

**Jace:** Yes, I'd like that too. Thanks.

There's a lot more, but they just go on to talk about the bar and sports and guy stuff. They even talked about The Freeway Station. And from what I can see, it turns out they hit it off really well. I'm so relieved.

But I still need Tanner to fill in the blanks for me.

When he gets up, I make him give me the play-by-play of their conversation.

"Keri, I can't possibly remember everything I said."

I give him the evil eye as he takes his phone from me and pulls up Jace's texts.

"I told him you're like family to me and I asked what his intentions were concerning you. Then he didn't really answer my question, so I asked him flat-out if he wants anything romantically or physically from you."

My eyes go wide. Then my heart sinks. That must have been when he said he loves Morgan.

Tanner says, "After he told me that although they aren't together, he still has feelings for her, I asked him if he has feelings for you. Then I think I asked him to respect your request to only be friends and not push you on it. Then I told him I'd hurt him if he ever hurts you." He looks up at me with raised eyebrows. "Satisfied?"

"So, it looked like you guys got along okay, I mean from what you talked about the rest of the night."

"Yeah, he seems like a decent guy. He loved the stories I told him about us back at Freeway. What does he know about that anyway? Did you ever tell him about our hookup?"

I shake my head. "No."

"The guy is going to be pissed when he finds out, Keri. He thinks we're just friends."

"We *are* just friends, Tan. Just like Jace and I are *just* friends. He would have no right to be pissed, now would he?"

But I secretly wouldn't mind if the news made him a little jealous.

"Whatever, Keri. You guys can blow smoke up each other's asses all day long. The bottom line is you want him, and he obviously wants you, too. So be careful. I don't want to see you get hurt."

~ ~ ~

If anyone had asked me three months ago if I would be smiling while driving up to the chemo center, I would have said they were crazy. But here I am, pulling into the parking lot, not only thinking about this being my last cycle, but about the fact that I will see Jace today when I'm done. He said he would meet me here afterward.

I'm as giddy as a schoolgirl as I float up the front walk for my thirteenth and final cycle.

My heart swells when I enter the double doors. There is Jace, sitting right next to my designated spot, in a visitor's chair, holding a bouquet of flowers.

"You came!"

I can't mask the excitement in my voice or the sheer happiness I feel because this man wanted to be here to support me during my last session.

"And you're early. You're never early."

I sit down and he hands me the flowers and pulls out his phone.

**Jace: Well, I can't be your inspiration if I don't show up, can I?**

I want to tell him he's my inspiration every second of every day. That his picture, his voice, his whispers, his texts … all got me through this. But I don't, I just say, "No, I guess not. Thank you so much for being here."

**Jace: I wouldn't miss it for the world.**

We play the same game we did last week, only in reverse, with me trying to guess where we're going after, but he won't give me an inch.

**Jace: Just promise me one thing, Keri. Promise me you'll remember what I told you last week. When I said no matter what you told me about your past, it wouldn't change the way I feel about you? I need you to remember that today.**

I'm about to ask why he would tell me that when I suddenly recall how those words helped me. So, I tell him what happened with Tyler. I tell him it was his words, his understanding, his compassion that allowed me to share my experience with Tyler and ultimately get him to open up to me. I tell him I didn't realize that what I went through could help others.

**Jace: You helped me. Even before you knew me, you helped me. And you helped Tyler. And you help the other kids at Freeway every day. This is what you are meant to do, Keri. If any good can come from your horrible past, it's that you will help countless kids in your life.**

"Thank you, Jace," I whisper to him.

He leans over and whispers back, "Ditto," repeating the word I spoke to him long ago when we admitted our feelings for the first time.

The main doors open, and a woman walks in with her young son. I think she must be the new patient Stacy told us was arriving today.

I wonder what kind of cancer she has. I immediately look at her breasts and notice she's well endowed. She's also very well dressed, her arms adorned with bracelets—which is not allowed when you get chemo.

My heart sinks when I look at the boy and realize they are here for him, not his mother. Jace must realize this, too, and I see his heart breaking along with mine.

"Group, our newest member has arrived. This is Dylan. He will be here for twelve cycles. And this is Dylan's mom, Helen."

Stacy proceeds to introduce them to everyone before she gets Dylan situated in Jace's old spot.

I have to hold back the tears. This boy can't be more than ten years old. Jace reaches over, squeezes my hand and doesn't let go.

The entire group watches in silence as Dylan gets his workup and then gets hooked up to the IV line.

John, who's in the seat next to Dylan, talks to him and his mom a bit and then hands the TV remote to the boy. We all laugh when he settles on SpongeBob SquarePants—much better than The Travel Channel if you ask me.

I look over at Jace to see that he's been writing something on a piece of notebook paper.

He leans over to me and whispers, "Do you mind?" He nods at Dylan.

I smile when I realize he wants to go across the room to comfort the little boy who is obviously scared by what he sees in the clinic.

I remember how I felt coming in that first day and seeing the bald heads and pale faces of some of the patients. I imagine it must be so much more frightening for a ten-year-old.

Jace rolls his chair across the room and sits down in front of the boy and his mom. He hands the slip of paper to his mother, Helen. As she reads it, a tear falls down her cheek. She then nods at Jace and hands the paper to the boy.

After the boy reads it, a small smile crosses his face and he looks up at Jace. Jace writes something else for Helen to read, and then she gets out her phone and gives it to Dylan, who looks very excited to be entrusted with it.

For the next two hours, Jace and Dylan text each other. Dylan can obviously talk, but he doesn't, he uses him mom's phone the entire time. At one point he reaches out to touch Jace's bald head. Another time, Jace pulls the collar of his shirt down to show Dylan his scar.

While I'm watching them together, I think about how Jace had his sperm frozen so he could be sure to have kids one day. I can see now why he would want them. Even without a voice to speak to Dylan, Jace is great with him. There are not many single guys who are so at ease with children. I imagine he will be a wonderful father.

When Jace finally gets up, Helen stands and gives him a hug. Then he comes over and sits down next to me, sending me a text.

> **Jace: I'm so sorry. I didn't mean to ignore you the entire time. I came here to support you and I completely lost track of time talking to Dylan.**

I lean over so only he can hear me. "Jace, there is nothing in this world that would have made me happier than what you just did. I'm so glad you came today. You made that little boy not so scared and I'm sure it made all the difference. You're obviously great with kids."

> **Jace: No more than you are, Keri. It's no different than what you did with Tyler the other day. I guess we're just two of a kind.**

Two of a kind.

I smile at him. He keeps finding ways to penetrate the wall I've put up around my heart. The wall I need to keep firmly in place to keep him out. The wall that crumbles a little bit more every time I'm around him.

I pull out my phone and text him, because I'm not sure I can speak past this lump in my throat.

**Me: I need a side effect.**

He reads it and nods. He knows what that means. He understands how I feel. No explanations are necessary between us. He gets me.

Stacy's interruption is welcome, as she comes over to unhook me for the very last time. As she pulls the catheter out of my arm, I feel like I've crossed the finish line. I'm overcome by emotion as I look over at Jace. He nods at me again. He gets this, too. *Two of a kind.*

After I say my goodbyes and read the graduation card they have all signed, Jace walks me out of the clinic. But instead of walking me towards the parking lot, he pulls me in the opposite direction, towards the marina. My eyes get wide and my breathing accelerates. He rented a boat?

I stare at him and he shrugs, looking quite nervous. We walk down the dock, passing all kinds of boats. My excitement builds as I try to figure out which one we will go on. As we walk further, the boats get larger and larger. In fact, we've passed the boats and are now into the yachts. I think maybe we aren't going on a boat at all, but that perhaps he's taking me to the end of the dock so we can go fishing or something.

Just before we reach the end of the dock, he stops and stands by one of the nicest yachts here. It must be sixty feet long. He reaches down and squeezes my hand. Then he gestures towards the yacht.

I look at him in confusion before I turn my head to look at the extraordinary vessel. From what I can tell it has three decks. I take in the beauty of it, amazed that anyone could have such an extravagance. I wonder if he knows someone who has loaned it to him for the day.

Then I look at the very back of the yacht, where the name is, and my world comes crashing down. In a matter of seconds, it all makes sense. The spa day, the gifts to everyone at the clinic, my raise and the incredible tips I've been getting.

I think back on the hours upon hours of conversations that we had. Did he ever tell me his full name? Did I even ask? How have we known each other for months without it coming up? How can I have these intense feelings for him without even knowing his full name? The name that's obvious to me when I see the bright blue lettering on the back of the yacht.

## The Double J

I spin around and bark at him, "Jarrett? Your last name is Jarrett?"

Samantha Christy

# Chapter Nineteen

I walk over to sit on one of the benches that line the dock. I try to absorb the reality of the situation.

He's a Jarrett. The same Jarrett who owns the bar I work in. He's my *boss*. He's been playing me this whole time. Have I simply been his charity case?

Part of me wants to think our connection is real, based on the conversations we've had, his paintings, and my gut feeling. But why didn't he tell me? Why did he string me along and make me think he was a struggling artist?

*Oh my God.* I suddenly remember the times I told him about how poor my family was and how Tanner had to take on more jobs to pay my bills. My medical bills—the ones that were much lower than I thought they should be—I'm willing to bet he paid those too. I'm so ashamed.

His hand touches my shoulder as he reaches down to whisper in my ear, but before he can, I shake him off and start to walk away.

I won't be anyone's charity case. And I certainly won't be like Connor, being with someone just to have access to money.

Before I get very far, Jace grabs my hand and jerks me back. His eyes beg me not to run away until I've heard him out. I close my eyes and take a breath. I should run away. I should leave and not look back. Protect my dignity, protect my heart. But instead, I walk the few steps back over to the bench and sit down.

He's typing away on his phone as I try to steady my breathing and control the rapid pace at which my heart is beating.

**Jace: I don't tell people about my family, about my money, if I can help it. They look at me differently. They treat me differently. I never know if they like me just for me, or for my money. I never wanted to deceive you. The more I got to know you, the harder it became to figure out a way to tell you. What was I supposed to say? This doesn't change anything, Keri. I am who I am with or without money. It wasn't my choice to be born into money, just as it wasn't your choice to be born without it. I don't look at you any differently because you don't have money. Actually, that may not be entirely true. I think you not having money is one of the things I like about you. You don't have anything, yet you would give the shirt off your back to help another.**

I read his text and I get what he's saying. I don't tell people I'm an orphan because of the way they react to me. Is that any different than him not telling people about his wealth because he doesn't want it to define him? Still, that doesn't excuse the fact that he's spent so much money on me.

"But the money, Jace. I know it was you who got me the raise. You're my boss? And all the tips ... what, did you have people come in and put money in the tip jar for you?"

Then it dawns on me, that is exactly what he did. I remember two guys in particular, right after I told Jace where I worked, who came to the club and asked all kinds of questions and then left a ridiculously large tip.

**Jace: I'm not your boss. My dad owns the club. I merely suggested that Mike review your file, and when he did, he made his own decision to give you and Tanner that raise. It wasn't my call and you wouldn't have gotten it if you didn't deserve it.**

"What about the tips? What do you want from me? Do you expect me to have sex with you now, to pay you back for everything you've done for me?"

He looks at me in a panic and frantically types on his phone.

**Jace: God, no, Keri. I never give anything with strings or expectations. You deserved all of it, every penny. Money means nothing to me. I know that sounds conceited, but it's true. I don't want it. Yes, it's made my life easier, but it doesn't come without guilt. I never wanted to be like my parents. It's why I work at the foundation. My money can help other people, it can make them happy and make their lives easier, that's all I was trying to do for you. You**

**do things every day for people, never expecting anything in return. Look at what you do for the Freeway kids. What you did for Tanner. Do you expect them to be indebted to you?**

He has a point. I gave Tanner everything I had and never expected anything in return. Still, I don't want Jace's hand-outs.

"I appreciate what you're saying, and no, I never expect anything in return. But Jace, I don't want your pity. I don't want your money. I know you paid some of my medical bills. It makes me feel cheap, like I can't provide for myself and like I'll always owe you something."

**Jace: I'm sorry you feel that way. It was never my intention. But if it makes you feel any better, I paid some bills for everyone in our Monday morning group. Ask them if you want to. I also paid for Steven's funeral expenses and a few other odd things for people.**

I remember a few weeks ago when Grace told me she had won a trip to Europe. She was always talking about going there whenever she watched The Travel Channel, but she figured with her medical expenses, she would never get the chance.

"Grace's trip?" I ask him.

He nods.

"So, it wasn't just me?"

He shakes his head.

Then I look over at the yacht. "How can you say you don't like money and then have something as extravagant as this?"

**Jace: Yes, I'll admit it appears contradictory. But I don't own it. I mean, yes, it's mine. My parents gave it to me for my college graduation. They knew I would just donate it or sell it and donate the money, so they kept it in their name. I rarely even use it, unless it's for the foundation. But when you told me the story about you and your dad and the boat, I knew I had to bring you here. Please, let me take you out on her. There is nothing I want to do more.**

Damn it. I do want to go on it. I know it will remind me of my dad, and I really do want to feel close to him. But at what expense? I'm fighting an internal battle in my head when he sends me another text.

**Jace: One of the reasons I don't tell people who I am is that I never get to see people for who they really are. Do you think I want to give money to people who ask for it? People who tell me how much they deserve it? Those aren't the people I help, Keri. I help the ones who help others, who don't think they are themselves worthy. But do you know what? Those people are always the worthy ones, and the fact that they don't even know it, makes them so.**

I think about everything he has said. I go back and re-read the texts he sent me. I even start to believe he means what he says. Maybe his money doesn't matter, maybe it shouldn't matter, but in some small way, it does. And it's just one more reason why we could never be together. We come from different worlds. But I'm not sure I'm ready to lose him for good either.

I make a snap decision to make it not matter, to not treat him any differently—because he's done the exact same thing for me.

"So, why The Double J?" I ask, pointing to the name of the yacht. "And why The Triple J, and The J Spot for that matter?"

> **Jace: My dad is Jason Jarrett, Jr. He has three J's in his name, thus, The Triple J. I'm Jason Jarrett the third, I have two J's, thus The Double J. The J Spot is owned by his corporation. He tends to use the letter J in all his business ventures.**

"And his foundation? What is that called?" I ask.

> **Jace: It's not his foundation. It's mine. My parents try to appear philanthropic, and they do contribute to my foundation, as well as others, but I think it's merely for appearance sake. It's also a good tax deduction.**

He looks embarrassed for them.

> **Jace: I set up the foundation right after my college graduation, when I was awarded the trust fund my grandfather left me. Learning how to run a foundation is what I went to college for. I just picked up art along the way. I always thought of myself as different from my parents, different from my grandparents. I wanted to break the cycle of my family's**

**vainglorious existence. So, I named my foundation The Third Watch.**

*His* foundation? I'm dumbfounded. A young twenty-something man fresh out of college inherits God knows how many millions and immediately sets up a foundation to give it away to others.

How can I possibly hold a grudge against him?

A smile creeps up my face. "The Third Watch. Because you're Number Three, right?" I ask, referring to the nickname Jules gave him when they were kids.

He nods.

"Well, are you going to take me aboard, or what?"

He visibly relaxes as his eyes briefly close and a smile lights up his face.

But before I let him pull me up, I add, "Under one condition. You don't give me any more money. None, I don't want it. I will never be a Connor."

**Jace: A Connor? Sounds like there's a story there. Maybe you'll tell me someday. And Keri, I can't promise I won't spend money on you. I want to do nice things for my friends and you're going to have to learn to deal with it. But you should also know I don't live a large life, so it's not like I'll be flying you to Paris for the weekend. More like buying you a cheeseburger and a ticket to the movies. I do promise not to pay for anything else without you knowing about it first. Deal?**

"Deal."

I let him take my hand and lead me up the short ramp to the finest vessel I'll ever set foot upon. I vow to make the next few hours count, before I have to endure my final Monday Madness.

He gives me a tour of the yacht, which is even nicer than I imagined. It's adorned with rich oak and granite and is very tastefully decorated. He introduces me to the captain and then takes me down to one of the two large staterooms so I can change into a bathing suit. There must be a hundred bathing suits of all shapes and sizes, for both males and females, hanging in the closet. Alongside them are a variety of towels and cover-ups. Everything in here is still new with tags on.

Jace must see my eyes go wide because he texts me.

**Jace: I sometimes bring families associated with the foundation on board and I just want to be prepared. Some of the kids we help have never been on a boat and they don't even own a bathing suit, so I keep stocked up, just in case. So, take your pick.**

He brings kids on the yacht? I thought when he said he used it for foundation business, he meant fundraisers and that sort of thing. This man keeps surprising me.

As I peruse the selection, I hold up a bikini and see his face light up out of the corner of my eye. Yes, this is the one.

I smile and start to push him out the cabin door when I notice the painting on the wall. Another Jace Jarrett original. He hadn't shown this one to me, but I can tell it's new.

"Didn't it bother Morgan to see a picture of me here in one of the staterooms?" I ask.

**Jace: She doesn't come on the boat. Like I said, I
rarely take it out for personal use. And even if
she had been here, she wouldn't understand the
painting. Nobody would. Nobody but you.**

I study the painting. It's obvious to me what it is, and I wonder
how others can't see what I do. But the more I look at it, the more I
get what others must see. It's a woman sitting on a bench, like one
out on the dock, with many boats in the background. She's holding
what appear to be balloons. But I know better, and after I count
them, I'm sure. There are thirteen of them. IV bags. Bags of poison
for my thirteen cycles of chemotherapy. And there's that silly hat on
top of my head again.

Why he keeps painting me in that hat is beyond me.

"It's extraordinary," I tell him. "You are so talented, Jace."

He simply shrugs his shoulders and points to the bikini in my
hand. Then he walks out of the cabin and closes the door.

I don't change right away. I stare at the painting for another few
minutes. I'm still awestruck that he chooses to keep painting me.
Surely he must have paintings of Morgan here as well, or maybe he
removed them when she dumped him. I'll have to remember to ask
him about it. I really want to see more of his work someday.

I can feel the yacht moving before I emerge from the
stateroom. I climb the narrow stairway into the main living area to
find Jace wearing board shorts and a University of Miami t-shirt.

I take in a breath. I've never seen him look so casual. I've never
seen his legs before. His muscular calves and bare feet have my
internal juices flowing. Why are his bare feet so sexy?

I try to remember if I ever thought such things about James or
Connor.

I'm glad his back is turned to me so I can admire him without his knowledge.

He must hear me, and when he turns around, his jaw drops and he blinks repeatedly.

I look down at myself to make sure my bikini is covering the right places. I have a cover-up on over the bright-orange bikini, but the cover-up is sheer, and you can see right through it, and his eyes are burning a hole into my clothes as he takes me in.

I must flush bright red as he slowly lowers his eyes to my curves, all the way down to my feet.

Ordinarily, this would bother me, being devoured by a man's eyes in the same way a lion looks at a piece of meat. But all I can do is stand here and bask in delight, knowing my body affects him like this.

Then his lips move, as he whispers something not meant for my ears, and I think I see him discreetly adjust himself as he turns away and pulls out his phone.

**Jace: I'm glad you found one that fits. Are you hungry? Do you want lunch? I was always starving after chemo, so I have some things in case you are.**

"Yes, thank you. I could eat."

I half expect him to ring a little dinner bell and have elegantly dressed staff come out of nowhere to serve us from silver-domed platters. Instead, he pulls on my elbow for me to follow him into the galley.

He sits me down on a barstool, hands me a bottle of water and prepares our lunch. I should probably get up to help him, but I'm stunned. This man, with his multi-million-dollar yacht that has a closet full of swimwear 'just in case,' is cutting up different cheeses, breaking a loaf of French bread, and washing a bunch of grapes—all for me.

He puts everything on a tray and then pulls a bottle of champagne from the refrigerator, along with two chilled glasses. He picks up the tray and motions for me to follow him out to the deck.

After he has laid out our lunch on the deck table, he texts me.

**Jace: I thought we should celebrate your final cycle. I hope you like champagne.**

As he pours the champagne into the tall glasses, I kid, "What, no Cristal?"

He shakes his head, smirking. He knows I'm joking. He also knows that as a bartender, I know this is a thirty-dollar bottle of champagne. Not a two-hundred-dollar bottle most people might expect to be served in such a venue.

**Jace: I told you, I don't live a large life, Keri.**

Then he leans over and taps his glass to mine and whispers in my ear, "To the rest of your life."

It takes all my strength to recover from his sweet words and his hot breath on my ear.

"And to yours," I say, still melting on the inside from the unexpected pleasures he continues to bring me.

Over the next few hours, all thoughts of chemo and cancer fade away. He lets me drive the boat for a time and then when we sit on deck to absorb some sun, we find dolphins swimming and jumping right alongside us.

It's surreal.

It is exactly how I imagined it would be when my dad would tell me stories about our adventures back when I was little.

I notice that Jace hasn't removed his shirt in the warm sun, and I know it's because he still has the feeding tube. I can tell he has continued to put on weight, so I can't imagine he will have it much longer.

"When will you get the G-tube out?" I ask, hoping he won't be offended by my noticing his shirt has remained on.

**Jace: Next week, as long as I don't lose any of the weight I've gained.**

"You know, it won't bother me. I mean, if you want to take your shirt off and get some sun, it won't bother me to see it. You shouldn't have to stay covered up just for me. The sun is brilliant today and if I do say so myself, your pale skin could use some of it."

He silently laughs at me. He stares at me in contemplation. Then, he nervously watches me as he removes his shirt.

As I blatantly stare at his stomach, I realize how inconsequential the G-tube is. It's just a small plug that sits a few inches above and slightly off center from his belly button.

Moments later, I realize I've been staring at his abs. How does a man in chemo keep such toned abs? I notice that his shorts ride low and … *oh*, he didn't lose *all* his hair. There is a fine trail of hair running down from his belly button, beneath his shorts to the place that makes my face instantly heat up.

My phone vibrates on the table, pulling me from my fantasy.

**Jace: Are you objectifying me?**

"Uh …"

I'm mortified he caught me staring at him. I feel terrible that he probably thinks I was looking at his feeding tube. My mind races, trying to come up with something to say so he's not uncomfortable. However, when I look over at him, he has a smirk on his face.

**Jace: Thanks, Keri. I think you just gave me the best compliment I've ever had.**

We sunbathe together in comfortable silence, listening to music from his iPod. Music that is also on *my* playlist. How can two people from different worlds have so much in common?

When we hear thunder, the captain comes down to tell us there's a storm moving in and that we're going to head back to beat the weather.

We spend the next half hour watching the incredible lightning show far out at sea.

Then, there's a break in the clouds and sunshine peeks through, producing a glorious rainbow. Before I know it, tears are streaming down my cheeks and Jace's arms come around me.

"What is it?" he whispers, as he runs a hand soothingly up and down my arm.

"It's just that—this day, it's been incredible. You've given me something I never dreamed I would have. You've brought me closer to my dad. And now, seeing this rainbow … well, my dad used to comfort me during storms by telling me about rainbows. He said sometimes after a storm, a rainbow will shine brightly and that meant someone was reaching out from heaven."

Jace holds me as happy tears roll down my cheeks. And I know, despite what will happen to me later tonight, that this has been the best day of my life.

Samantha Christy

# Chapter Twenty

"Holy shit, Keri!"

Tanner covers his head with his hands and then runs them across his morning stubble. "You mean to tell me I threatened to kick a millionaire's ass?"

He shakes his head in disbelief and then turns his attention back to the laptop where he has been Googling all things Jarrett for the past fifteen minutes.

This morning, when I told Tanner everything I'd learned about Jace, he immediately went for his computer and started researching him, his family and his foundation.

"I can't believe what a normal guy he is," Tanner says. "I mean, he doesn't act like he has money at all. The stuff we talked about at the bar the other night was just the same crap I talk to all my buddies about. I can't believe he paid your medical bills and paid the bills of everyone else at chemo. Who does that?"

"I know, right?" I agree. "I was super mad at him until he told me he basically did the same for everyone else. It made me feel a little less like a Connor."

Tanner nods in agreement. He lived through it with me, so he understands what I mean. He knows I could never take advantage of someone for his money.

"So, what's wrong with the guy? He's too perfect. He's gorgeous, rich, nice, caring and he loves your best friend. There has to be a catch." He winks at me.

"There is. And her name is Morgan," I say sadly. "But I'm not going to let that stand in the way of our friendship. Even if I can't be *with* him, I can still be with him."

Suddenly, I realize what Jace's generosity means for Tanner and me, and a huge smile becomes plastered on my face. "Oh my God, Tan, you can quit your other jobs now! We can go back to being *us* and having fun with our friends. You no longer have to break your back for me."

"Keri, I never looked at it that way. I did what I had to do. And I would do it all over again. I can never repay you for what you did for me. This was barely a drop in the bucket compared to that."

He may say that, but I saw him being run ragged by the three jobs he was holding down. And he never complained. Not one time. He just kept filling up that tin can in the kitchen, and when it overflowed, he would deposit the money into an account earmarked for my medical expenses. Then he would start filling it up all over again. I don't even know how much he saved.

"Well, now you have some extra money. What are you going to do with it?" I ask.

"It's not my money, Keri. It was never my money. I don't want it, it's all for you. Buy a new laptop, get some new clothes, do whatever you want with it."

"No way, Tan. You earned it. I did nothing for it. I can't take your money. I won't."

"The hell you didn't earn it, Keri. You endured cancer and chemo, and you'll live in fear for the rest of your life that it might come back. By the way, when do you go in for your next scans?"

I go to the calendar on the wall and page forward three months to the date circled in red. That's the day. That is the day I will find out if I have to endure more chemo, or worse, surgery.

But I can't think about that now. I refuse to live under a cloud of doubt. I want to make the most of my life, however short or long it may be. I want to fill my life with people I care about. People who themselves are caring and compassionate and make life worth living. People like Jace.

And suddenly I know what to do with the money.

"Tan, if you're sure you won't keep the money for yourself, I think I have an idea of what to do with it."

"Throw it off a bridge if that's what you want. It's all yours. All ten thousand dollars of it."

I choke on my coffee. "Ten thousand dollars? Are you kidding me? How did you save that much in four months?" I eye him suspiciously.

"It's not what you think, Keri. We pretty much put our lives on hold. We stopped going out, stopped spending money. That, with my extra jobs and the awesome tips we got thanks to Richie Rich, all added up quickly."

I blow out the breath I was holding. It would kill me if Tanner ever went back to a life of crime just to help me. But I know he would do it if he thought he had to, and that scares me to no end.

Tanner gets up to get ready for his temp job. "I'll give them notice today and finish out the week. I promise I'll buy myself something nice with this week's paycheck if it will make you feel better."

I give him a sly smile and say, "Or you could just bring the extra money to Scrabble Night and try to make a killing."

He laughs at me. "Hell, I almost forgot about Scrabble Night. It will be great to get back to it after all these months. There's a guy at my day job who's been checking me out, maybe I'll bring him. Man, it will be weird to start dating again. Oh, and you should bring Jace. Or do you think it would be beneath him?" he teases.

Beneath him? I question if that man thinks anything is beneath him. He wasn't even embarrassed that he bought me a cheap bottle of champagne. I love his humility. Yes, I think I will invite him along.

But first, I've got ten thousand dollars burning a hole in my pocket.

~ ~ ~

After spending all of Tuesday recovering from my last chemo cycle, I stop by the bank to take care of the funds that Tanner transferred to my account yesterday. My phone vibrates in my pocket as I'm walking back to my car.

**Morgan: Hi Keri, it's Morgan. I hope you're doing well. I'm texting you to find out about Jace. How is he doing?**

Why is Morgan still texting me? She's a friend of his family and should be getting information from *them*. The last thing I want is to be communicating with his ex.

> **Me: Morgan, don't you think you should be asking his family? They probably know more about his medical condition than I do.**

It's a lie. I know they don't know much at all, except for Jules. I know his parents don't know how much weight he lost and how much he gained back. They never asked about his Monday Madness or offered much help in any way. They never showed one ounce of support. At least Morgan bothered to show up a few times.

> **Morgan: I've tried to stay away. I know they must be furious with me. I can barely stand to be with myself these days. I don't deserve to be kept informed about his situation. But I thought you might tell me anyway.**

I think back to what she said the last time she texted me. I think about when I first met Jace and he told me all the wonderful things about her. I've since talked with other people at chemo and I've learned that there are more people than you'd think who simply can't deal with a loved one's cancer.

I'm trying not to hold it against her. But it would be so much easier if Jace didn't still love her.

> **Me: He's doing well, actually. He's still gaining weight. He's happy to be done with chemo. He's still waiting to see if he will be able to speak again, but I guess that just takes time.**

> **Morgan: Thank you, Keri. I really appreciate it.**

**Me: Now that I've cooperated with you, will you give me an honest answer to something?**

**Morgan: Of course.**

**Me: Are you going to come back to him when he's better? When he gets his feeding tube out and when his hair grows in. When he is talking again. Will you get back together with him?**

I press send and then realize my hands are shaking and I'm holding my breath awaiting her response. I don't know if it's merely my imagination, but it seems like she's taking her time texting me back. Does she not know the answer? Does she even have any idea that the woman she is texting is in love with him? Or maybe that's exactly why she is texting me. Keep your friends close and your enemies closer.

**Morgan: I don't know. I mean, I know I'm a horrible person for leaving him that way. It wouldn't be fair of me to ask him to come back to me after what I did. But I just don't know. All I know is that I still love him. That's as honest as I can be, Keri.**

# Chapter Twenty-one

At work on Saturday, I'm still thinking about Morgan's text. She still loves him. He still loves her. Of course they will get back together. I know deep down, I hope she'll walk away and he will eventually get over her. And sometimes I'll have an amazing day with him, like on the yacht last week, and I see a glimmer of hope and those walls around my heart start to break open and let him in. But then I realize he hasn't texted me, not since he checked on me Tuesday, and I slowly build those walls back up again.

My heart is on a roller coaster ride and at some point, I fear it will spin out of control.

My phone vibrates in my pocket, pulling me from my trance.

**Jace: What does it take to get a drink around here?**

I look up and glance around the bar to see Jace sitting down in the middle of the bar near both Tanner's and my sections. I delight in my power to conjure him up at will.

After I finish serving a few customers, I walk over, peeking in the mirror behind the bar along the way to make sure I look presentable. I'm glad I wore one of my best Triple J shirts and my almost-too-tight shorts that give my butt a nice lift.

"Hey, how are you?"

**Jace: I'm great.**

He has a smirk on his face and is looking at me like he knows a secret. I notice how happy he looks. Not that I haven't seen him happy before, I have. Like when we were on his boat, or when he was talking to Dylan, the kid at chemo, or when we went for coffee. Then I frown as I remember … or when he was with Morgan. I shake it off.

"What can I get you?"

**Jace: How about a draft beer. Anything is fine.**

"Coming right up," I say.

His eyes follow me as I get a frosty glass from the cooler. He watches me the entire time I tap his beer, and when it overflows all over my hand, he silently laughs.

I'm sure my face is turning red as I quickly wipe down the glass and place it on a coaster for him. As he reaches for the glass, his fingers momentarily touch mine making my skin tingle.

"Hey, man, how are you doing?" Tanner says over my shoulder as he reaches a hand out to shake Jace's.

I watch the two of them as they talk and text back and forth like old buddies. I'm glad that Tanner hasn't let Jace's revelation of riches interfere with their budding friendship.

**Jace: I don't have to ask you how it feels to know you don't have to go for chemo on Monday. We should celebrate.**

I pull out my own private bottle of tequila. Tanner and I each keep one under the bar for those rare occasions when you just need a shot, like when we got a raise a few months ago.

I pour us each a shot, slide his over to him and say, "Don't tell the boss." Then I clink his glass and take my shot. He downs his as well and smiles while shaking his head.

**Jace: Thanks, but that's not what I meant. We should go out and celebrate our renewed freedom. You know, someplace fun, knowing we won't get sick after ... at least not from chemo. Where we can just enjoy ourselves and be regular people for a change. What do you say, Keri?**

I'm excited by the fact that he wants to continue our friendship, however twisted it is, but at the same time I'm bummed that we'll never take it to the next level.

"Jace, I'm not going on a date with you."

No matter how much I want to, no matter how much my body is screaming for it.

**Jace: Not a date, Keri. I'm going to respect your wishes. There are no expectations here. I just think we need to celebrate.**

Yes, I can do that.

Maybe.

I think.

But I draw the line at going out by ourselves. It blurs the lines of our friendship. We need to go somewhere with lots of other people. Someplace public. Then I remember what Tanner said earlier this week and a smile crosses my face.

"Are you free Monday night?" I ask him.

**Jace: Sure, what do you have in mind?**

"Scrabble."

He looks at me like my head isn't screwed on properly. Like I thought he would look at me when I said it. Nobody gets it, our silly Scrabble Night. The one night we all get together and cut loose because the rest of the time we have to be responsible bartenders or waitresses as we watch other people have fun.

**Jace: Did you really just say Scrabble?**

I laugh before I explain our Monday night tradition. His face lights up as I tell him all about it. About the food—everyone brings a dish. About the betting—one quarter per point. About the fun— bring your own liquor. We rotate the location and we play in teams based on how many people show up.

"You really have to experience it to understand it," I say.

**Jace: I can't think of a better way to spend my Monday night. I'm in.**

I can't keep the smile from my face as I go about helping other customers.

It's starting to get busy as the night goes on, and the club is filling up.

Two attractive women sit at the bar, flanking Jace's barstool. They giggle and say things I can't hear. And then Jace texts them.

My spine stiffens and the smile falls from my face when I realize he must know them to have their phone numbers. Of course he does. What, do I think he doesn't have attractive women falling all over him everywhere he goes?

I guess I've never really seen him out of the context of chemo, or the few times we've been out just the two of us. He probably has a harem of women waiting to be with the rich and gorgeous Jace Jarrett.

He waves me over to them. *Oh, God,* I've been so busy avoiding them that I forgot I should be serving them.

I hurry over and say, "Sorry, ladies, what can I get for you?"

They spout their orders at me while Jace is texting. My phone vibrates and he motions for me to look at it right away.

**Jace: Keri, this is Brittney and Carly, old friends of mine.**

I reach over the bar to shake hands with them. Well, I try to shake their hands, but they barely touch me, like my working-class hands might bleed poverty all over their highly manicured fingers.

They share a look with one another, then they look back at me and assess me from head to toe while I make their drinks. The way they're looking at me is not the way you might take in a new acquaintance, more like the way you size up a bug while trying to decide if you're going to use your shoe or a magazine to squash it.

**Jace: Ignore them, Keri. Please understand that I use the term 'friends' very loosely when referring to them. They're just some girls from my parents' country club. They don't know what it's like to work a day in their lives. I didn't know they were going to be here. I'm sorry.**

I'm relieved a little after reading his text. But these girls are just one more reason we could never be together. I look at their designer clothes and their Prada purses and realize I wouldn't even begin to fit into his world. Even though he's not like that, in his Levi's and polo shirt that were probably purchased at the local mall.

I get busy with drink orders, but I still notice Bottle-Blonde and Bottle-Blonder talking, flirting, and hair-flipping their way through a few drinks with Jace. He, however, stops at two drinks while his 'friends' continue to imbibe.

I look at Jace and he rolls his eyes as if he's bored and has heard their stories a million times over. He catches me watching him in the bar mirror and makes ridiculous faces at me. He texts me silly one-liners that keep me smiling.

Eventually, Mike walks by and notices Jace sitting at the bar. They shake hands and then a smiling Jace texts me to tell me he's going to Mike's office to be 'rescued' from the giggle twins.

It doesn't escape me how Brittney and Carly have been assaulting me with their eyes. I wonder what Jace told them about me or if they even bothered to ask.

I go to freshen up their drinks when Brittney says to me, "So, Jeri, was it?" Like I don't know that Jace texted her my name when he introduced us.

"It's Keri, actually. With a 'K'."

She snorts and waves off my comment. "Whatever," she says. "Are you having fun being Jace's latest project?"

"Project?" I question her.

"Yes, project. You know what a nice guy he is. How he likes to give to the less fortunate. Surely you realize what's going on here, right?"

*Project?* I'm his project? Like one of his charities? I absorb her words, but I don't want to believe them. He isn't like that. Surely they're just jealous because he wasn't giving his full attention to them.

Carly laughs and says, "Oh my God, you think he really likes you. Oh, you poor dear." She shakes her head and gives her friend a look. "You could never compete with Morgan. You must know that. Even if they don't get back together, there are so many more women he can choose from. His possibilities are endless."

"And I suppose you two would be first in line."

I try not to appear hurt by their words, the words that cut through me like a serrated knife. The words I know are true. There are plenty more suitable candidates for Jace. What would he ever want with a bartender who comes from a broken past?

Brittney pipes in, "Oh, we wouldn't lower ourselves to stand in any line. We would never throw ourselves at him like a commoner." She laughs and then covers her mouth in mock surprise. "Not to say that's what *you* are doing or anything." She rolls her eyes at Carly.

"No, of course not," Carly says. "That would be pathetic, even for a bartender. Well, we have better things to do on a Saturday night." They get up to leave and she turns around and spits out, "See you around, Jeri." And then they walk out, not even bothering to pay for their expensive drinks.

Tanner's arm comes around my shoulder. "I only heard the end of your conversation, but Keri, don't let those bitches get to you. It's exactly what they want. They must know Jace has feelings for you and they're jealous. That's all that was, nothing more."

I nod and try to hold my head high, but a tear betrays me and falls down my cheek just as Jace walks back up to the bar.

**Jace: Are you okay? What happened? Where did Brittney and Carly go?**

"I'm fine, the keg kicked back on me when we changed it and I got some foam in my eye. The girls left a few minutes ago, you just missed them."

Tanner shakes his head at me in disappointment that I didn't rat Jace's so-called-friends out to him.

I know what Tanner is thinking—where's the Keri he met back at Freeway. Where's the girl with a backbone. The girl with the thick skin who couldn't be penetrated by inconsequential words from shallow people. The girl who could stand up for herself when she needed to and even throw down if she had to.

But that was different. Back at Freeway, we were all on a level playing field. Here, with girls like those, I'm completely out of my element.

Jace and I talk for a few more minutes. I give him Shana's address for Scrabble Night, then he gets up to leave, throwing a hundred-dollar bill on the bar. I stare him down.

**Jace: I know they didn't pay for their drinks, Keri. They never do, and I'm not about to short**

**the till. I'm sure when you work it out, you'll see I've left you an appropriate, not over-the-top tip.**

He walks to the end of the bar and waits for me to come over. He pulls me close and whispers, "See you Monday."

Then he walks out, leaving me a quivering mess. A mess because of his hot breath on my ear and his sexy whisper along with that scent I've come to love so much. A mess because his friends confirmed for me what I know to be true, that he is way out of my league. A mess because I am a stupid, stupid girl who continues to get trampled on by fantasies of more-than-enough love.

# Chapter Twenty-two

It was nice to be able to volunteer at Freeway on a Monday again. The feeling I got when I woke up this morning was incredible. No more chemo. After thirteen weeks of waking up and knowing exactly what was in store for me that day, it was so nice not to have it all scripted out. Especially tonight, I have no idea what tonight will bring.

I've changed my clothes no less than four times. It's not a date. I keep reminding myself of that, but this is the first time Jace will see me when it's not related to chemo or work. I want to make a good impression, yet still seem calm and casual.

I settle on my favorite jeans and a blouse that, when coupled with my push-up bra, has the buttons stressing just a tiny bit, drawing the slightest attention to my artificially augmented cleavage.

I've learned to embrace my breasts through all this, both literally and figuratively. God blessed us with them not only to feed our young but to appeal to men. Since I don't have any young to feed, I'll gladly use them for their secondary purpose as long as they shall remain attached to my body.

Of course, it's not all men that I'm trying to appeal to. In fact, I could care less about all men. *One* man, that's all I care about. One man among the billions of men on Earth.

I ride with Tanner over to Shana's. Greg, the guy he met at his temp job, is meeting us there, as is Jace. I wanted to arrive a little early to explain to those I haven't seen in a while that Jace is not my boyfriend and that he needs to text instead of speaking out loud.

I spend the next twenty minutes checking and re-checking my appearance. I decided to go natural, letting my still-thinned-out wavy hair flow down my back. I may have used a bit more mascara than usual, and my pocket is holding a tiny container of Tic-Tacs—just in case he sits close enough to whisper to me.

Every time there's a knock on the door, my heartbeat races so fast that Nurse Stacy would probably be calling 911.

Finally, he arrives, precisely on time. He carries a six pack of beer under one arm, a bag full of quarters in one hand, and a tray of sectioned deli subs in the other.

Tanner and I share a look and giggle. What did we expect … a bottle of Johnnie Walker Blue along with a tray of caviar?

I love the way Jace continues to surprise me with his taste for simple pleasures.

The first thing I notice is that he has what appears to be a five o'clock shadow. Not only on his face, but on top of his head. Oh, his hair is coming in! I want so badly to walk the few steps over to him and run my hands across his cheeks and on his head. How I long to feel the scruffiness of fresh stubble under my fingers from the hair that promises to come.

I introduce him to everyone here. "Jace, this is Shana and her boyfriend, Kevin. She and Ashley over there are waitresses. This is

Austin, one of the weeknight bartenders. You know Tanner and that's his date, Greg. Ashley and Austin have come stag as well, so we're in good company."

Everyone shares a look as he goes around and shakes their hands. I know what they're thinking. It's the same way the people at chemo looked at us. I shake off their raised eyebrows and direct Jace to the kitchen to deposit his contributions.

"Do you think they know you're the boss's kid?" I ask him.

**Jace: Didn't you tell them?**

"It's not my story to tell," I say, with a smug little smile, throwing his own words from a few weeks ago back at him.

**Jace: Then, no, they probably don't know. If we can keep it that way, I'd prefer it. They seem like a great bunch and I don't want to make them uncomfortable thinking they have to behave a certain way around me. I like to get to know people for who they are, not who they pretend to be when they find out who I am.**

I get it. I don't doubt that once people find out who he is, some of them may ask him for money. Others, women mainly, probably try to get him into bed. I think back to what Brittney—or maybe it was Carly—said about him having a line of women waiting to be the next girlfriend of the most eligible bachelor in South Florida.

"Okay then, grab a beer and let's head out so you can get a rundown of the rules along with Greg."

**Jace: I'm not drinking tonight. But I didn't want to come empty-handed. And, it's Scrabble, doesn't everyone know the rules?**

I laugh at him and say, "Oh, you thought this was regular old Scrabble? Come, my young Padawan."

I start to walk out but he pulls me back to him, then he types out a text.

**Jace: Keri, you just quoted my favorite movie of all time. Lead the way, Obi-wan Kenobi. Wait … we're not playing Strip Scrabble, are we?**

He looks up at me with a smirk on his face that makes me blush. We grab a couple of sodas and head out to the table with eight chairs crowded around it. Shana lays out the rules for Greg and Jace who are the only two here who haven't played before.

"Gentlemen, this is a drinking game. However, in the name of responsibility, since most of us work in a bar, you may choose to drink soda and watch the rest of us get smashed, or you can utilize one of the cab companies we have conveniently listed on the kitchen counter. But everyone's car keys go in that drawer over there and nobody gets them back without the approval of the OSP."

"OSP?" Greg asks.

"The Only Sober Player," Shana replies. "We have one every week. It's like a designated driver. This week, Keri has graciously volunteered her services."

I see Jace whip out his phone.

**Jace: Keri, why don't you have fun with your friends? Let me be the SOB, or OPS or OSP, whatever. I probably won't drink anyway.**

I laugh at his text. "No, it's already been decided per the rules of the game. Plus, I just finished chemo last week and I want all that crap out of my system before I really tie one on. Maybe you can be the OSP next week, if we lose that is," I say, hopeful that he will be returning to become a part of our Monday night group.

**Jace: You have a deal. But I never lose.**

"As I was saying," Shana says, rolling her eyes at our private conversation that interrupted her rule-telling, "here is a copy of the rules." She hands them each a printed slip of paper. "In a nutshell, if you use more than five tiles for a word, the other teams have to take a drink. If you use five tiles or less, *your* team has to take a drink. If you can't make a word, the team with the most points pours you a shot—their choice. If you use a word that doesn't exist on Wikipedia, you take a drink and lose your turn. Any tiles you have left at the end of a game, you take that many drinks. Oh, and dirty words always score double word points and all the other teams must take a shot. We usually keep playing over and over, adding up the cumulative scores until someone passes out. Questions?"

Greg raises his hand like a kid in school, making the rest of us giggle. "Yeah, what does the winner get?"

"I'm glad you asked," she says. "The winning team gets to pick next week's OSP from the losing team. But usually anyone on the losing team was so drunk that they are still hung over the following week, so they really don't care. Oh, and the winners also get the quarters. It's one quarter per point on the words you play, not counting doubles or triples, just face value, I mean we only work in a bar, we don't *own* one."

My eyes go wide and I look at Tanner. He shakes his head at me to let me know he didn't say anything. I look around to see everyone laughing and realize her remark was purely coincidental.

Jace shrugs off the comment as well and then leans close and whispers, "Lost your last game, did you?"

"Big time," I reply. "As in, I'm still recovering almost four months later."

"Not tonight," he whispers.

Oh, he's competitive. I like that in a man.

We take our seats, all squished in around Shana's small table. There is barely room for eight chairs, let alone eight people, and I'm very aware that my thigh is firmly pressed up against Jace's. I'm also aware of the very large smile on his face.

An hour into the game, things get exciting. I find I have just as much fun being the OSP and watching the others get silly drunk, as I do participating in the drunkenness.

Jace seems to be enjoying himself as well. Everyone has their phone in front of them so he can text them and participate in the conversation. He's getting to know everyone at the table, as the more they drink, the more secrets they reveal about themselves.

It's quite funny when we find out that Greg was actually a drag queen at a bar in Vegas one time when he couldn't find a job and make rent. We all laugh when we gather around Shana's computer and watch a YouTube video of one of his performances.

As the night goes on, the words get funnier and dirtier. Shana looks proud of herself when she puts down the word 'fagshag.'

We all look at her with raised eyebrows.

"What?" she pouts. "I'm half British, I can use it. You know, fagshag, when you sleep with your gay best friend, like Keri and Tanner over here."

Shana giggles like it's the funniest thing she's ever said. Everyone else at the table momentarily bursts out laughing until they see Jace doesn't find it amusing. Then all eyes go between Tanner, Jace and me.

If Jace weren't here, I would probably be laughing with the rest of them. Even Greg finds it funny. But seeing the look on Jace's face, like someone just told him his puppy dog died, makes it not so funny.

Tanner holds up his hands in surrender, looks Jace straight in the eye and says, "Seven years ago. One time. I swear."

Jace gets up from the table and goes to the kitchen. I follow him and watch as he pulls one of his previously untouched beers out of the refrigerator and drinks it. The whole thing. In one drink.

Then he looks up at me and I'm not sure what to say. It's not that I was hiding the fact that we had a hookup, it just never came up.

When Jace asked early on if Tanner was more than my roommate, I simply left out that tiny little detail. After all, Jace and I didn't know each other very well back then. Now, looking at his face, I feel guilty for not telling him. I feel bad he had to find out this way, in front of other people.

**Jace: I get it. You don't go around advertising it. That is something I understand. It's in your past, Keri, and I have no right to hold it against him or you. Hell, I have no right to be pissed even if you were sleeping with him or any other man right now. But even though I know that, I**

**can't help but stand here and want to beat him and every other man who has touched you into a bloody pulp.**

I laugh at his text and he gives me a questioning look. "How do you think I felt every time I saw Morgan?"

He nods at me in understanding. Then he grabs another beer, takes a calming breath, and leads us back into the other room.

With each beer Jace drinks, I find we are getting more comfortable with each other. He keeps kicking the heel of my shoe with the toe of his. He knocks his knee into mine repeatedly, the whole time smiling as if he's enjoying a private joke. Sometimes our hands brush together when we both reach out to grab a tile at the same time. And when he leans over to whisper in my ear ... well, I'm just glad we're stuffed in like sardines or I might fall right out of my chair into a gooey puddle of hormones on the floor.

Every touch, every knee bump, every whisper, is making my body hum and the little hairs on my neck stand at attention.

I'm grateful I'm the OSP tonight or I might have ended up making some very bad choices. I make a note to myself that one of us must always remain sober when Jace and I are together. He is my weakness. My kryptonite. And I'm beginning to think that I might very well be his.

After one o'clock in the morning rolls around, the liquor has dried up and the yawns come out. I assess all the people here. Ashley is going to sleep on Shana's couch. Greg stopped drinking before eleven and has sobered up. Tanner, Austin and Jace are what we bartenders call completely wasted. Greg has offered to take Tanner and Austin home. I will drive Jace home in Tanner's car, and Jace can come back to Shana's for his car in the morning.

We say our goodbyes and head out to the parking lot. Jace sends me a text. I have to read it twice to understand his drunken words.

**Jace: take my caar that way have escuse to see you tmorrow.**

I shake my head at him. "You want me to drive your car, so you can see me tomorrow?"

He nods.

**Jace: you cn drive home nd bring it bak tomorrow.**

My blood pumps harder at the idea of driving the kind of car he would own. "Which one is your car?" I ask, looking around for a Ferrari or Maserati, but I don't see one.

He gives me the keys and I press the unlock button and I spy the flashing lights a few cars down. As we approach, it's easy for me to see it under the streetlights in the parking lot. It is a BMW M3 Coupe. It looks very sporty, which I would have guessed, and it looks like a very nice car, one I would never be able to afford. Still, it's not the uber-flashy car I would expect a multi-millionaire to drive.

"Is the Aston Martin in the shop?" I tease as I take him around to the passenger side, very aware that in his drunkenness, he's holding on to me quite tightly.

Thirty minutes later, I'm waking him up, which means removing his hand from where he placed it on my thigh when we got in the car. I'm a little concerned about how I'm going to get him up the stairs to his loft, but once he comes to, he seems slightly less inebriated than when we left Shana's apartment. He's able to manage the stairs with me next to him providing balance.

I use his keys to unlock the loft door and help him onto the couch. I'm overwhelmed, once again, by the mixture of fresh paint and that rugged spicy smell that is all Jace. I take a moment to breathe it in. After all, he's not going to notice.

I stare at the painting of me over the fireplace and remember the last time I was here, the time we found out about our deeper connection. I wonder if that could be enough, if it could ever be enough to make us right for each other.

As I head into the kitchen to put on a pot of coffee, I pass by an easel that's half covered by a sheet. It's obviously another one of me, but this time, I see *him* in the background.

I step closer to study it when my phone vibrates in my pocket, scaring the living daylights out of me. It's Tanner wanting to make sure I got to Jace's place okay. I have a brief conversation with him while I go in the kitchen in search of a coffee maker.

When I come back with a cup of strong, black coffee for Jace, I find him snoring on the sofa. I take his shoes off and put his legs up on the couch and reach for a blanket to cover him with.

Then, suddenly, I'm pulled down on top of him. He holds me tight and takes in a deep breath. "Lavender," he whispers in my ear. "My favorite."

Before my mind can catch up with what's happening to my body, he's running his hands up and down my arms and across my back. Explosions of desire are dotting my skin everywhere he touches it.

He reaches up and pulls my hair to the side, staring directly into my eyes as he whispers into my mouth, "I want you."

Then his lips crash into mine. Or mine crash into his. It's all blurred together now, along with the lines of our friendship. But all I can think about as his lips explore mine is how much I want this. How much I need him. How I want his hands everywhere on my body. I reach up and stroke his strong jaw when I feel the burn of his stubble on my face. I don't care that my cheeks will be red and raw; I just delight in the feel of his hair growing in because it's a sign of his renewed health.

He breaks our kiss only to feather new tiny ones up my jaw to my ear where he whispers, "You taste so good."

My hands run down his strong arms and I take a minute to explore the biceps that I've only dreamed of touching. Then he flips us over so he's towering on top of me as his lips, once again, come together with mine. His tongue comes out and swipes across my bottom lip, begging for entrance. I quickly oblige and our tongues tangle for the most incredible dance that has my heart singing.

While my body screams for more, my mind pleads with me to stop. But I don't know if I can, it feels so right to be with him. Maybe I shouldn't think about the consequences, about what will happen tomorrow.

He reaches down to cup my breasts and the sensation overwhelms me. A few months ago, I wasn't sure a man would ever get to touch them again. I'm frozen in the moment, taking in every tingle of pleasure he gives me by caressing my breasts and running his thumbs over my stiff nipples through the fabric of my thin blouse.

"I want you so much," he whispers.

I've never felt this way in my entire life. I've been with three men, slept with them even, and not one of them even came close to making me feel the way Jace is with merely his lips and his soft touches. I shudder to think what it would be like if he made love to me.

He breaks our kiss and leans up to whisper in my ear again. "I love you, Keri."

My breath hitches, my heart soars, I practically sprout wings and fly on the high running through my body. He kisses me with as much passion as I've ever experienced and then he whispers, "I love you so much, Morgan."

My wings fail and my world comes crashing down around me as my happy tears turn to sad ones. I abruptly pull away.

*He did say my name first, didn't he?*

Maybe I was hearing things, hearing what my mind so desperately wants to be true. Does he think I'm Morgan? Oh God, what if he's so drunk, he thinks he's back together with her?

I push him off me until we're both sitting up on the couch. He looks at me with cloudy eyes and I say, "Jace, this can't happen. I have to get out of here."

He doesn't even protest, he falls back on the couch and from what I can tell, he passes out.

Once I've calmed my nerves enough to stand on my own two feet, I grab the coffee that is now getting cold and take it to the kitchen to dump it out.

On my way, I stumble into the easel next to the kitchen, toppling it over. As I stare at the fully-revealed painting on the floor, I know he did, in fact, say my name—as sure as I know he did, in fact, say hers.

There it is as plain as day. A painting of the two of us, Morgan and me. We both look beautiful, even in the abstract way he's painted us. And behind us is a man, with outstretched arms, being torn apart by the two women.

I quickly put the painting back the way it was. Then I go downstairs and call a cab to take me home.

# Chapter Twenty-three

I lie in my bed, going over the events of last night. He loves me? He really said it. He loves Morgan. He really said that, too. And the painting of him being stretched, torn between two women—I can't get it out of my head.

People say things when they're drunk. Things they may not mean to say. I'm a bartender. I see it all the time. I'm not naïve. But in my experience, they do tend to say things they mean. I'm just not sure what to do with this information. I'm terrified of what this will do to our friendship.

My phone rings and I smile at who's calling. "Hey, Jules. How are you?"

"I'm good, just feeling like a bad friend because I haven't asked you to lunch sooner. Are you free today?"

I check my mental calendar. I still haven't been put back on the official volunteer schedule at Freeway. Chaz thought I needed to have a week or two to recover before pushing myself. Thinking of this reminds me that I need to have Mike put me back on full rotation at the club as well.

"Yes, I'm free. It will be great to see you again."

She gives me the address of the pricey place where she wants me to meet her for lunch and tells me it's her treat. A chemo graduation lunch.

We hang up and I'm left wondering if Jace is sending Jules to break up with me—if friends can even do that. Maybe he called her this morning and told her he can't hang out with me anymore. Maybe he said he feels guilty about having feelings for me when he still loves Morgan.

A few hours later, I pull up to the restaurant that only offers valet parking. I can't afford that. So I drive four blocks away, park on a residential street, and hike back in my three-inch heels, grateful the hot Florida sun is not out in full force today.

I walk around the corner and see Jules waiting for me out front. She smiles at me and I realize that seeing her does nothing to take my mind off Jace.

"Keri, I'm glad you could come. We have so much catching up to do."

She grabs my arm and pulls me into the restaurant—the restaurant with white linen tablecloths, crystal glasses, and no less than three sterling silver forks at each impeccable place setting. Yeah, way out of my league.

"Don't look at me like that," she says. "It's one of my dad's places, otherwise I wouldn't be caught dead here. And neither would my brother, for that matter. But I think you already know that."

I cock my head to study her. Why isn't she asking me about last night?

"I guess I do, but he and I haven't spent much time together, so I don't know where he likes to dine," I say, trying not to sound too disappointed about it.

We get settled at a table and order some iced tea. Jules puts her hand on mine. "I just had to talk to you. Last week, I happened to read some of your conversations on Jace's phone when we were at my parents' house and I knew we needed to have a powwow."

I raise my brows at her. "Just *happened* to see them, huh? Like the phone fell into your lap and opened our texting thread?" I shake my head.

"I told you, Keri. All up in your business. Get used to it."

Then I realize she said she saw our texts from sometime last week. Not last night.

"So, you're not here to talk to me about last night?"

Her eyes snap to mine and she looks at me suspiciously. She puts down her glass of iced tea she was about to take a drink of. "Oh, now you *have* to spill. What happened last night? Were you with Jace?"

I'm not sure what I should tell her. She's been friends with Morgan since they were kids. Yet, I felt instantly at ease with her when we first met. And she's never led me to believe she doesn't like me. In fact, she's gone out of her way to make me feel comfortable. I do wonder how much she knows about my past, and if that would change her opinion of me. I'm sure Jace didn't tell her since 'it's not his story to tell.'

She grabs my hand. "Keri, we're friends, right?"

I nod.

"You should know that even though I'm all up in your business, whatever you tell me stays right here. I know you're worried about me being friends with Morgan, but you shouldn't be. I love her and think she's a great girl. She will make someone else a fine sister-in-law, but I don't want her as mine. She's not right for Jace. Not like you are."

Her smile is so sincere it's hard for me not to believe her. She wants *me* for a sister-in-law? Whoa!

"Don't look so surprised, Keri. I know my brother better than anyone. He wants to settle down and have kids, and the fact he hasn't done it with Morgan means she's not the one for him. I see your texts and I've seen the way he looks at you. I've seen his texts with Morgan, too. There is no heat, no passion there."

I have to trust she is being genuine. I need to talk to someone about last night. Tanner is great and all, but he's a guy, and even a gay guy can't understand some things. So I tell her. I tell her all about it. About how he was mad when he found out about my hookup with Tanner. About our impromptu make-out session on his couch. About his declarations of love ... for both Morgan and me. About the disturbing painting.

Jules is smiling from ear to ear by the time I get done with my long narrative of last night.

"He said he loves you?"

I frown at her giddiness. "Yes, about two seconds before he called me Morgan and proclaimed his love for her as well."

She shakes her head. "Don't be sad. This is a good thing, Keri. Of course he loves her. He will probably always love her in some way. They share a childhood. They basically grew up together. He's been telling her he loves her since before I can remember, even when we were kids. It's probably instinct by now, like putting the cap back on the toothpaste without realizing you're doing it."

I perk up a bit at her reference to him loving her being like an old habit. I know from experience that habits are hard to break. Maybe he's just so used to being with her that he doesn't know and can't imagine anything else. Any*one* else.

"My brother is stubborn. I'm sure you've learned that by now. He won't let anyone tell him what to do and he won't take no for an answer. It's his stubbornness that's keeping him from acknowledging his true feelings for you. But he has to come to this conclusion on his own. I can't tell him. You can't tell him. The only question is, are you willing to stick around long enough to see how this plays out?"

As I ponder her question, my phone vibrates on the table. Jules brazenly picks it up and squeals, "Oh, it's Jace!" She shoves it at me and pulls her chair around the table so she's sitting next to me.

"Really?" I eye her.

"Don't worry. I got your back." She winks at me and nods at my phone.

**Jace: Mornin.' Or should I say afternoon? Now I remember why I don't drink much. God, Keri, I hope I didn't embarrass you. And please tell me I didn't drive myself home. Oh, and don't yell at me in your text, I'm not sure my head can take it.**

Jules laughs after reading the text. "Oh my God, he doesn't remember a thing! He must have really been jealous over the whole Tanner revelation. My brother does not get drunk, Keri. Nice job."

He doesn't remember? I'm not sure how I feel about that. On one hand, I want him to remember the words he said to me about wanting me. Loving me. However, I don't want our friendship to get weird, or worse, end, because of what happened. I conclude it's definitely for the best that he doesn't remember.

**Me: No, you were quite the gentleman. I drove you home in your car, followed by Greg who took me back to my place. I'm sorry your head hurts.**

Jules snorts, "Liar." Then she squeezes my arm and whispers into my ear as if he can hear us, "This is going to be so much fun."

**Jace: Thank God. Your friends are great. I hope they don't mind if I go with you again sometime.**

I smile at his comment and Jules gives me a high five. I feel like I'm in high school. Only the better version of it this time. Not the one where I was the orphaned freak who didn't get asked to any dances. Or the one where I ate lunch alone in the breezeway behind the gymnasium.

"You're in," Jules tells me. "You are so gonna marry my brother someday."

I eye her like she's crazy, but she shakes it off and rolls her eyes at me.

Marry her brother. She has to stop talking like that. She can't get my hopes up and make me lower my defenses just to have my dreams squashed again every time he slips up and calls me Morgan.

**Jace: Are you free tomorrow?**

Jules elbows me with another squeal as my stomach flutters with anticipation.

**Me: What did you have in mind?**

**Jace: Just some foundation business I thought
you might enjoy since you like working with
kids so much. But, Keri, I need you for the whole
day.**

He *needs* me. For the whole day.

I try not to text him back too quickly. That might make me
seem desperate. Spend the entire day with him *and* work with kids?
I'm brimming with excitement.

The waitress comes by, and I take an extra-long time placing
my order. Jules smiles at me and shakes her head at my antics.

**Me: I would love to help you with foundation
business. But right now, I need to get back to my
lunch with your sister. Text me the time and I'll
be ready.**

After reading my text, Jules laughs as she scoots her chair back
to its original position. "Well played. I really like you, Keri. Just in
case I haven't told you that."

We eat lunch, telling stories about our childhoods. I even open
up to her about my parents and my time at Freeway. She, like Jace,
is very understanding and doesn't seem to hold herself in any higher
regard than she holds me.

I come to find out Jules is a bit of a slut. And I mean that with
not even a hint of condescension. She has analyzed her own sexually
permissive behavior and chalks it up to her parents. Just as they did
with Jace, they seemed to be grooming her to marry the perfect man;
the son of a senator and his socialite wife who are close friends with
her parents. Apparently, this was her way of rebelling against them.

"Oh, speak of the devils." She nods her head towards an impressively dressed couple walking through the front doors of the restaurant.

I stiffen and my heart pounds in my chest as I take them in. He has on an open-collared shirt paired with khakis. She has on a tailored sundress, fitting her perfect curves and her store-bought bosom, I presume. No fifty-year-old woman would have breasts that stand at attention like that under a strapless dress. Her wrists are adorned with platinum bracelets, and her ears, large tear-drop diamonds. Their faces break out in smiles when they spot Jules. They head straight for us.

Her dad leans over and gives her a kiss on the cheek. "Jules, wonderful to see you."

Her mother puts a hand on Jules' shoulder. "Hello, Julianne dear."

"Mom, Dad, this is Keri Brookstone."

Her dad smiles sweetly at me. He offers me his hand which I shakily take into mine, while trying to dismiss the fact that this will, more than likely, be the richest man I will ever touch in my lifetime.

I stutter, "I-It's so nice to meet you, Mr. Jarrett."

"Please, call me Jason."

Her mother offers her well-manicured hand as well. "Brookstone," she says. "What an unusual name. I feel as if I've heard it before. Are you and your family members of the club?"

I assume she's referring to her country club, not The Triple J where I work. Oh, Lord. *I work for them.* Do I tell them? Would they think it beneath their daughter to be having lunch in this nice place with the help?

Thankfully, Jules rescues me. "No, Mom. Keri and I have recently become friends. She's a friend of Jace's. They met at chemotherapy." She winks over at me, even though I'm about to die because she told them I know Jace.

"Oh, how dreadful," her mother muses. "You don't look any worse for wear. You're a pretty thing, aren't you?"

She's eyeing me as if she is trying to place how she knows me. I don't think I've ever seen her, so I don't know how she could.

"Please tell my son and his beautiful girlfriend that I hope to see them soon, will you?"

Her words are directed at me. I suppose to remind me that Jace has someone in his life and she doesn't want me to forget it.

They say their goodbyes and go off to a table in the far corner. I don't miss the fact that every time I look over at them, Mrs. Jarrett is staring at me.

"Don't pay her any attention," Jules says. "She's had Jace married off to Morgan since before they were out of diapers. She probably feels that a gorgeous girl like you could threaten that. It's all about climbing the social ladder for her. Knowing the right kinds of people to make her more important. Don't get me wrong, I love my parents, but I could swear I'm adopted."

I choke on my tea. "That's exactly what Jace said."

As we're leaving, we make plans to have lunch again next Tuesday. I'm sure she suggested that day so she can get another play-by-play of Scrabble Night. I walk back to my car, smiling at the fact that I've just made a wonderful friend.

# Chapter Twenty-four

As I wait for Jace to pick me up this morning, I count the things I'm excited about. First, I get to see Jace. No explanation necessary. Second, I'm going to find out first-hand how a multimillion-dollar charity foundation can help kids. And third, I get to interact with said kids.

He gave me no clues as to where we're going. I'm not sure why he's being so mysterious. All he said when he texted me last night was that he would pick me up at eight in the morning and to dress casually. And that he couldn't think of a more perfect person to bring with him on this project.

*Project*. There's that word again. The word Brittney and Carly used that night. I try to brush it off for the hundredth time, thinking how I didn't feel anything like his project Monday night when he was whispering in my ear and getting jealous over Tanner.

There's a knock on my door at precisely eight o'clock. I make myself get up slowly and take small, hesitant steps toward the door.

I don't want him to know I've been waiting here for an hour, anticipating the day ahead and fantasizing about how it will go.

He smiles brightly at me when I open the door. His eyes graze over my body and he laughs when he sees my Jar Jar Binks t-shirt.

I shrug. "You said casual. Did I overdo it?"

**Jace: Don't change a thing. It's perfect! Did you just happen to have that lying around, or did you go buy one after our conversation the other night?**

"Oh, I have an entire collection. Maybe I'll show you someday."

I never thought my being a closet Star Wars fan would come in handy. Tanner teases me all the time about my choice of nerdy t-shirts. And I sometimes make him sit through all six DVDs with me when I'm feeling depressed. Now, I will never look at those movies the same way again. I'll never be able to watch them without thinking of Jace.

**Jace: I would very much like to see it, but we need to get going. We have a bit of a drive.**

"Are you going to tell me where we're going, or do I have to guess, like at chemo?"

He shakes his head and types out a text.

**Jace: We're going to Best Buy, Toys R Us and Target. Then we're going to The Angel House, a children's home in Orlando. Are you ready to have a blast spending some foundation money?**

My eyes go wide. "We're going on a shopping spree? *For kids?* Are you kidding, it's like my wildest dream come true! Wait, I thought foundations have staff who just order stuff and have it delivered. Why are *we* going?"

**Jace: I like to keep personal tabs on foundation business. For the most part, we do a lot of bulk ordering and distributing. But this particular house is close to my heart. And knowing how much you love the kids at Freeway, I thought you might want to share in this experience with me.**

"Of course I do. Thank you. Lead the way."

As we go down to his car, the one I drove him home in the other night, all kinds of memories explode in my head. From his hand on my thigh, to his lips on my skin, his fingers on my breast, and the 'I love you' he whispered in my ear. I push them aside and tell him, "I really enjoyed driving your car. Are you going to let me drive it again today?"

**Jace: Sure, if you like you can drive home, but I'll get us there since you don't know the way.**

"You'd let me drive your car? I mean, when you're not drunk? Most guys wouldn't dare risk a silly female driver with their 'baby'," I air quote.

**Jace: It's just a car, Keri. You may drive it whenever you like. On one condition.**

Of course there's a catch. There's always a catch. I roll my eyes at him and ask, "What's that?"

**Jace: You tell me about Tanner. And about Connor, I'm guessing he was another boyfriend? How many have there been, Keri? Or maybe I don't want to know.**

I was wondering when he was going to ask me about Tanner.

"Fine," I say. "But it's a short list, just them and one other. And I'll expect the same in return."

**Jace: Deal. Short list, too. Let's get going. You can tell me in the car.**

I spend the next hour telling him about Tanner and I and the bridge at the train yard. It was under that bridge where he took my virginity. It was an awkward moment, and if we hadn't been such good friends, it might have ended us. Fortunately, we were able to laugh about it. Tanner teases me to this day, saying I turned him gay. Jace laughs at the story, but James' and Connor's he doesn't find so amusing.

James took me in shortly after I left Freeway and would buy me things in exchange for sex. I didn't know any better, and when I finally caught on and stood up for myself, he locked me out. Literally changed the locks, saying he had bought everything, so it was all his, except for the one small trash bag of things he left on the front porch.

I had only recently turned eighteen, and the survivor's fund hadn't made its way into my hands with all the red tape, so I slept on Tanner's couch until Connor invited me to stay with him.

Connor was the one who broke my heart. He said all the right things and made me fall in love with him. But then after I gave Tanner my money from the survivor's fund, Connor went ballistic. He even slapped me and called me stupid. He threw me out in a rainstorm, along with the magazine articles and newspaper clippings he had collected about me. I later found out he had scammed other women out of money.

I tell Jace I swore off men after that. That I decided to become a strong, independent woman who didn't rely on others for anything.

Jace can't really respond, he just nods and smiles compassionately. When we stop at a traffic light in Orlando, he takes a moment to text me.

**Jace: Keri, you did become a strong, independent woman. I'm sorry you ever had to deal with assholes like that.**

We finally pull up to our first stop. Best Buy. Jace turns to me with a huge smile on his face and leans over the console. He whispers, "Ready?"

"So, how does this work?" I ask, as we walk into the store.

He grabs my hand and pulls me over to the Customer Service counter. It's a simple gesture and I'm sure he doesn't mean for it be romantic, but, oh, the feel of his large hand encompassing my small one. It's like being wrapped in a thick, warm blanket on a cold night.

He gives his business card to the lady behind the counter.

She smiles and says, "Mr. Jarrett, we've been expecting you. We have a courier on stand-by to deliver your purchases. Please, take your time."

I feel him squeeze my hand, so I speak for him. "Thank you, we'll just get started then."

Jace smiles at me and walks us over to get a cart. He pushes it around the store as naturally as … say, a bartender might do it, not a multi-millionaire. I laugh when he immediately takes us to the video game section and looks at Star Wars Xbox games. He gives me a wink and then he texts me.

**Jace: This one's for me. You up for a challenge?**

I can't help the excitement in my voice when I reply, realizing he's making more plans for us to hang out. "You're on!"

**Jace: Okay, now for the fun stuff. I know about the guys, but you need to tell me about the girl stuff. Think about what you wish you had when you were at Freeway. Nothing's off the table.**

My eyes go wide once again. "Seriously? Are you giving me carte blanche?"

He nods and laughs at what I can only imagine is a kid-in-a-candy-store look on my face. Then he leans close and whispers, "Lead the way."

Thirty minutes later, we've filled no less than three carts with gaming systems, iPods, iPads, e-readers, DVDs, video games, and even two laptop computers. I can't even imagine what the total came to—thousands probably.

Leaving the store, I'm on a high from the experience. And there is still more to come on this extravagant shopping spree. That, along with the knowledge of how the kids will react when they see all this stuff, is one hell of an incredible feeling. I get why he does this. I imagine this is the feeling he got when he bought all those things for the chemo gang.

The next two stops bring more of the same; walking down aisle after aisle of toys and games and being able to choose any of it—all of it. We fill another five carts at the toy store and four at Target.

Jace looks to me for direction, especially for the teenage girls. The electronics and the games are great, but I also select everyday things such as decorative bed pillows, picture frames, wall hangings and magazines. I also get some flat irons, even though I can't use them myself due to the smell, but I know most girls really like them. I pick all the things that make a girl's room feel like a home, not like a temporary stay at a hotel.

Jace gives me a look of awe and adoration.

**Jace: In the five years I've run the foundation, no one has ever suggested these things. You have a rare insight, Keri, a connection to these kids that nobody else has. Picture frames and pink fuzzy pillows ... genius.**

I pick up one of the pillows and throw it at him.

After our shopping spree, we stop for lunch. When he pulls into the parking lot of a Burger King, my jaw drops before I shake my head and laugh at him.

**Jace: What? I love Whoppers. And look, they're BOGO today!**

*He loves Whoppers.*

I once read about a restaurant in New York City that serves a hundred-dollar cheeseburger. Of course you also get white linen service, a bottle of high-end wine, and a dessert. But here sits a man who could get the hundred-dollar burger every day for lunch, yet he chooses Burger King—and is excited because of the BOGO special.

As we sit and eat our Whoppers, enjoying our meal that, combined, came in at under ten dollars, he tells me about his past relationships. Just like he promised he would do. I didn't even have to ask.

> **Jace: I was sixteen when Crystal took my virginity. She was a senior. She was the school slut. She taught me everything about sex. I'm also pretty sure she's the one who gave me HPV.**

I've decided I now hate Crystal. Not only did she take his virginity, but she gave him cancer. I'm wondering how many others I will hate by the time he's finished telling me.

> **Jace: The answer is three.**

I look up at him, confused. "What?"

> **Jace: Three women. Morgan, Crystal and a girl named Chelsey in college. Three, same as you.**

How does he continue to read my mind like that? I don't think I want any more information. I already have to deal with visuals of Crystal 'teaching' him about sex. And of course, Morgan. I don't need to know about Chelsey as well. But there *is* something I want to know about.

"Has Morgan gotten in touch with you? Do you text her at all?"

Embarrassed by asking him this, I play with a french fry instead of looking him in the eye.

**Jace: No, she hasn't contacted me directly and I don't text her. But I've been questioned by mutual friends about her, about our relationship, and about the status of my health.**

I nod. "She contacted me again last week. She wanted to see how you were doing."

**Jace: Did you tell her? You have every right not to talk to her, you know.**

"I know, but she cares about you. If the tables were turned, I'd want to know how you were doing. It'd be horrible not to know."

**Jace: You would never be in her position, Keri. You care about people too much. You would never turn your back on someone who was sick or in need. It's one of the qualities that has drawn me to you. You're a giver. And speaking of giving, what do you say we go make the day of a dozen great kids?**

I get the idea he doesn't want to talk about Morgan anymore. He doesn't ever want to bring her up around me. I know it's because he still loves her. I wonder if he still feels guilty for loving her while spending so much time with me.

I shake my head in an attempt to rid my brain of all things Morgan. I need to focus on today, on the incredible experience we're about to take part in. "Absolutely!"

It's only a short drive to our destination. We pull up to an old, large house, bigger than The Freeway Station, but similar in the way that it looks just like any other residence with the exception of a passenger van in the oversized driveway. As we park at the curb in front of the house, I notice the sign over the main entrance. It is a beautifully painted sign that reads ANGEL HOUSE, adorned with a couple of floating angels on either side. It's not an abstract, but the tone of the painting is familiar.

"Your work?" I ask him, nodding to the sign as we go up the front walk.

He shrugs his shoulders nonchalantly. Then he grabs my hand before we reach the front door. He looks in my eyes, silently trying to convey a message to me. His thoughtful stare is scaring me a little.

*What's in the house?* He's preparing me for something without actually using words. He is imploring me to do this with him. I give him a smile and a nod after our telepathic exchange. He takes a deep breath, closing his eyes momentarily before opening the front door.

The house is quiet even though it's almost three o'clock and kids of this age should probably be getting home from school. We're greeted by an older lady who pulls Jace into a hug.

"Oh, sweet boy, I'm so glad to see you. And who have you brought with you?"

"Hi, I'm Keri Brookstone," I say, offering her my hand.

She pushes my hand away and wraps her arms around me. "Well, Keri, around here, we hug. It's nice to finally meet you, I'm Gracy Fowler."

I instantly like this woman. Then I realize what she said. *Finally* meet me?

"Nice to meet you too, Gracy. What a nice house this is. I'm so excited Jace has brought me here today to help him out."

"Well, we are glad to have you, dear. Jace tells me you work with kids at a home over in Tampa. It's so nice to see young people taking an interest in these types of places."

"Oh, I more than take an interest. I hope to one day run a place for kids. It's what I go to college for."

Gracy pulls me in for another hug. "Bless you, Keri. If only there were more people like you and Jace in this world." Her eyes well up with tears. "Oh, don't mind me," she says. "If the wind blows in the wrong direction, I'll cry."

She laughs at herself and takes my hand in hers. The she grabs Jace's hand and walks us toward the back porch.

On the way, we pass by a large living area with three couches, some beanbag chairs, a television and a PlayStation console that looks long outdated. I smile knowing what's about to get delivered to the house in an hour or so.

Then I stop in my tracks, jerking back both Gracy and Jace so that they look at me with questioning eyes.

Hanging on the wall of the living room is a picture of *me.*

I release Gracy's hand and walk slowly over to it. This one is different from the paintings he's done lately. It's clearly me, but not the me of today, not the me he knows so well and captures in his paintings. On either side of my yellow hair, up in the sky are two angels. I turn to him with an inquisitive look.

**Jace: Your guardian angels.**

I look back up and study the painting. It hits me that the angels are different, one is male, and one is female. My parents. *But how?* I step closer and look at the date in the corner of the painting. It was dated a few years after my parents died. He painted this over five years ago. I look at him in disbelief.

**Jace: I told you. You were my inspiration. And there wasn't a place in the world more fitting to hang it than in this very house. Come, you'll see.**

We walk out on the back porch to see children playing in the massive backyard. There is a swing set far off in the corner. There's a volleyball net, an old basketball hoop—I smile knowing a new one is on the way—some outdoor furniture, and some odd toys strewn about.

The children are running around and playing with each other, interacting just as if this were a family gathering, not an orphanage or children's home.

Some of the kids hear the backdoor slam shut and come running. That's when I see it. That's when I know why this house exists. That's when my heart breaks and swells at the very same time.

Children of different ages are running towards us and shouting out Jace's name like he is Santa Claus on Christmas Day. Children who all have brilliant smiles on their faces, despite the fact they all have varying degrees of burns covering their faces, necks, arms and legs. Children who Jace pulls into hugs, planting kisses on their burned and disfigured faces just as if they were his own flesh and blood.

I fight back the tears that threaten to fall, knowing these children do not want my pity. And as I continue to watch Jace greet every one of them as if each one is his favorite person in the entire world, the wall around my heart crumbles and I'm certain I won't be able to build it back up.

# Chapter Twenty-five

Gracy introduces me to all the children once a few stragglers come down from upstairs. They range in age from eight to sixteen years old. While Jace is still saying hello, she pulls me aside and explains things to me when she sees I'm clearly surprised and Jace had obviously not prepared me.

I learn that all these children were orphaned by fires in which their parents died. Just like me. Only these kids didn't come away physically unscathed like I did.

I glance over Gracy's shoulder as she gives me the history of the house. I look at the kids to see the range of burns. Most have burns covering part of an arm or leg, but some of the children have been severely disfigured. The worst being a young girl who has lost some of her hair and half of her face is distorted with severe scarring.

Gracy must see me staring at the little girl.

"That's Lilly, she's ten. She lost her parents late last year. She'll be having reconstructive surgery soon, thanks to Jace's foundation."

"Has Jace told you why he wanted to bring me here?" I question her.

"No, dear, he hasn't. All I know is that he met a wonderful woman who works with children at a home in Tampa. You know Jace, he doesn't like to tell other people's stories. That man was sent straight from heaven."

I see the kids are still busy with Jace, so I decide to tell Gracy how we met and why Jace brought me here. She is, of course, crying as she holds my hands while listening to my story.

She hugs me and says, "Then you are a gift from God as well. I think you will accomplish great things in your life, Keri. Your parents would be proud. Now let me go fix a snack for the kids while you get to know everyone."

There isn't even a question of who I'm going to talk to first. I walk over to the little girl and say, "You know, lilies are my favorite flower in the whole world."

She smiles brightly at me and asks if I want to see her room. Some of the other kids tag along and show me their shared rooms as well. As I look at the barren walls and outdated décor, I smile at what is to come.

I instantly form a bond with Lilly. The other kids have gone downstairs for a snack, but Lilly is showing me how to make a bracelet on her Rainbow Loom.

"Lilly, did anyone ever tell you about rainbows?"

I spend the next ten minutes telling her my story and by the time I finish, she's sitting on my lap and we both have tear-streaked faces.

She raises her head up to look at me. "I love you, Keri."

My heart bursts with warmth and tenderness as it forges an attachment to this child that I doubt will ever be broken.

"I love you, too, Lilly."

I rub the side of her head that still boasts long, brown ringlets of hair.

I hear a soft knock on the door frame. I turn to see Jace standing frozen in the doorway, watching us with tears welling up in his eyes, and I wonder how long he's been there.

As I hug the little girl, Jace and I look into each other's eyes. I see so much emotion, so much compassion, so much love. I know he loves these kids. I can see it so clearly. He truly is sent from heaven.

Hours later, after we've set up all the electronics and spent time with each child, helping them pick out new things for their rooms, Jace and I get ready to leave.

I pull Lilly aside and quickly teach her how to call me on one of the new iPads or laptops using Skype.

"Will you come visit us again?" she asks, hope gleaming in her gorgeous blue eyes.

"A hurricane couldn't keep me away," I say, giving her one last hug as we head for the door.

I glance over my shoulder and take a peek at the painting in the living room on our way out. Then I look down at the rubber-band bracelet adorning my wrist, courtesy of Lilly and her Rainbow Loom. She made it with all the colors of the rainbow. She said it's to remember my daddy.

On our way down the sidewalk to the car, I ask Jace, "Do you ever sell your paintings?"

**Jace: No. I only donate them. Can we sit for a minute before we leave?**

He points to a bench along the sidewalk in front of the house.

"Of course," I say. I can see his mind is spinning and he has something he wants to tell me. He almost looks nervous, so I start talking to ease his tension. "Thank you for today. I can't remember a day that has ever meant more to me. You do incredible things with your foundation. I'm in awe of you, you know."

I look at him as he texts me. He has a smile on his face that produces that adorable dimple in his left cheek.

**Jace: In awe of me? You have no idea, Keri.**

He shakes his head as he continues to text.

**Jace: It was you. You made today possible. This was all because of your donation.**

I look up from my phone in utter disbelief. "What? How?"

**Jace: I run the foundation, Keri. I have a hand in everything. I see the checks that come in, even the ones marked for anonymous donation. You are a phenomenal woman. Most people who suddenly come into ten thousand dollars would blow it on frivolous things, maybe take a nice vacation. But you, who clearly could use the money, you donate it. You continually amaze me.**

I can feel the blush sweep across my face. "It was the least I could do after your generous donation to Freeway." I raise my eyebrows at him. "What, do you think I didn't figure that out as well?"

He laughs.

**Jace: You were astounding with the kids. I watched you all afternoon. They are drawn to you. You treat them like you would any other kid. You see them as perfect children despite their scars. And they pick up on that. You also have a knack for understanding what they want and need because you have rare insight from being in a home yourself. I want to offer you a job at the foundation.**

I snap my head up to look at him after reading his text. "What? Are you insane? I could never work for a foundation. I have no training, no experience. I haven't even graduated yet. I'm a bartender for heaven's sake."

**Jace: You have the best kind of experience, Keri. Life experience. I could really use someone like you to make sure the charities the foundation supports are getting run properly. That they are appropriately staffed, are meeting the kids' needs both physically and emotionally, and that they have all the material things kids need for a normal upbringing. The Angel House is just one of many such places the foundation supports. You could work with the kids whenever you wanted to. And we can train you on foundation business.**

I try to absorb what he's saying. It does sound like my dream job. But I haven't even been a paid counselor for Freeway yet. I really am grossly underqualified. Is he doing this out of pity? I can't possibly accept a job that he's creating just for me. I'm not going to be one of his foundation charity cases.

"Jace, I can't. I mean, I appreciate the offer, but I really need to work full-time at Freeway before I can even consider something like that. I need to build up my confidence. I need to learn the ins and outs of a children's home before I can possibly tell others how to run one. But, thank you for believing I could do it."

He simply nods at me.

**Jace: Okay, but the offer stands. Whenever you're ready for it, Keri. Now, let's head back.**

He pulls his car keys out of his pocket and tosses them to me. I catch them with a huge smile on my face, one that mirrors his own, and I find I have to keep my hand from reaching out to touch that dimple on his cheek. The cheek with the still-darkening stubble that continues to grow, just like the new hair on his head.

He can't talk, of course, on the hour-long drive back home, so we take turns picking music to listen to. We like the same music, and when I absentmindedly sing along to a favorite song, he reaches over to give my hand a squeeze.

As the miles pass, I find myself deliberately singing more and more, just to feel the heat of his fingers when they reach out to grab mine.

# Chapter Twenty-six

The past few weeks have been spent getting my life back to normal. I've resumed a full-time rotation at the bar. Chaz finally agreed to give me a few volunteer day-shifts at Freeway, and I've been finishing up my last few classes in school. He has also put in a request to hire me full-time once my graduation is official.

Jace went with me to The Freeway Station to meet all the kids. He was great with them, just as he was at The Angel House. He and Chaz seemed to get along very well, even going off to talk in Chaz's office. I wonder if Jace was considering making another donation.

There had been a few new intakes recently at Freeway, so I spent some time getting to know Kelsey and Curtis. And I said goodbye to Anthony, who went home to his parents.

Kimberly is doing well and has been patient with her new friend, Adam.

Tyler has been in much better spirits lately. His mom is divorcing, and has pressed charges against, his stepfather. But these things take time as the court system is backlogged. Tyler will be staying for another month while he and his mother re-build their relationship.

Today was a special day for me as I took the last of my exams. I am officially done with college. It feels incredible.

Tanner and I are on our way to Scrabble Night. My skin tingles knowing I will see Jace shortly.

Jace and I have seen each other a few times a week, and he's been joining us every Monday night. He has really fit in with the gang from the bar. Even after they found out who he really is, they didn't treat him any differently which I imagine is refreshing for Jace.

We open the door to Austin's apartment and are greeted with, "Congratulations!"

There's a banner on the wall. And when I look around, I see Jace and all my other friends smiling and clapping for me.

I hug each of them in turn and when I get to Jace, he pulls me into a guarded hug and whispers, "I'm proud of you."

As we break apart, he plants a kiss on the top of my head. It's like a kiss you would give a child, and I find disappointment coursing through my veins.

It's not lost on me that this is the first time he's touched me since our drive back from The Angel House weeks ago. He didn't touch me when he came to Freeway, or the time we went to lunch last week. He hasn't even touched me the past few Scrabble Nights. Not one time. And my body misses it. My body craves it. I try to shake it off with the help of the shots of alcohol everyone is shoving at me as they toast my graduation.

As the night rolls on, Jace and I fall into our familiar pattern of flirty banter, probably fueled by alcohol on my part.

He is the OSP tonight, due to our pitiful performance last week. I think he prefers to remain sober anyway, and I have been most grateful that we haven't had a repeat performance of his drunken slip-of-the-tongue.

As usual, our words become funnier and sexier as the night rolls on, and Jace and I crack each other up when we make words on our tile holder that only we can see. Words such as LUST, YEARN and ACHE.

I perk up when he starts to kick my foot again, the way he did that first night. My blood pumps fast through my body when our fingers touch as we reach for the same tile.

I know it's probably the alcohol, but when Jace gets up to hit the bathroom, all I can do is sit here and think of an excuse I could come up with to get him to take me to his loft tonight.

I'm ready to give in to these feelings if he will have me. I'm ready to have him remove the cobwebs from my much-neglected girl parts.

*No!* I admonish myself. I can't do that. It will ruin everything. I pick up my phone and text Tanner.

**Me: Tan, do NOT let me leave with Jace tonight. No matter what!**

I hear Jace's phone vibrate on the table next to me. Oh, crap. I must have accidentally texted him instead of Tanner. I quickly pick up his phone to delete the text before he returns to the table.

My heart falls into the pit of my stomach when I see that, no, I did not accidentally text him. Can I blame it on my inebriated state if I open his new text that isn't from me? I know it is so wrong. I'll be crossing the boundaries of our friendship if I do it. But as my finger draws closer to the screen, I have no willpower to keep it from tapping open the text.

**Morgan: I just wanted to tell you I ran into Chris and he told me to say hello to you. Hope you are having fun at your game night.**

*His game night?* He's been talking with her? But when I asked him, he said he hadn't heard from her. And he told her about Scrabble Night? I've already gone too far, so I scroll down and read the thread.

**Morgan: I had lunch with your parents yesterday. It was so nice to see them again. I've really missed them.**

**Jace: I'm glad you went. You know they love you.**

**Morgan: I miss you, too, Jace.**

**Jace: You, too, Morgan. I have to get going. I have a game night to get to.**

**Morgan: Oh, right. Scrabble was it? Well, have fun and tell Keri I said hello.**

She saw his parents. She misses him. He misses her. He told her about me and Scrabble Night. My mind flashes back to when I found out he told her about spilling the latte on me. He shared everything with her then. *Oh, God,* are they back together? My heart breaks.

I hear Jace coming back down the hall from the bathroom. I stand up and hold his phone out for him to see. "Your girlfriend texted you," I spit out, drunkenly.

His face pales as he walks toward me, holding out his hand for the phone. He doesn't look pissed that I violated his privacy, he looks frantic.

I know he can't defend himself without the phone, so I hold it captive while I continue to speak.

"Don't bother texting me with more lies. You're a liar, Jace. I know you lied about talking to her. Are you going to lie and tell me you're not screwing her, too?"

His eyes go wide and he shakes his head. I know I sound like a jealous girlfriend. I know the alcohol is fueling my inappropriate behavior. I can't believe what I'm doing, what I'm saying. But it's done, it's out there now. I can't take it back. He's never seen this side of me. *I've* never seen this side of me. I see his face turn to anger.

He grabs his phone from me and types on it.

**Jace: What the hell would it matter if I was?**

I read his text and my blood boils. I have no right to be angry. I have no claim on him. He has never given me any reason to think he wants me and only me. But that doesn't keep me from yelling, "Get the hell out of here! Leave!"

He winces at my harsh words.

**Jace: But I'm the OSP.**

"No, Jace, you're the asshole. Now just leave. We'll be fine without you. *I'll* be fine without you."

He looks at me like I've punched him in the gut.

The others have all seen my inglorious display of emotion. Austin cuts in and says, "It's okay, Jace, I've got this. Keri can sleep here, and I'll make sure the others get home safely."

Jace looks at Austin with daggers shooting from his eyes. Then he turns and looks at me with what I can only describe as a look of disgust. He's mad at me for reading his texts and calling him out. He's mad that I found out about his reconciliation with Morgan. I guess he's also mad that he didn't get a chance to get me into his bed before I figured it all out. Well, I'm not that stupid. He turns and walks out the door. I turn and take three shots of whiskey.

~ ~ ~

When light blinds me and I get my bearings, I realize I'm in my own bed, not in Austin's apartment. I think back in horror over what I remember from last night. Did I really call Jace an asshole? As I re-live the entire embarrassing scene in my head, Tanner comes in and sits down on my bed, giving me a hug.

I cry into his shoulder. "He's a liar and a cheat." Tanner rubs my back as he listens. "Except he's *not* a cheat. He was never with me so how can I even say that? We were friends and he was probably just trying to protect my feelings. Tan, I'm such a bitch."

I spend the next week mourning the fact that Jace is not in my life. He hasn't texted me. I haven't texted him. I keep myself busy with work and volunteering. I wonder if he will have me fired now. I guess it doesn't really matter since I'll go full-time at Freeway soon. But I was hoping to keep a shift or two at The Triple J for extra money, not to mention keeping in touch with my friends.

Jules calls me, wanting to get together for coffee. I can only imagine what Jace has told her. We meet at Starbucks. I walk in with my tail between my legs.

"Jules, I ruined it. I said awful, hateful words to him. I had no right to say those things. He has every reason to be with Morgan. I was a jealous bitch and I don't think he will ever forgive me."

She laughs and shakes her head at me. "It's nice to see that you're as miserable as my big brother. Listen, I'm not supposed to tell you that. He made me promise, so I'm breaking the sibling code. He wanted you to stew over it, but I didn't want you to go do something stupid. I think you did hurt him, Keri, but he wasn't completely honest with you so maybe he deserved it."

"He's miserable?" I'm not sure I really heard any words she said after that. "How can he be miserable about our fight if he's back together with Morgan?"

"He and Morgan are not back together. Yes, she contacted him. And they have been texting, but you have to remember they've been friends forever and I'm not sure that will go away just because they aren't together."

"But he said—"

"I saw his texts. He was mad. You were mad. You both said stuff you didn't mean. He's still unsure of where his feelings stand, Keri, and you need to give him more time. But based on his behavior the past few days, well, let's just say smashing a phone was kid stuff compared to it."

"I don't understand why he's so unsure of himself. He seems like such confident guy. When he deals with the foundation, with the kids, he is this pillar of credence. He's the stability others look to for guidance."

"Oh, Keri, you have no idea."

She blows out a deep breath and has some kind of internal battle in her mind while sizing me up at the same time.

"I'm being a shitty sister today, revealing all his secrets, but I hope you know I do it with the best intentions. I really do believe you two are meant for each other." She takes a long drink of her coffee. "Oh, hell … here it goes. Jace is afraid to speak. Nobody but me knows this, and he won't talk to anyone else about it. And I only know it because I was with him at his pre-op appointment. The appointment where they told him not to speak at all for two or three weeks after surgery, but then after that, he could start to whisper and slowly build back up to talking normally. They told him there was a slight chance he would lose the ability to speak altogether since his vocal cords were involved in the surgery. But more than likely the only negative outcome would be a more gravelly voice. But, Keri, he's terrified that he won't be able to speak again. He would rather not speak at all than try to speak and fail. I made an appointment with his surgeon who told me that since Jace has gone so long without talking, he will probably have to go to speech therapy if he ever wants to speak normally again."

I'm stunned. It's been almost five months since his surgery. He hasn't tried to speak for *five months?*

I close my eyes and think of the young me, right after my parents died. Back when I was afraid to feel. I wouldn't allow myself to feel any emotion. Not happiness. Not even grief. It was almost a year of a numb existence before I started shoplifting just to feel something, anything. And then Tanner came into my life and taught me how to heal.

Then it dawns on me. This strong, gorgeous, millionaire is just like the kids at Freeway. He's just like me and every other person who has ever had some kind of existential struggle. And suddenly our worlds inch a little closer.

"I won't ask you to keep this a secret since I didn't, Keri. Do whatever you want with this information and I'll deal with the backlash. Heck, maybe you will be the one who can help him when nobody else could. Don't shut him out because he made a mistake and didn't tell you about Morgan. He loves you. I know he does. Please, just hang in there."

I give her a hug when we leave, grateful she broke his confidence to tell me these things. I can hardly wait until I get back home to text him. I think about it the whole drive home. What will I say? What can I possibly say to excuse my behavior? I really can't come up with anything except the flat-out truth.

**Me: I was drunk.**

**Jace: I know.**

**Me: I'm so sorry.**

**Jace: I know.**

**Me: Can you ever forgive me?**

**Jace: If you meet me for breakfast tomorrow, the answer is yes.**

I smile as my entire body relaxes for the first time in a week.

# Chapter Twenty-seven

I decided not to let on that I know about his voice issues. It's something he needs to work out for himself. I can be supportive as his friend, but nobody can be pushed to do anything they aren't ready for.

As soon as Jace sees me at the restaurant, he pulls me into a hug. A hug that has meaning. A hug that says *I'm sorry* and *I forgive you*, all without words. A hug that has my insides melting and my blood pumping.

We get a table and place our order. I tell him I have to be done by ten because Chaz has asked me to help him at Freeway today even though I'm not on the schedule. Jace gives me a dimpled smile like he has a secret. Then he turns all serious and texts me.

**Jace: I know I owe you an explanation. Morgan calls me occasionally, but she doesn't leave messages. I think she just calls to listen to my voicemail greeting. I was getting sick of seeing**

**her number displayed, so I texted her and asked her to stop it. She texted me back and we just started talking. We're not back together and there hasn't been any talk of it either. We simply text as friends, nothing more. Keri, you should know that what I said wasn't a lie. When you asked me at The Angel House if I talked with her, I didn't lie to you. I hadn't yet texted her to stop calling, and we weren't yet communicating. Then afterwards, I guess I just didn't know how to tell you we had started texting. I knew it might cause some hurt feelings.**

"But you stopped touching me. After Angel House, you didn't even hug me or take my hand. It all seemed to make sense, that you wanted her back."

He looks at me for a moment while he gathers his thoughts. Then he starts and stops texting several times. I'm starting to get worried about what he's trying to tell me.

**Jace: When we were at The Angel House, I realized how wonderful a person you are. I mean, I knew you were incredible before that, but seeing you with those kids. It touched my heart. You touched my heart. And after hearing you sing on the way home—all I can say is it was a very powerful day for me, and I was finding it extremely hard to be around you and still respect your wish to just be friends.**

I touched his heart? I think back to that day and remember him standing in the doorway while I comforted Lilly. The way he was looking at us, I thought it was about the kids, about Lilly. Could it have been about me? He wants us to be more than friends? But what about Morgan?

"What about Morgan? Do you still love her? Do you … want her?" I ask shyly.

I hold my breath the entire time he types out his reply. I hold it right through the waitress bringing us our breakfast; right through his contemplative thought process. I think I might pass out if he doesn't send it soon.

> **Jace: I'm not exactly sure how to answer that right now. Do I still love her? I've loved her for a long time, since we were kids, so yes, I guess I do. Do I still want her? That's another thing entirely. She left me. Even though I have tried to understand her reasons why, she left me when I needed someone the most. I'm not sure she deserves a second chance even if I wanted to give it to her. And I'm not saying I do, but I am saying it may take time for me to readjust my thinking about her, to live my life without her so deeply ingrained in it.**

I appreciate his honesty. But I'm not sure he answered the question. He loves her but he doesn't *want* her? Or he doesn't *want* to want her? He must sense my frustration over his text.

> **Jace: Keri, all I can say is after that day at The Angel House, I was in need of a side effect. I don't think I had ever needed one more.**

His revelation softens me a little and I hesitantly ask him, "And now, do you still need one *now?*"

**Jace: No. I don't, Keri. I don't want to push away my feelings anymore.**

I'm stunned speechless and rendered incapable of words.

**Jace: Can I ask you a question?**

"Of course," I reply, recovering my power of speech.

**Jace: Why don't you ever call me? I mean, I know you did the one time when I missed chemo. But I've never seen your number on my phone after that unless you're texting me. I'm pretty sure I know how you feel about me, Keri, so why don't you want to hear my voice like Morgan does?**

I look at him guiltily. "I'm not going to lie and tell you I haven't thought about it. I've even picked up the phone to do that very thing. But then I think about how selfish that makes me. I mean, what if I had lost my breasts and all my boyfriend wanted to do was stare at old pictures of them?" I realize what I said, and heat rises up my face. "I mean, not that you're my boyfriend. Well, um ... you know what I mean. Ugh."

He laughs silently and then looks directly into my eyes as he types his next text.

**Jace: Yes, Keri. I know what you mean. I know exactly how it feels to crave something I can't**

**have. Are you ever going to agree to go out with me?**

I read his text and then stare at him. He craves me. Just like I crave him. He wants to go out with me. He doesn't need any more side effects. He's not sure he wants Morgan, but he loves her.

I want so desperately to yell, 'Yes, yes!' but I don't. Instead I say, "Jace, I need more time. I need to know you won't go back to Morgan, and right now I'm not sure you wouldn't. I don't even think *you* are sure you wouldn't. Can we just be friends for now?"

He closes his eyes briefly while nodding his head.

**Jace: Of course we can, and I hope we always will be, no matter what. But I can't promise you I won't keep trying to wear you down.**

I laugh at his comment as I hear a man's voice behind me. "Hello, son."

I turn around and Jace's dad says, "Keri, nice to see you again."

"Hi, Mr. Jarrett, Mrs. Jarrett."

"You don't mind if we join you, do you?" his mother asks, eyeing me with condescension.

I sneak a peek at the time, and I'm relieved we have to go in just a few minutes.

The hostess quickly sets two more place settings at our table and his mom and dad settle in. Jace and his dad have a texting conversation while Jace's mother makes small talk with me.

I don't know how to relate to these people, so I quietly eat the remains of my breakfast and hope this will be over quickly.

When Jace finishes his meal, he excuses himself to use the bathroom. Then Jace's dad gets a phone call and leaves the table. I'm left sitting next to his mother, at a complete and utter loss for what to talk about. But it seems I don't need to pick a topic of conversation as she already had one prepared.

"So, Keri Brookstone." She spears me with her eyes. "I knew I had heard that name somewhere, so I did some checking around. And low and behold, you are the same Keri Brookstone from that fire all those years ago. The same girl who Jace convinced us to donate a sizable sum of money into a survivor's fund for. And the same girl who used said money to pay off a drug debt for her drug-dealing boyfriend."

My mouth falls open. I'm stunned into silence for the second time this morning. *They* donated the money? *She knows about me?* My hands start shaking and I try to find something to say, but how can I reply to her when everything she's just said is one-hundred-percent true?

"Did you think we wouldn't do a background check on someone our son is spending time with? In the future, you would be wise not to write checks to known drug dealers, Keri. There is always a paper trail. I would like you to tell me exactly what your intentions are with my son. Do you or any of your shoplifting friends have another debt to pay?"

Tears well up in my eyes. But before I can answer her, before I can defend myself, Jace comes back to the table. He clearly senses something is wrong based on what I can only imagine is my face that must be devoid of color.

He looks at me with great concern and pulls out his phone, but I quickly say to him, "Jace, can you please tell your dad I wasn't feeling well? I think I'm going to head out. Nice to see you Mrs. Jarrett."

I almost topple over my chair in my hasty exit.

I hear his mother mumble something to him and then I hear footsteps follow me out to the parking lot. Tears are now streaming down my face as he catches up to me and puts a gentle hand on my shoulder.

When I turn around and he sees how wrecked I am, he pulls me into a hug and lets me cry against him.

He whispers, "Shhh, shhh, shhh," in my ear. Then he walks me over to a bench along the sidewalk.

### Jace: What did she say to you?

I look up at him and he nods at me like he knows his mom just chewed me up, spit me out, and ground me into the pavement with her shoe.

"She knows everything about me, Jace. My name seemed familiar to her when she ran into me when I was having lunch with Jules, so she ran a background check on me. She knows about my record. She even knows what I did with the money. The money that *your* family donated. Oh God, Jace, that's just one more thing your family's money has done for me. I'll never be able to repay you."

Jace catches another tear before it falls from my cheek. Then he rubs my back soothingly.

"But that's not the worst of it," I say. "I haven't told you everything. The money … the money I gave to Tanner was to pay off a drug dealer."

I lower my head in shame. "Tanner had gotten into trouble before we met. He did drugs and ran up a large debt, and to pay it off, he started dealing himself. One thing led to another and he just dug himself in deeper. He got clean, but he still owed a lot of money to someone who started coming after him. They couldn't touch him when he was at Freeway, but when he got out, the threats started again, and he feared for his life. He feared for *my* life since we were so close. So as soon as I got the money, I paid off his debt."

Jace stops rubbing my back. I'm afraid to even look at him. I can't imagine what he must think of me now, knowing I was involved in such criminal activity. I keep my eyes closed tightly when I say, "The thing is, everything your mom said about me is true. Every word. There was nothing I could say to defend myself."

My phone vibrates in my hand and I realize he had stopped rubbing my back so he could text me.

**Jace: You have to ignore her, Keri. I don't care what you and Tanner did when you were seventeen. You are different people now. I'm sorry she made you feel like that money came with strings attached, that you had to use it a certain way to be righteous in her eyes. But please know that I never have expectations about how donations are used. In my opinion, it did go to a good cause because it got Tanner cleaned up and out of trouble. And because of that, he was able to return the favor and help you through some very tough times in your life. It was money well spent if you ask me. Please don't let her get to you. I don't share her beliefs, not one little bit of them. I told you—I think I'm adopted ;-)**

The little winky face in his text makes me smile.

"I thought you would hate me. I thought you would hate both Tanner and me when you found out."

He leans close and whispers, "Never." Then he texts me.

**Jace: Come on, we've got someplace we need to be.**

"I can't. I told you I promised to help Chaz with something for the day," I say.

Jace simply smiles at me again and types out a text. Then he pulls on my hand, dragging me towards his car.

**Jace: Yes, I know you did, and he sent me to make sure you get there. Come on, I'm driving.**

We drive through town, past the turn that would take us to The Freeway Station, and I eye him and the smirk on his face suspiciously.

When we pull up to the marina, I look over to the chemo clinic and wonder just who of our gang is left in there and how the rest are doing. I make a mental note to check up on them. Then excitement washes over me as I recall the first time Jace took me on his yacht. I turn to him. "I thought you only use it for foundation business."

**Jace: Sometimes I like to mix business with pleasure.**

He comes around and opens my door for me and offers his hand to help me out of the car. As we walk towards the dock, I realize he's not let go of my hand, and my eyes close as I take in the warmth of his strong fingers around mine.

When we get closer and closer to the end of the dock, I see there are people gathered on his yacht. I realize who they are and look at Jace. He just squeezes my hand and shrugs his shoulders. I look at the faces of all the kids I know and love from Freeway.

When we get close enough to climb aboard, they all yell, "Surprise!"

Confused, I look at Jace and I walk over to a table adorned with party decorations and a cake. The writing on the cake says, 'Congratulations Keri.' I turn around in surprise and see Chaz, Todd and Tanner coming from the galley with drinks and snacks. All the kids are in bathing suits that I recognize from the closet down in one of the cabins. I know what's in store for today and I'm so happy these kids will get to experience it.

**Jace: We thought it fitting that you get to celebrate with the very people your degree will benefit on a daily basis. We are all so proud of you.**

"Welcome back, Keri," the captain interrupts, when he comes to ask Jace if we're ready to depart.

He and Jace start a conversation, so I head down to get changed, hoping the orange bikini is still here. I'd hate to waste another one. A few minutes later, I emerge donning said bikini, and I go up on deck, feeling the motion of the boat as we head out.

Kimberly's eyes go wide when she sees me. "Oh, Keri, you look just like the girl in the painting."

I panic for a split second as I didn't think anyone else could tell I was the subject of Jace's work. However, when she finishes pulling me into the salon, I realize why she said it.

There on the wall is a painting of me, in this same orange bikini, sitting on the edge of this very yacht. My eyes get teary when I realize he has painted a rainbow in the background, and the lower part of the rainbow is wrapping around my body like a blanket. It's beautiful.

I'm touched at how he seems to remember every detail of every conversation we have.

"Do you like it?" he whispers in my ear, causing me to jump and sigh at the same time.

"Oh, I love it! It's wonderful. But then again, I love all your paintings." I go over each of them in my mind. "Okay, except maybe the one with me grabbing my boobs," I whisper, so Kimberly doesn't overhear.

When I turn around to look at him, I have to keep my jaw firmly in place to keep the saliva from drooling out of my mouth. He is gorgeous.

I belatedly notice that his hair has grown out some more. It's all spiky and haphazard and I'll bet it's almost two inches long. I would love to run my fingers through it. The last time I did, it was just a shadow of what exists now.

But it's the drool-worthy body that has me swooning. He's in those same board shorts again, sans top, and I notice the tiny scar where his feeding tube used to be. I know I'm staring, but the man has obviously been working out and his abs are definitely worth staring at.

He smirks at my more-than-apparent admiration of his impeccable body and I try to recover by quickly saying, "You got the feeding tube out, that is fantastic."

But he just shakes his head at me and laughs, so I roll my eyes at him and walk away, leaving him and Kimberly alone in the salon. But before I'm entirely out of earshot I hear Kimberly's innocent words. "Jace, you think Keri is pretty, don't you? Do you think you will marry her?"

And for the first time, I'm completely bummed that he doesn't have a voice, because I would give anything to know his reply.

# Chapter Twenty-eight

The past several weeks have been wonderfully busy. My full-time appointment was approved, and I've officially become a Residential Support Counselor at Freeway. I work three ten-hour shifts plus one overnight. I've managed to keep my job at The Triple J despite the fact that the owners hate me—or at least the owner's wife hates me. I imagine Jace had a hand in me keeping the job. I only work two shifts a week, but I really wanted to keep up with my friends and I genuinely do love bartending.

Jace treated us to another day on the yacht with people from our chemo group. Dylan was delighted to get to 'drive' the yacht, and the others were all just as floored as I was to find out that Jace comes from such money.

Tanner and I went to Jace's loft a few times to play the Star Wars Xbox game he bought last month. Turns out, I'm pretty good at killing storm troopers.

Jace even hosted Scrabble Night, which gave everyone the opportunity to see what a regular guy he really is, living in a loft and not a mansion as I'm sure they'd pictured.

Jace has respected my boundaries, and although still quite flirty, he has not pushed me to date him. I can only imagine it's because he is still struggling with the Morgan thing.

We go out to lunch once a week, but I make sure it's never at a nice place, ensuring we won't have another run-in with his parents.

He visits Freeway occasionally as it has become another project in his foundation. I try to get to The Angel House when I can, to keep up with Lilly and the other kids there.

It's Lilly I'm thinking about now, as I tidy up around the Freeway house. She's having an operation next month to get hair implants and fix the appearance of her face. She will never look like other ten-year-old girls, but they are hoping for great improvement to enhance her quality of life.

Most of the kids here have gone for a beach day. Even Kimberly went along, fully clothed of course, but at least she joined in the fun.

Tyler and I were unable to go because Social Services is sending someone by to interview him about the situation with his mom and soon-to-be-ex-stepdad. They interviewed his mother last week, and they feel if Tyler is showing signs that he's ready to go home, they're willing to allow it.

Tyler and I have formed a strong attachment and I've gotten to know his mom quite well when she comes to sessions here. I will miss that boy so much, but I'm happy he will go home and lead a normal life now. Well, as normal as life can be after the abuse he endured.

Jules and I are chatting on the phone when the doorbell rings. I motion for Tyler to go let in the Social Services rep.

I'm telling Jules what days I have free for lunch when I hear some commotion in the front hallway. I turn towards the sound and look in horror when I see a man holding a gun to Tyler's head.

"Oh, God, no … Please no!" I shout, right before my phone drops and smashes onto the floor, sending pieces of it flying across the room.

"You're the bitch who took him to the police to report me," says the gunman.

The blood has drained from Tyler's face and the crotch of his pants is soaking wet. I can only assume he lost control of his bladder over the shock of what's happening.

"Did you think I wouldn't find out? I'm a cop, or didn't the brat tell you that?" He winces. "Or at least I was until the two of you got me fired. Now I don't have a job. I don't have a wife. I don't have a home."

He walks Tyler over to me and stands so close I can smell the alcohol on his breath. "You fucked with the wrong man, lady. Now let's take a little trip upstairs, shall we?"

He forces me to walk in front of him, all the while holding the barrel of the gun against Tyler's head. I don't know what to do. The only thing my mind can grasp is that I'll never see Jace's face again. I'm going to die today, and I will never get to tell him I love him. I'll never get to feel his hands on me or run my fingers through his new hair.

I try to clear my head and look for a weapon. Anything I could hit him with that might make him drop the gun. If he takes us to Curtis's room, there will be a baseball bat in the corner. Shelly's will have a baton, and I try to figure out if that would be hard enough to take down such a large man.

But he takes us into Tyler's room, and I wonder how he knows it's his.

"You. Get over on the bed," he says to Tyler.

Tyler's eyes grow wide in terror, and then he leans over and throws up on himself. His stepfather backs away in disgust. Then he hits Tyler over the head with the barrel of his gun, sending him to the floor, unconscious.

He turns to me and says, "Boy, girl, it don't make no difference to me. Now get your pretty little ass over on the bed."

I look at Tyler, lifeless on the floor. I can tell he's still breathing and for that, I'm relieved. But then thoughts of what's about to happen to me race through my head and I start to bat my hands around at Tyler's stepdad.

He laughs it off and surges at me, taking me with him down onto the bed. He turns me around so I'm lying on my stomach underneath him and he reaches around to try and rip the button from my jeans.

As he's fumbling with my button, I'm completely helpless and I start to feel a panic attack come over me. I flash back to when I was sixteen, and I remember now. It all comes rushing back to me. I remember being in my room and waking up coughing. I saw smoke pouring into my bedroom through the crack under the door. I froze in my bed. Then, knowing I was going to die, I rolled off the bed and crouched in the corner farthest from the door, hoping for just a few more seconds of life. And the last thing I remember hearing before I passed out was my mom yelling at me, "Keri! Keri, get out. Jump, baby. You can save yourself!"

I hear her words as clear as day in my head right now and I make a decision. I will not let this moment define me. I won't let it control my life like before. I won't panic, I won't freeze and hope a fireman will rescue me. Nobody is coming. I have to do what my mom said. I have to save myself this time.

All of a sudden, my training kicks in. The self-defense training that all counselors have to go through before they can work or volunteer at Freeway. But his body is heavy on me and I'm not sure how I can get him off me. *Think!*

I press my head as deep into the mattress as I can, then with everything inside me, I snap it up and back with all the force I can summon and crack it into his face behind me.

He screams out in agony as I feel him roll off me and bring his hands to his face, dropping the gun off the other side of the bed in the process.

I don't wait to see what he will do next. I brace my elbow with my body, and I jump up, bringing it down with full force right into his groin. This has him screaming once more.

He rolls off the bed and even loses consciousness for a few seconds. I stare at him, wondering if he's dead, when he grabs my leg and mumbles something through his bloody teeth about killing me.

Then Tyler yells behind me, "Let her go or I'll put a bullet in your head, you bastard."

He releases my leg and begs Tyler not to shoot him. I see Tyler's eyes. These are not the eyes of an innocent fourteen-year-old boy. They are the eyes of a killer. He's going to shoot this man. This is going to be the moment that defines him.

I jump in between Tyler and his stepfather and plead with him. "Tyler, don't do this. Don't be like him. He doesn't matter. He's going to be punished for this and for what he did to you. But if you do this, it will change you, it will define you and your life will never be the same. Right now, you can walk away. Do you hear the sirens? Someone is coming to take him. To lock him up so he can never hurt you or anyone again. Please, give me the gun. Make me proud of the man you're becoming."

He looks from his stepdad to me and then down at the gun he's holding. A tear rolls from his eye as he holds it out to me just as I hear the front door burst open and people running all around the house.

"Up here! It's okay, we're okay!" I yell as my shaky hands hold the gun on Tyler's stepdad, making sure he doesn't make a move.

~ ~ ~

Hours later, after we've given our statements countless times to countless people, Tyler and I are free to go. I walk out to the front of the police station and fall directly into Jace's arms.

Chaz and Tyler's mom take Tyler back to Freeway. I'm grateful he has nothing but a bump on the head.

Jace and Tanner drive me to the hospital to get my head stitched up as the paramedics who came to Freeway simply put a bandage over my wound to stop the bleeding. Apparently, when you headbutt someone in the teeth, there is a good possibility of getting a large gash in your skull.

Tanner sits in the waiting area out front while Jace accompanies me into the emergency room. He helps me set up the new phone he picked up for me when I was at the police station. He was able to recover my SIM card from my old, broken phone so thankfully, all my pictures were saved.

I learn it was Jules who called the police when she heard me shout and then couldn't get me back on the phone.

Ten stitches later, I'm good to go.

When the three of us head out to the parking lot, we see Morgan carrying a large stuffed bear with a balloon emblazoned with 'It's a girl.'

*Great.* What are the odds of running into her here?

She spots us. "Oh! Hi, Jace. Keri."

She takes in Jace and it's obvious to me that she hasn't seen him in quite a while, possibly since their breakup. She eyes him from head to toe appreciatively then she just stares at his hair and smiles. "You look great, Jace. Wow!"

Jace texts her. Then she turns to greet Tanner as Jace must have introduced them.

"We should get together for lunch sometime," she says to Jace. "I miss you."

He texts her back. Then she texts him back. This goes on for a minute and I'm aware that Tanner and I are standing here not privy to anything they're saying. It's very awkward and my heart hurts thinking that maybe they're making plans to meet for lunch, or worse, get back together.

Finally, she hugs him goodbye, whispering something in his ear before she waves to all of us as she enters the hospital.

We drive back to my place in silence. Tanner must know what I'm thinking. Jace keeps glancing over at me with a look of sympathy like he knows he's about to destroy me, especially after what happened to me today.

After Tanner is sure I'm okay, he leaves us alone and goes back to his room.

Immediately, Jace pulls me into a hug. "Keri, I was so scared," he whispers.

He knows the whole story. He was there at Freeway the first time I talked to the police. Apparently, Jules also called him, and he rushed over, arriving shortly after the police did.

But right now, despite what happened earlier, all my thoughts are on Morgan. I pull away from him a little and ask, "Did you get back together with her just now?" He gives me a strange look, so I ask him again. "Morgan. Did you get back together with her at the hospital? She seems to really miss you. And then the way you were looking at me in the car." I frown.

> **Jace: Your life was in danger. You saved a child. You got ten stitches. And what you want to talk about is if I'm getting back together with Morgan? Keri, I was concerned about you in the car. You had kind of a bad day by anyone's standards.**

I laugh at his remark, but he still didn't answer my question.

"Today, at Freeway, when that horrible man was pushing me up the stairs while he had a gun on Tyler, all I could think about was you and your hair. How weird is that? Of all the things I could think about when I felt I was about to die, I was thinking about your hair." I look down at the floor.

Then he shoves his phone at me and taps the screen a few times to pull up his conversation with Morgan. I look up at him, but he motions down to the phone, so I read it.

> **Jace: Thanks, you look nice, too. This is Tanner, Keri's roommate.**

> **Morgan: Oh, he's cute. I'll bet they are more than just roommates! So, lunch?**

> **Jace: Morgan, today was a very bad day for some people who are very close to me. I can't really think about making lunch plans.**

> **Morgan: Oh, I'm sorry to hear that. I can't believe how quickly your hair has come in. I**

almost forgot how handsome you are. How
about we go to your dad's restaurant. Thursday
maybe?

Jace: We need to go. I'll have to let you know
about lunch.

Morgan: Okay, I hope everything is alright. I
can't wait to see you Thursday.

He takes his phone back, but I'm still unsure if they made a date
or not, because obviously Morgan thinks they did. Was he simply
brushing her off, or is he really going to meet her on Thursday? Jace
puts his hand on my arm as my phone vibrates with a new text.

Jace: After I got the frantic call from Jules and I
was on my way to Freeway, all I could think
about were your lips. I know we've only kissed
the one time, but all I thought was how I would
miss them. There's so much I want to say to you.
I don't know what I would do without you, Keri.
You have no idea how proud I am of what you
did today. You saved Tyler. You saved yourself.

I think he's leaning over to whisper in my ear, so I close my
eyes and wait for that feeling of his hot breath flowing over my neck.
When I feel his lips on me, it's a shock. But I surprise myself even
more when I push him away.

"Jace, I want this. I really do. But today was one of those really
intense days that sometimes has people making the wrong choices. I
see the way Morgan looks at you. She's not done with you. And I
can't move on unless I know you're done with her."

He goes to text me, but I grab his hands to stop him. "No, don't say anything about it now. Can we just watch Star Wars or something and forget today even happened?"

His lips turn into a big smile that brings out the dimple I love. He gets up and walks over to the TV and finds Episode II, which he knows is my favorite. We sit watching it, holding hands through the entire movie. Well, he watches it, I watch our clasped hands.

It's the best movie I've ever seen.

# Chapter Twenty-nine

I've spent the last several days wondering what Jace was going to text me that night and feeling stupid for not letting him do so. We've both been so busy with work we've barely gotten a chance to talk much since then.

I volunteered to work the day after the 'incident' just to help with all the questions and anxiety around Freeway. It was an emotional day for Tyler and me and we spent a lot of time talking through our feelings about what happened.

It turns out the police found the social worker bound and gagged in the trunk of her car out in front of Freeway shortly after they searched the grounds for evidence. So they had another representative come out yesterday to interview Tyler, and it was decided he would reunite with his mother next week.

Unfortunately, Tyler and I now have one more thing in common, but I think it has cemented a life-long bond between us.

Now, as I sit and wait for Jace to pick me up and go with me to find out the results of the PET scans I had a few days ago, I finally allow myself to think of what will happen if they find anything. The past few months, I've pushed it out of my head. I focused on anything and everything except what I would do if my tumor didn't go away. What if it has only shrunk and I need more chemo? What if it's gotten bigger, or worse, spread to my lymph nodes? I'm driving myself crazy with all the questions I've suppressed for the last twelve weeks.

Jace holds my hand the entire way to my doctor's office. Then when we get there, he occupies my mind while we wait for my appointment.

**Jace: I know you've only been a full-time counselor for a month now, but have you given any more thought to the foundation job?**

"Jace, I really don't have enough experience. Are you just trying to get me out of harm's way? Because you know I want to work with the kids. I'd never give that up. Not even after what happened."

**Jace: I know better than to ask you to give it up. I wouldn't be able to stay away either. But I just wanted to bring it up again, so you know I'm serious. The foundation will even pay for you to get an advanced degree. Now, before you say anything, it's not charity, Keri. You are good, great in fact, and I want to snatch you up before everyone else realizes it.**

I *have* thought about his offer. I've thought about it a lot since he mentioned it. But I wasn't about to bring it up in case it was a heat-of-the-moment kind of thing. Now that The Third Watch has taken on Freeway as one of its charities, it means I would be able to oversee it and still interact with the counselors and the kids that I love so much.

I still think I'm grossly underqualified. The idea that they would pay for my master's degree and let me continue to do what I love— it seems too good to be true. So, I'm scared that it is.

"I need more time to think about it. Are you okay with that? I mean, if you need to hire someone else, then maybe you should. I don't want you to wait around until I think I'm ready."

**Jace: Keri, there's nobody else I would hire. The job is yours when and if you want it. Take all the time you need. I just wanted you to know I'm dead serious about it and that I don't go using foundation money where it's not going to do a lot of good.**

Somehow, I believe him. Maybe it's knowing him and seeing that he doesn't throw money around frivolously or even spend it on himself. This makes me feel like he really does trust in my ability to do the foundation job.

My name is called and Jace gives my hand a squeeze as we stand up and head into the office.

"Keri, so nice to see you. You're looking well," Dr. Olsen says.

I introduce him to Jace and tell him Jace can't speak due to his own cancer and the surgery he had.

"Is that how the two of you met? It's so rare to see two young people with cancer who know each other so well."

I explain to Dr. Olsen how we met at chemotherapy and that Jace has accompanied me here to support me when I get the news of my scans. I tell him he can speak openly in front of Jace.

"Well then, I won't make you wait any longer," he says. "You'll have to come back every four months for scans for one year, and then twice a year for a while after that. But I'm pleased to say that as of right now, you appear to be tumor-free, Keri."

I look over at Jace and back at Dr. Olsen. I see them both smiling, so I'm pretty sure I heard him correctly. But I ask him anyway. "Doctor, can you please say that again?"

He laughs at my request. "Keri, you are tumor-free. We don't throw around words like *remission* until you've had a second clean scan, but you're a lucky girl. Now, go live your life and I'll see you back here in four months."

His words are still reverberating in my head when Jace pulls me up by the hand that was already holding mine. He pulls me out of my chair and directly into his arms. Then, without even thinking about it, our lips collide.

It must be the excitement, the adrenaline, the high we got from hearing the words 'tumor-free.' But here we are kissing, crying, and laughing at the news, right here in front of my oncologist.

I don't know what Dr. Olsen thinks of this display, and I don't even care. All I hear is the click of his office door closing as he leaves the room to give us privacy.

Somehow, some way, we end up driving back to Jace's loft a short time later. I lose track of time as I keep re-playing Dr. Olsen's words in my head along with re-living what happened in the moments after.

I call Tanner to give him the incredible news.

The adrenaline and the high still course through my veins as we race up the stairs to his loft. Jace opens the door and I throw my bag on the entry table as he picks me up and carries me over by the couch to finish what we started at the doctor's office. He puts me down in front of him and stares at me for a long moment. He cups my face with his hands and looks into my eyes. We stare at each other with such intensity I think I can actually see his soul.

When he finally lowers his face to kiss me, I feel like I'm being re-born. Like I've been lost my entire life, and in this moment of clarity, I've been found. When his lips softly touch mine, my heart explodes with insurmountable joy and my skin tingles with excitement. After only moments of kissing, I'm already addicted to the taste of his lips and the smell of his breath mingling with mine. I know there isn't another man in the world who could feed this addiction.

When his lips urge mine apart and I open for him, our tongues weave a web of tangled pleasure as our hands explore each other's faces, necks and hair. He's careful not to touch the stitches in the back of my head, but I have no such boundaries with his.

His hair is just long enough now that my fingers can twist through it and tug on it, eliciting a whispered moan from Jace's throat. He breaks our kiss and starts to explore my neck with his lips, planting a trail of kisses up one side of it to right beneath my ear, stopping to lick and suck on a spot that makes me quiver and produce my own pleasurable sounds.

I try to quiet the voice in my head. The one telling me I still don't know where Jace's heart is and that I might end up hurt. The voice that screams I don't belong in his bed or his world. It tells me I could never measure up to the kind of woman it would take to be on his arm forever. That his mother would never even give me the time of day and his friends may never accept me in their lives.

There are a million reasons why I shouldn't be doing this. Reasons I shouldn't allow him to crawl any deeper inside my soul than he already has. A million reasons why I should walk away. But there is one reason that keeps my hands wandering his body, my lips tasting his mouth. And it's this one reason that I decide will trump all the others. *I love him.*

I pull away and let him know with my eyes that he's won. That I've let down every single defense I've had. I know he understands my message. I know he gets me. He has always gotten me, from the day he spilled the latte all over my favorite jeans. And I get him. We're connected by a bond nobody can sever. We can communicate without words. I don't need his words. I don't need anything but him and now.

I rise onto my toes and whisper, "I want you, Jace."

He tightens his grip on my hips and lowers his mouth to my ear. "Oh, Keri," he whispers, as he eases us down onto the couch behind us.

He pulls me onto his lap, and I lean over and explore his face with my lips while my fingers continue the assault on his hair.

I tenderly kiss the scar on his neck. It's a part of him and I love it just as I love the rest of his magnificent body. He runs his hands up and down my sides as his quickened breath flows across my face. In a bold move, I reach down and pull the hem of my shirt up and over my head.

I swear he stops breathing. He stares at my breasts with blinking eyes, admiring the very things that caused me such pain in the months before. When I reach around to unclasp my bra and release them from their confinement, his breath hitches. He brings his hands up to cup them. He caresses them gently at first and then kneads them, gradually increasing the pressure as desire builds inside him.

He stops what he's doing and pulls my head down so my ear is next to his mouth. He whispers, "They are lovely, Keri." And then he kisses that place beneath my ear and whispers, "But you would be beautiful even without them."

The world falls away as I give my heart to him as I have no other. I want him on me, I want him *in* me. I want to be as close to him as two people can get without being one person. I can feel his arousal pressing against me as I straddle him, and I instinctively grind my hips into him, causing both of us to close our eyes in shared euphoria.

I run my hands all over his chest, feeling every ridge, every ripple. I untuck his shirt and pull it over his head. Then I continue my exploration of every inch of bare skin on his torso while he continues his own pleasurable torture on mine.

He tugs on my nipples and a moan escapes my throat. "Oh God, Jace."

I reach my hand down to the button of his jeans, but he grabs it. He clasps my hands in his, taking them around my back as he wraps his arms around me. He whispers to me, "Let's go slow."

"Jace, I want you. We've waited so long. I want this. It's okay," I beg him.

He closes his eyes and gently helps me off his lap and onto the cushion next to him. Then, before he pulls out his phone, he leans over to trail more kisses up my neck to assure me I'm not being rejected.

> **Jace: Believe me, Keri, I want this, too. More than anything. I want you more than anything. But I think we should take it slow. A lot has happened this week. Today. We have all these emotions flying around and I want to make sure we do this for the right reasons. I want you to be sure.**

"I'm sure, Jace," I say to him, still breathing heavily and riding waves of want and passion.

**Jace: And I am too. So, if we are so sure, then we will still be sure tomorrow, or the next day. There's no need to rush this.**

I nod and reach down to the floor to retrieve my bra and our shirts. As I put mine back on, I know he's right. I know my emotions are out of control right now. I just found out my tumor is gone. I've recently had a brush with death. That's a lot to process in the course of a few days.

No matter how much I wanted to and would have continued down the path we were on tonight, he has endeared himself to me even more with his willpower and wisdom.

"Okay. You're right. I know you're right. There is no need to rush this." I look down at his shirt in my hands. Then I reach over and place a kiss on his cheek as I run my hand down the prickly stubble. "But if I can't have you, I'm keeping the shirt."

**Jace: It's yours. But, Keri, I need to take you home. I don't trust myself now that I've seen what I'll be missing. Now that I've had a good long taste of you. If you stay, I won't be able to keep my hands off you. So even though I want you to stay, I want you to stay more than you know, I'm going to drive you home now.**

I smile as I tuck my top into my pants. Jace nods to the bathroom and holds up his finger for me to give him a minute. I walk over and gather my purse from the entry hall table.

That's when I see it. A pretty pink envelope addressed to Jace with a heart drawn in the corner. It isn't sealed, the flap is merely tucked in, so I decide, in a very un-Keri-like moment, to peek inside. I open it just enough to see the closing words and the signature.

*Please come back to me. I love you, Morgan.*

I panic. I close the envelope and stash it away in my purse before Jace walks down the hall, smiling and completely oblivious to what I've just fallen upon.

I try to look happy and smile brightly back at him, but my heart has splintered into a thousand pieces and the shards are stabbing my insides.

Jace mistakes my behavior for sexual frustration when he texts me.

**Jace: Keri, don't worry, it will happen. I don't think I've ever wanted anything so much in my life.**

He gives me one last passionate, earth-shattering kiss before he walks me downstairs and drives me home.

# Chapter Thirty

I open a bottle of wine. I figure I'm going to need it when I sit down to read the letter. Tanner has a shift at the club, so it's just me in the apartment. Just me and the love letter from Morgan. The letter I stole from Jace's vestibule. The letter she obviously placed inside his loft by using a key she still possesses.

Today has been such a roller-coaster ride of emotions for me. First it was the anxiety leading up to my appointment, then the incredible news that my tumor is gone, and then the aftermath of it with Jace. And now, I fear this letter will send the roller-coaster spiraling down to a fiery death while I sit in the very front seat.

I take a large gulp of wine before I remove the letter from the envelope. I close my eyes and take a calming breath. Then I read.

My dearest Jace,

Words cannot express what I felt when I saw you the other day as you were leaving the hospital. I didn't even realize I missed you this much until I saw your face. I've tried to stay away. I have tried to push my feelings for you aside knowing I don't deserve to ask you for a second chance. I hurt you. I hurt you so deeply during a time when you needed my support. My harsh words were inexcusable. My actions were unforgivable. But I'm asking you anyway. Forgive me. Love me. Let me back into your life.

I miss you. I miss your parents. I miss Sunday morning walks in the park and Wednesday night ice-cream runs. I've even found myself going to animal shelters to find that one perfect dog you always talked about rescuing.

Do you remember when we were seven years old and we would play dress-up and pretend to get married? We said always and forever—that's how long we would be together. Even when I went away to boarding school and you went away to college and we couldn't be together. Even when we dated other people, I never could see myself with anyone else.

I'm begging you to give me another chance to be the woman you know I can be. I can be stronger for you. I promise I will never give you another reason to doubt me.

Please come back to me. I love you.

Morgan

I drop the letter as if it has burned me. Then I chug the rest of my wine and pour another glass.

When Tanner gets home, he finds me next to an empty bottle of wine along with the letter that is exactly where I dropped it hours ago.

He hugs me with excitement because, of course, he thinks I'm celebrating the news I called him about earlier today. But when he sees my tears and the direction of my gaze, he picks up the letter and reads it.

"Oh, Keri. Did he show you this? What's he going to do? Did he blow you off?"

"He hasn't even seen it, Tan. I stole it from his entry table when I saw it after we almost made love."

Tanner holds up his finger and runs into the kitchen to grab another bottle of wine and a glass for himself. Then I tell him everything that happened right up until he walked in the door.

"Why are you so upset? Do you think he'll go back to her, after the day you had? He practically declared his love for you. He said he never wanted anything so much in his life. Well, Morgan was a pretty big part of his life and he just said he wanted you more. There's your answer. He chooses you."

He pats my leg and holds out the bottle to refill my glass.

"But he didn't know she wanted him back when he said all those things. It's different now, he has a choice to make when he didn't earlier. I was his *only* choice then. I won by default, Tan."

He stays up for hours with me, hearing me out and giving me advice on what to do. I love Jace, that's for sure. She loves him, too. They have Sunday morning walks and Wednesday night ice-cream. They have a long history together. They got pretend-married at age seven for heaven's sake.

How do I compete with that?

~ ~ ~

I think I fell asleep from exhaustion somewhere around four in the morning. I tried to come up with reasons to fight for him and then I tried to rationalize walking away. I even prayed for a sign. Something ... anything to let me know how I should proceed.

Today should be a happy day. I should be celebrating my prognosis. But instead, there is a letter on my coffee table. It's a small thing, but it carries the weight of the world as I contemplate what to do with it.

Jace is out of town on foundation business all day. Do I sneak back over and leave the letter for him? He deserves to read it. It was unfair of me to take it from his loft. He would be so upset with me if he knew I was this underhanded. I'm pulled from the world of will-I-or-won't-I when my phone rings. I see an unfamiliar number on the screen and decide to answer it.

"Hello?"

"Keri, this is Mrs. Jarrett, Jace's mother."

"Oh, yes ma'am. What can I do for you?"

*Oh, God, why is Jace's mother calling me?* If she's calling to reprimand me again for the way I spent her money, I don't know if I can take it. Would Jace be upset if I hung up on his mother?

"Well, it comes down to what you can do for my son, dear. You see, it has recently come to my attention that he may have feelings for you and that you might share those feelings."

"Yes ma'am."

What is she getting at? My hands shake and my breathing accelerates.

"Well, I also happen to know his girlfriend, Morgan, would like very much to get back together with him."

It's not lost on me that she called her his girlfriend, not his *ex-girlfriend*. I brace myself for what's going to come next. She needs something from me. I know exactly what is coming. I implore myself to hang up so I don't have to hear it. If I don't hear the words, I don't have to acknowledge that this is the sign I was praying for just hours ago.

But instead of hanging up I say, "What does that have to do with me, Mrs. Jarrett?"

"Well, if you are the saint that my son says you are, I have to believe you will do what's in his best interest and graciously walk away. Allow him to live the life he was destined for. To marry someone of social status and means who will help his foundation grow. His foundation will help countless children with their combined resources. What could *you* possibly bring to the table? It's my understanding that you're a kind-hearted person who helps children. Well, Keri, if my son marries Morgan, she will bring insurmountable wealth to his foundation. You wouldn't want to keep that wealth from your precious Freeway house or that Angel home, would you? My son and Morgan have been destined to marry since they were small children. I know you feel a connection with him because you both have cancer. But, Keri, once that isn't an issue, if you both get better, what will you have then? A strong relationship needs a foundation, a history to build upon. He has that with Morgan. You and Jace don't have it. You couldn't possibly fit into his world. Morgan does. She belongs with him. If you love my son, please do the right thing and walk away."

I can't talk through the lump in my throat. Through the tears pouring from my eyes. I knew what she was going to ask, but I didn't think she would make such a compelling argument.

"I h-have t-to go," I stutter. I don't even wait for her reply as I hang up the phone.

I stare at the ceiling for hours, thinking of the words in Morgan's letter, and I know what I have to do.

I pick up the phone, my finger lingering over Jace's name. I contemplate texting him, but I need to hear his voice. I need to hear it one more time. The voice I have craved for so long but have kept myself from.

I let myself think, one final time, how perfect yesterday was. The feel of his lips on my lips and his hands on my body was better than I could have imagined; better than in my dreams. He whispered all the right things to me, things I wanted to hear, things he had alluded to before. Things I refused to succumb to until last night. He was so gentle, not pushing me for more than he thought I could handle after the up-and-down week I had been through. I know I would have let him make love to me if he hadn't stopped us.

That's why making this call will be hardest thing I've ever had to do. I don't fit into his world. Morgan, she fits in. She's the one he belongs with, the one who is perfect for him. I guess I knew it all along, I just didn't allow myself to believe it. Not until I got that phone call this morning. I love him too much to make him spend his life with me, with someone who is not his equal.

I dial his number, resolving to get through my message without breaking into sobs. He has to understand that I mean what I say. It's the only way this will work. As I listen to the sound of his voice for only the second time in my life, tears well up in my eyes and my broken heart falls from my chest out onto the floor, to be trampled on by my own feet.

I take a deep breath and tell him what I must.

"Jace, it's Keri. I've done a lot of thinking and I've decided that being with you is not good for me. Maybe you just waited too long to say the things you did. I've realized you are not the man I need in my life to become the person I want to be. I'm cured. And I got what

I wanted from you, for you to pay my bills. Last night was a mistake. But it doesn't matter anymore because you couldn't give me what I needed, so I went out and found someone who could. Someone who is right for me. Someone who is better for me than you are. I've made my decision. Go back to Morgan. Please don't contact me ever again."

As I hang up the phone, sealing my fate with my lies, tears stream down my cheeks and fall onto the shirt I hold in my hands. The shirt with his scent on it. The shirt I will never launder as long as I live.

# Chapter Thirty-one

I dry my tears. I have things to accomplish this afternoon. I quickly head over to Jace's and slip the card from Morgan under his door. Then I contact Austin and Jordan from the club and get them to cover my two shifts this week, assuming I will even have a job there once Jace gets my message. Then I pack a bag and go to Freeway. I tell Chaz that Jace and I had a falling out, and that I'm volunteering for all the overnights this week so I'm not at home where Jace will expect me. Just in case he was to go looking for me.

But as I lie here in bed at Freeway, one week later, I realize how unnecessary all of that was as Jace never contacted me. Not even once. He never texted me, never knocked on my door, never sent an inquiry. Just as I requested. Not only that, but I haven't heard from Jules either. She became a casualty of war. I never intended for that to happen, but it makes perfect sense that she remain loyal to her brother and not the backstabbing never-was girlfriend he befriended.

My tears dried up long ago. Now I busy my days by staying occupied at Freeway. I try not to let my mind wander to the what-ifs and could-have-beens. I try to rejoice in my new-found health and embrace it as the miracle it is. I pray Jace will be able to embrace his own renewed health in a couple of months when he gets his new scans. I'm so sad I won't be there to support him, but I know Morgan will be, and I need to accept the fact that everything has worked out as it should.

At Freeway we are preparing the house for the construction that will begin soon, thanks to Jace's generous donation. As Chaz and I remove some of the wall hangings I ask, "Do you think Jace will pull the funding we're getting from The Third Watch now?"

"No, I don't think so. When I talked to him the other day, he seemed to indicate it was business as usual."

*He talked to him?* This is news to me.

"You talked to him, Chaz? Why didn't you tell me? Did he ask about me?"

Chaz looks at me with sorry eyes. "I'm sorry, Keri, but no, he didn't ask about you. We simply talked about the expansion and the plans to fund another position or two."

I know this is what I asked for. I know I hurt him. I guess I just never fully expected it to work. Maybe in the back of my mind, I thought he would see through all the crap I was feeding him in my message and ride in on his white horse and whisk me away to live happily ever after.

But there will be no happily ever after for me. I know I'll never find another man like Jace. I was happy once, before him, wasn't I? If I can just get back to the way things were before Jace. Before cancer. I was fine living a life filled with Tanner, my other friends, and the kids at Freeway. That will be enough. I will make it be enough.

But then I think of my mother and her words about finding my more-than-enough love. I've let her down. I know I've let her down and maybe that makes me saddest of all.

~ ~ ~

Jules finally contacted me after a few weeks and we're going to lunch today. I prepare myself for her reprimands. I will sit and take whatever she dishes me. I deserve it. The main reason I'm going, other than the fact that I really like Jules and I miss our friendship, is I'm hoping she will give me some sliver of information about him. Is he okay? Is he back with Morgan?

Part of me hopes he's leading a miserable existence of a life, just as I am. But the other part, the part that loves him to the depths of my soul, hopes he is happy and will eventually live the life he was meant to live, with the person he was meant to live it with.

"Keri, I've missed you so much." Jules pulls me in for a hug and I hold onto her for dear life as a tear rolls down my cheek.

"I've missed you, too. Thanks for contacting me. I wasn't sure you would."

I look at her and wonder if she can see the abundance of guilt I carry on my shoulders.

"The truth is, he asked me not to, but I couldn't stay away," she says.

And if it's possible, my heart breaks even more, becoming a hollow, lifeless organ that resembles my robotic existence.

"I like you, Keri, and we can be friends, but you hurt my brother, so I should tell you I'm not here to talk about him if that's why you came."

How can I fault her for that? I dug my own grave. I'm getting exactly what I asked for.

"Maybe I did come to find out if he's okay, but that's not the only reason. I miss you. I value our friendship and if talking about him is off the table, I can be okay with that. But I have to ask one thing. If I keep in contact with Lilly and the kids from The Angel House, do you think that would seem too much like me stalking him?"

My question extracts a laugh from her. "Keri, if you cut off contact with those precious kids, then you aren't the kind of friend I thought you were. Whatever your issues are with my brother, nobody can fault you for being a good humanitarian."

I smile knowing I've gotten her blessing to continue to see those great kids, and especially Lilly, who is having her surgery in a few days.

We spend the next hour figuring out we have more in common than just her brother, which is good, because I wasn't sure we would be able to find anything else to talk about.

We make plans to get together for lunch next week. She even said she might come to the club Tuesday night, my slow night, just to keep me company—after assuring me I still have a job there.

~ ~ ~

A few more weeks have crawled by at a snail's pace. Lilly had her surgery and I went to the hospital to visit her on two occasions, after checking with Gracy to make sure Jace wasn't there.

Tyler and his mother are happily co-existing at home, and his ex-stepdad is resting not-so-comfortably in jail, awaiting trial for a myriad of charges.

Scrabble Nights are back to normal—sans Jace. Tanner still brings Greg, and they graciously allow me to be a third wheel on some of their dates.

I think I'm wearing grooves in all my Star Wars DVDs that have always been my go-to movies in times of depression.

I'm grateful I took pictures of all Jace's paintings along with the ones he sent me. And I have some candid shots from the times he took the Freeway kids and our chemo friends on the yacht. I scroll through them every day.

It's pitiful, I know, but I almost wish we were back in chemo, tumors still invading our healthy bodies, poison still dripping into our veins. At least then we would be together.

I still love him.

I'm not sure I'll ever stop loving him.

My heart hurts from not being able to see him, touch him, feel his whispers. I keep expecting the pain to die down, to go away. But every day when I wake up and realize he's gone from my life, I have to force myself to get out of bed and go through the motions of living.

I finally break down and pull out my laptop to Google him just to see him again. What I see astounds me.

His life did not stop when mine did. He didn't seem to miss a beat. I see an article about him and how he took a child with cancer to meet the boy's football hero. I recognize Dylan from the picture, and I laugh because his hero is the quarterback for Tampa Bay, and there is Jace, wearing a Buc's cap right along with him. Then I see pictures of him with some of the familiar faces from The Angel House right alongside Mickey Mouse and Donald Duck. Apparently, he took them all to Disney World.

There's another place his foundation supports that he never spoke of much called The Stopover in Ft. Lauderdale. It's a shelter for women and children that puts women through training for jobs like nursing assistants or massage therapists—jobs that only require a month or so of training. There's a picture of Jace and a barrage of women and children at a ribbon-cutting ceremony for the new facility built by The Third Watch.

But it's the final picture I find that has my heart battling with my head. There is a picture of Jace, all dressed up in a tux and looking like I've never seen him before. His hair has grown out more and is starting to flop over to the side in a fresh-out-of-bed look that probably has women falling at his feet. And standing right next to him, with her hand on his chest, is Morgan, dressed to the nines in a magnificent evening gown. Next to them are Jace's parents. They look like the perfect family. I read the caption that says the picture was taken at a charity ball. Three days ago.

So that's it. The question has been answered. He's back together with her. He looked happy even.

I close the lid to my laptop and go lie on my bed. I tell myself this is exactly what I wanted; exactly what I wished would happen. So why then, does it feel like my heart has been through a meat grinder? Why do I lie here trying to feel nothing? Because feeling nothing would surely be better than the pain. The pain that is different from anything I've ever experienced. Different even from when I lost my parents, different from when I found out I had cancer, different from those horrible Monday nights I spent in my bathroom. Different from when I had a gun pointed at me.

No, this pain … it's like part of my body has been removed. It's like I've been stabbed in the chest with a knife and each painful memory cuts deeper than the last. It's like my soul was ripped in half and shredded to pieces.

It's the pain of knowing I will never have that more-than-enough love.

# Chapter Thirty-two

Tanner has been my rock. He makes me laugh when I think laughing is no longer possible. He gets my ass out of bed when all I want to do is wallow in self-pity. And bless him, he watches Star Wars with me whenever I ask him to.

He took away my laptop last week after he found me Googling Jace. He told me it was unhealthy and that I just needed to give it time and everything would work out in the end. For whom, I wonder?

He's taking me somewhere nice tonight. He said six weeks of commiseration was all he could bear, so he made me put on makeup, dress up, and paint a fake smile on my face in the name of fun.

He won't tell me where we're going. He says it's a surprise. But he must really think it's great because he's had a shit-eating grin on his face the entire drive.

We pull up to the curb alongside the road in a trendy district of downtown Tampa. Tanner, being all gentlemanly, comes around to open my door and leads me up to the glass front door of some kind of art gallery.

"What are we doing here, Tan?" I ask, with a suspicious stare, knowing he has about as much appreciation of art as a blind baboon.

"Just come in, Keri."

He holds the door open for me and we walk through into an empty gallery. It's so deserted that the clicks of my heels echo off the gleaming white tile floors and concrete walls.

A woman comes over to me holding a silver tray with a single glass of champagne on it. She hands me the champagne and says, "Right this way, Miss."

I start to walk with her when Tanner says, "I'll be right over here on this couch if you need me."

He winks at me then he gives me a push toward the opening of another room.

I'm utterly confused. Why am I being lured into an art gallery and handed champagne if I'm the only one getting to enjoy it?

The woman turns around and disappears somewhere. And then my heart thunders as I look up and see the painting on the wall in front of me.

It's the painting that used to hang over Jace's fireplace. The one he did of me being pulled from my burning house the night my parents died. The one that was his inspiration.

*Why is it here?*

Has he decided to sell his art since he got back together with Morgan? But why would Tanner bring me here, unless maybe he thinks I want to buy it. All sorts of things are racing through my mind.

The art gallery is apparently laid out to keep people moving from one exhibit to the next by using partitions and strategically placed walls. A light clicks on, illuminating another painting in the next area. I walk over to look at it and see it's the painting that was at The Angel House with my guardian angels on it.

Then I see another light and walk around the partition to see the painting he did of us on the bathroom floor. This was the first one he painted after we met at chemo.

I'm beginning to see a pattern here as the paintings are being displayed in the order in which he made them. If that's the case, the next one will be the one of me cupping my breasts. I walk over to where the next light shines and I see that, yes, it is in fact the one.

My steps quicken over to the next painting, and I reach it even before the light turns on. I hear someone snicker when I stand in front of it and wait for it to be illuminated. I look around, wondering if Tanner is somehow watching me.

The light turns on and it's exactly the one I thought it would be. The first one from the yacht, the one in the cabin of me with the thirteen 'balloons.'

I move on to the next one, the lights coming quicker now to keep up with me. But I'm stunned to see it's not the painting I suspected it would be, this one I haven't seen before. It's a painting of me under the old bridge at the train yard, the place Tanner used to take me in order to clear my head.

I know Jace must have visited the place because he painted it dead-on. I take extra time to look at it, even though the light has already clicked on to illuminate the next painting.

The next one I recognize. It's the rainbow painting from the salon on his yacht. I smile remembering the graduation party he threw for me the day I first saw it.

A few steps over, I see another unfamiliar one. This one causes the tears welling up in my eyes to spill over. It's a picture of Lilly and me, hugging on her bed at The Angel House.

I look around but don't see any more lights. I don't know what to do. I'm still not sure why I'm here. My heart tells me it's because of Jace, but my head won't let me believe it yet.

The gallery is eerily dark, only illuminated by the glow of the lights that still shine on each painting.

I take a shaky sip of my untouched champagne. Then someone comes out of the shadows and my heart skips a beat. It skips ten-thousand beats.

He is gorgeous.

I've never seen a more handsome man. He has a light-grey suit on. He's not wearing a tie, and the collar of his white linen shirt has the top button undone. His hair is much longer and is perfectly messy. There's a smile on his face revealing his wonderful dimple. The smile touches his eyes making me understand he's here for me.

Jace points in the direction of a still-darkened painting. "There's one more, Keri."

My heart comes out of my chest. *He spoke!* From across the room he spoke to me. Oh, my God. His voice is deep and gravelly and sexy and wonderful and perfect. It makes me wonder if he really did speak or if I just dreamed it. Maybe I'm dreaming *all* of it.

He walks over to me and takes my hand. He leads me towards the darkened painting. "Here, let me show you."

A light turns on, shining on another new painting. It's me, sitting at a table with Scrabble pieces strewn about. There's a man's hand in the painting, his fingers touching the tiles that sit in the tile holder. I look at the tiles to see that they spell two words.

**I'M SURE.**

I set my glass down on a nearby table and turn to him. "But I hurt you. I said those awful things. Why would you still want me?"

"You don't really think I believed a word of your voicemail message, do you, Keri?" He smirks at me as I swoon over his rough, delicious voice. "I know why you did it. I saw the letter and I know my mom called you. But I didn't think you would understand at the time that I wanted you and only you. Things were too fresh. We had just seen Morgan and you had read her pleas to me. I knew if I tried to get you then that you would run away. I had to give you time and space."

"But the picture of you and Morgan at the charity event—"

"Was planned months before that," he interrupts me. "Even before Morgan and I split, I had committed to it. It was platonic, I assure you, and very unfortunate that they snapped the picture while her hand was on my chest. She probably planned it that way. You should know she says she still wants to get back with me."

I shake my head at him. "You never went back to her?"

He smiles at me. "I never went back to her. I told you that night, Keri. I told you I was sure. I'm still sure. It's you. You're the one I want. You may not have been my first love, but you are the love of my life."

I briefly close my eyes and rejoice in his words before I say, "And you are the love of mine."

I lift my hand to his jaw and rub it across the rough bit of stubble. "Your voice … you got your voice back."

He grabs my hand and pulls it to his mouth to kiss the palm of it. "It was you. You were my inspiration, Keri. You have been since I was nineteen. I've never met a stronger, more beautiful woman— inside and out. And I just had to get my voice back. I've worked so hard these past weeks with a speech therapist because I had to be able to tell you how I feel." He takes my hands in his and looks me in the eyes, his own tears welling up, when he says, "I love you, Keri."

"Thank you." It's all I can manage to say through my tears as he pulls me to him and crashes his lips against mine.

Minutes later when we reluctantly part our swollen lips, he impatiently pulls me towards the front door of the gallery. I look at our surroundings. "Where is Tanner?" I ask.

"He left a while ago." He smirks at me.

"Kind of a foregone conclusion, was I?" I roll my eyes.

He laughs and my insides melt at the sound of the low sexy grumble.

"No, Keri, you are anything but predictable. But I didn't want you to have an out, a way to leave before I had the chance to tell you how I felt."

"And he was okay with that—with leaving me here with you?" I question, knowing how Tanner has always been so protective of me.

"We've been communicating for weeks. Everyone was in on it, even Jules and Chaz." He looks at me guiltily as I raise my eyebrows to scold him. "Keri, I needed to know if you were going to do something drastic like date another man. I wouldn't have been able to stand it if you did. I was fully prepared to scrap the entire plan and whisk you away the moment you turned your head for anyone else."

I can't help but smile at his jealously and possessiveness.

"I'm sorry I put you through that," he says. "I know the past weeks have been hell on you. They've been hell on me, too. Not seeing you, not touching you—I'm starving for you, Keri. And I fully plan to make it up to you if you'll let me."

"Oh really?" I smile at him suggestively. "And just how do you plan on doing that?"

"If you'll come back to the loft with me, I'll show you."

Thoughts of what almost happened the last time we were at his loft run through my head. And desire floods my body at the anticipation of getting to touch him again. Then suddenly, I'm the one pulling him through the front door of the gallery.

We talk the whole way back to his loft, my ears dancing with pleasure at the sound of his gravelly voice. By the time we reach our destination, my skin is humming with passion as he has seduced me with only his voice—his enticingly spoken words.

We both giggle as we quickly bypass the living room, almost running to reach the bedroom at the far end of the loft. We need to finish what we started six weeks ago. We need it like we need air. He pulls me into a heated kiss. I thread my fingers through his hair, then run my hands down his back, pulling him almost painfully close to my body.

We break apart and he cups my face, rubbing his thumbs back and forth on my cheeks as he stares into my eyes. No one has ever looked at me the way he does. Like I'm the only person in the world. Like I'm the only thing that matters to him.

"You own me, Keri. Every piece of me. Let me make love to you. I want to make love to you with my voice and my body."

His spoken wishes and passionate words cause my body to tremble with warmth and need. "Jace ... yes. I'm yours," I say, my proclamation laced with lust and want for him.

He removes his clothes and then slowly undresses me, taking time to appreciate every single part of my body as he exposes it. The way he looks at me has me aching. My body is on high alert, responding instantly wherever he touches it.

"You are so exquisitely beautiful," he says, laying me down on the bed beneath him. He leans down to kiss me and my eyes close as he lets out a growl of desire when our naked bodies touch, igniting my incessant greed for him.

"Look at me, Keri," he says with panting breaths. "Watch me as I love you. See how you make me feel."

And as he enters me and we become one for the first time, I cry out at the pleasure of him filling me gently, perfectly, and completely, unlike any other person ever has. As he moves within me, he whispers declarations of love and devotion, and when he kisses me, I feel the truth of every word he has spoken.

My body tightens around him, lights explode behind my eyelids and euphoria bursts within me as I arch my back through the incredible release. My body continues shuddering as his own climax pulses through him. Then, as we lay tangled together in breathless bliss, I realize that I am truly his—wholly, deeply, and unconditionally.

Happy tears stream down my face as he pulls me into a kiss. A kiss that trumps all other kisses. A kiss so sweet and full of meaning that it would have sufficed in the absence of his words. A kiss with promises of more-than-enough love.

# Epilogue

*One month later ...*

I'm still riding high from his grand gesture of love. Jace finally wore me down and I have agreed to take a position at The Third Watch. But only with the condition that I get to remain heavily involved with day-to-day operations, and most importantly, that I still get to interact with the kids.

I'm both scared and excited to begin my master's program in the fall. Luckily, I can go to school part-time and still fulfill my duties as the new Residential Coordinator for the foundation.

In celebration, Jace is surprising me with a night out. After a few minutes of driving, I smile because I know where he's taking me. We both love going on the yacht, and every chance we get, we come up with some kind of charity function that will allow us to utilize it without feeling any guilt.

We pull into the parking lot and he comes around to open my door. He grabs my hand and we walk blissfully over to the sidewalk.

However, when we get there, he leads me in the opposite direction, back towards the darkened entrance of the chemo clinic.

"Do you want to live out an old fantasy and make-out with me in front of the clinic?" I tease.

He laughs. I still can't get over his laugh. I've made it my mission every day to hear it at least a dozen times. But it's not hard. He makes me happier than I ever dreamed.

"Something like that," he says, winking at me. He goes to push the door of the clinic open.

"Jace! What are you doing? It's dark in there. They aren't open. Do you want to get arrested?"

"Oh, lighten up and live a little, Keri. Come on."

He pulls me through the double doors. He walks me into the main room of the clinic and a light flickers on.

I'm surprised to see who's here. I look around at all the faces of those who went through chemo with us. There is Grace, Mel, John, Ann, Peggy, Eileen, Jenny, and even Dylan. Most are in the same seats they used during treatment. With one exception. Steven's seat has been left conspicuously vacant and I take a second to remember him before I see who else is here.

Lining the walls behind the large leather chairs are our nurses, Stacy and Camille, along with Trina, the masseuse. And rounding out the bunch are Chaz, Tanner and Jules.

I smile big when I see everyone. I can't believe he's arranged yet another surprise party for me. And all because I've agreed to work with him at the foundation. I'm touched that all these people would show up for this.

"Wow, thank you all for coming. I'm so flattered you're here. It's nice to see you all."

I start to walk over to them to greet them individually when Jace grabs my hands and pulls me to the middle of the room.

"Keri, this is where I first met you. It's where my life changed. I had to bring you here. There isn't any other place I could imagine bringing you on this day."

His eyes become glassy and I begin to think the purpose of this little gathering is not, in fact, a surprise party at all. My heart races, blood pounds in my ears, and tears threaten to fall as he continues to speak to me.

"When I was first diagnosed with cancer, I felt like someone ripped the very ground out from under my feet. I couldn't help but think 'why me?' I would sit in my loft and stare at the painting of you that I'd painted all those years ago. I would draw courage and inspiration from it. It was you—that painting—that got me to come here, and it was here that I met you. So, I no longer ask 'why me.' Instead I say 'thank God.' Because now I know that no matter what my prognosis is in a few weeks, I know you will be by my side."

His voice cracks and he whispers that he's still getting used to using it, making me laugh.

"You are the best side effect of chemo, Keri." He smiles at me as we laugh at our private joke through our tears. "I can't imagine spending the rest of my life with anyone else. You are ashamed of your past, but your past has made you who you are today. It has made you into the woman I love. You're the strongest person I know. When life took your parents, you turned it into a career for helping children. When life gave you cancer, you said 'screw you' and cupped your breasts. You gave up the man you loved because you unselfishly thought it was the best thing for him. And you stood between the barrel of a gun and a monster to save a boy from a lifetime of regret. That is the woman I love. She is the one I want to spend my life with. She is the woman who can teach our children to be amazing—just like she is."

My ears tell me we are not the only two people shedding tears of joy in this room. But I can't pull my eyes away from Jace to look at anyone else. We share a moment that etches itself forever into my soul. Then he smiles and drops down on one knee.

"I have a question to ask you, Keri. I'll whisper it, I'll text it, I'll scream it from the mountain tops ... as long as I get the answer I want. The answer I need to bring happiness to the rest of my days."

He reaches into his pocket and produces a ring. It's the most beautiful thing I've ever seen. It's not a huge diamond, one that will weigh down my finger and make me feel pretentious. It's a perfectly sized diamond. But it's positively, undoubtedly, absolutely ... more than enough.

"Keri, will you do me the honor of becoming my wife?"

Even through tear-blurred vision, he is the most handsome man I will ever lay eyes on. I can't imagine a more romantic proposal, topping even the art gallery gesture of last month. I know this man will love me and continue to surprise me until we cease to exist on this earth. I believe our love may even transcend this world and follow us into the next.

I pull out my phone.

**Me: Yes! A million times, yes!**

# Acknowledgments

First and foremost, I have to thank my family for putting up with a crazy wife and mother during this process. Bruce, you have always given me the freedom and support to follow my dreams and for that I can never have enough gratitude. Dylan, Austin, Kaitlyn, and Ryan, you had to endure month after month of your mom being locked in the office, typing away on the laptop while you fended for yourselves. I couldn't have asked for more wonderful and responsible children and I'm so proud of you all.

I can never fully express the appreciation I have for my editors, Jeannie Hinkle and Ann Peters. Without the two of you, my books would never see the light of day. Thanks for your honest, and sometimes brutal, opinions and guidance.

To my beta readers, Tammy Dixon, Lisa Crawford and Stephanie Smith, your feedback kept me writing and your words of encouragement kept me from burning my manuscript in frustration.

When the idea behind this book came to me, I wondered if I could write a book about chemotherapy without having actually been there myself. I did a lot of research and read countless internet blogs on the subject. I can't go without thanking Gwen Schell and Marty Danko for sharing their very personal experiences with me, giving me some insight into the world of cancer. I certainly have a new appreciation for you and everyone else who has been touched by this awful disease.

Samantha Christy

# About the Author

Samantha Christy's passion for writing started long before her first novel was published. Graduating from the University of Nebraska with a degree in Criminal Justice, she held the title of Computer Systems Analyst for The Supreme Court of Wisconsin and several major universities around the United States. Raised mainly in Indianapolis, she holds the Midwest and its homegrown values dear to her heart and upon the birth of her third child devoted herself to raising her family full time. While it took time to get from there to here, writing has remained her utmost passion and being a stay-at-home mom facilitated her ability to follow that dream. When she is not writing, she keeps busy cruising to every Caribbean island where ships sail. Samantha Christy currently resides in St. Augustine, Florida with her husband and four children.

You can reach Samantha Christy through her website www.samanthachristy.com.

Made in the USA
Las Vegas, NV
25 April 2021